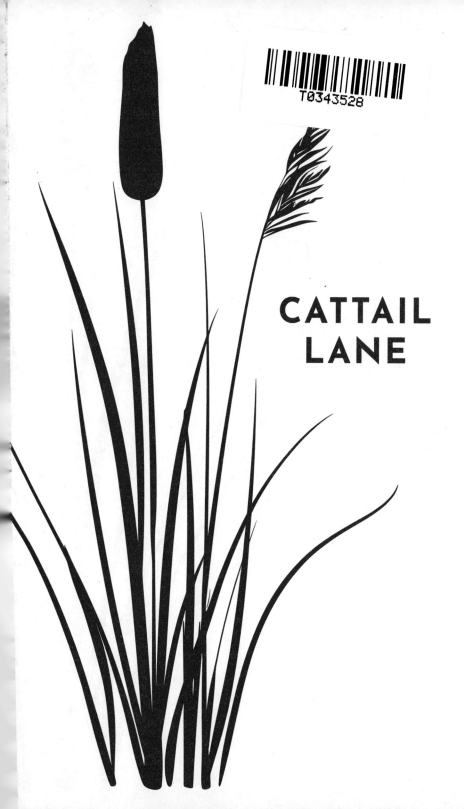

CATTAIL
LANE

FRAN KIMMEL

CATTAIL LANE

Editor for the Press: Jen Knoch
Copy editor: Jen Albert
Cattail image: Gfx Expert Team, stock.adobe.com

This is a work of fiction. Names, characters, places, and incidents either are the product of the author's imagination or are used fictitiously, and any resemblance to actual persons, living or dead, business establishments, events, or locales is entirely coincidental.

LIBRARY AND ARCHIVES CANADA CATALOGUING IN PUBLICATION

Title: Cattail Lane : a novel / Fran Kimmel.

Names: Kimmel, Fran, 1955- author.

Identifiers: Canadiana (print) 20240495977 | Canadiana (ebook) 20240495985

ISBN 978-1-77041-787-8 (softcover)
ISBN 978-1-77852-374-8 (PDF)
ISBN 978-1-77852-373-1 (ePub)

Subjects: LCGFT: Novels.

Classification: LCC PS8621.I5449 C38 2025 | DDC C813/.6—dc23

This book is funded in part by the Government of Canada. Ce livre est financé en partie par le gouvernement du Canada. We acknowledge the support of the Canada Council for the Arts. Nous remercions le Conseil des arts du Canada de son soutien. We would like to acknowledge the funding support of the Ontario Arts Council (OAC) and the Government of Ontario for their support. We also acknowledge the support of the Government of Ontario through the Ontario Book Publishing Tax Credit, and through Ontario Creates.

Canada Council   Conseil des arts
for the Arts   du Canada

ONTARIO ARTS COUNCIL
CONSEIL DES ARTS DE L'ONTARIO
an Ontario government agency
un organisme du gouvernement de l'Ontario

Ontario

ONTARIO CREATES

PRINTED AND BOUND IN CANADA   PRINTING: MARQUIS   5 4 3 2 1

Get the ebook free!*
*proof of purchase required

Purchase the print edition and receive the ebook free.
For details, go to ecwpress.com/ebook.

for my angel mother,
Irma

Chapter 1

It wasn't much of a letter, just four lines.

Dear Nick,

You have a son.
His name is Billy.
It's time for you to come get him.
He's a good boy.

Sincerely, Evelyn Peat

Enough to thrust Nick Ackerman kicking and screaming into fatherhood.

When Nick first laid eyes on Billy, he felt a gurgle of relief in the back of his throat. It was all a whopping mistake. Anyone with half a brain could see the fourteen-year-old kid was not his. Where Nick was ruddy cheeked, stocky, weight planted low and built for defence, Billy was anemic pale, like he was allergic to the world, tall and weak and shaped like an out-of-control dandelion. Billy was the type of boy that Nick would have avoided at school. His voice too soft, eyes startling green, his face a kaleidoscope of expressions waiting to sync up.

Nick fought it far longer than was decent. After three months of waffling, DNA tests (two, to be sure), and heated conversations with the doctors and social workers, he still couldn't build his case. Billy was his problem, and the woman came with him. Evelyn Peat, Billy's grandma. She'd written that letter years ago, tucking it in a folder named *About Billy*. The social worker found it in a dusty filing cabinet during a house visit. In the folder was her letter. Her last will and testament. Her power of attorney documents. Nick named inexplicably on them all.

Billy wouldn't leave without Evelyn, so Nick had the privilege of hauling them both out of there. A pig pile of a package deal.

They got off to a rocky start. By the time they had ransacked Billy's house in Chetville, the truck was hillbilly stuffed. Nick had been expecting Billy's things and a few dresses and toiletries for Evelyn.

"Billy, she's only got a small room," he kept repeating.

"It's her life, not yours," Billy grumbled, piling the last bag on the stack.

Nick put Evelyn in the back seat for the drive into Rigsbee, hoping to break ground with the kid, but Billy kept his head turned away and his mouth shut. It was a long and sullen three hundred kilometres.

He was exhausted by the time they pulled up to Prairie View Manor. At five stories, the building was the tallest in his mostly one-storey town; even the hospital and the school spread out, not up). It stood like a sentry tower at the northern town limits, guarding against the gophers in the fields beyond.

Billy looked up at the balconies and their rows of hanging plants, coloured flags and pinwheels, butterflies on metal sticks.

"Your grandma's room is on the main floor," Nick said. If your brain and body still worked, you got sent to the top floor rooms with balconies. If you needed help with your socks or your bath, you were given floor number two. If you were inclined to yell for no reason or wander in your underwear, then it was the main floor for you, behind the heavy locked door. There was a depressing inevitability to the downward slide, a game of snakes and ladders played backwards.

Nick turned to Evelyn, who was rifling through her purse. "Ready to see your new place?" Billy didn't move.

"I can't find my key," she said with panic. "The ice cream will melt, and I can't find my key."

Billy whipped around and said, "It's okay, Grandma. I found it." He produced an irrelevant key from his pants pocket and showed it to her.

"Should we check it out then?" Nick tried to sound hopeful as he got out of the truck. By the time he got to the sidewalk side, Billy was out too. Nick opened Evelyn's door, and she smiled and dropped some change, a quarter and a dime, in his palm.

"God, Grandma." Billy kicked his runner against the tire. "You don't have to give him money."

"Don't be silly," she said. "You must always tip."

"Why don't we show your grandma her room before we unload?" Nick said. Billy ignored him, pulling stuff out of the truck bed and piling it on the grass.

Nick helped Evelyn step from the truck and grabbed the old lamp from the back seat. When he turned, she was heading across the lawn.

Billy tossed a stack of blankets and pillows onto the sidewalk, which was starting to look like the dregs of a garage sale. Evelyn had wandered to the far side of the green space to examine something on the ground. Nick started to go after her, the lamp cord dragging like a leash missing its dog, when a man stepped out from behind the sliding door and yelled, "Excuse me. We have to keep this sidewalk clear."

Nick backtracked. "Sorry. Moving day. Is there somewhere else I should park?"

"And who are you?"

"Nick. Nick Ackerman. And that is my . . . that is Billy, Billy Peat. Evelyn Peat's grandson." Billy disappeared behind the back of the truck.

The man studied his open binder, pulled a ballpoint from his pocket, and placed a check on the page. He looked at his watch. "We were expecting you this morning."

And I was expecting not this, Nick thought irritably. "Who are you?" he asked the small man.

The man looked around, as if someone else could tell him who and where he was. "Lewis Clifton. Interim manager."

Odd. Nick had met the interim manager less than two weeks earlier when he'd signed permission forms for Evelyn. A rattled woman who added a sorry to every sentence.

Lewis Clifton squinted as he pointed at Evelyn. "Is that the new resident?"

Nick squinted too. "Yes, it is," he said, unable to move his feet.

"Well, perhaps someone should go get her."

The two men stood stupid side by side and stared into the sun. There in the distance was Evelyn, plucking white clover from the grass beneath a resident's window. Billy came around from the back of the truck, hissed between his teeth, and went to fetch her.

Clifton led them single file, swiping his fob to let them into the dementia unit, and stopped in front of Evelyn's room. "I'll let you get settled, Mrs. Peat," he said too loud and slow. He disappeared, as if he couldn't get out fast enough. Nick could relate.

"Come on then." Nick herded Billy and Evelyn into her room and shut the door behind them. He'd bought her a bed and a couch, a shower curtain and wastebasket, toilet paper and toothpaste, sticking to the list the nurse had given except for a few framed prints he'd picked up in the city.

"Do you like it, Evelyn?" Nick asked.

"Oh yes, this is very nice." She moved across the room to look out the window. The view included a skinny strip of mowed lawn, then patches of thistle and scrub brush, then the road out of Rigsbee.

He walked up beside her. "I hope the bed is comfortable." Nick turned and said, "Got you the same one, Billy."

"Great," Billy muttered sarcastically. He was opening every cupboard, finding toilet paper rolls by the dozen.

A pulsing screech started up from outside the door.

Nick yelled above the racket, "It's the door alarm."

"Can't we stop it?" Billy moved towards his grandma, who had covered her ears and squeezed her eyes shut.

"We'd have to know the code," Nick said. "A nurse will shut it off."

Billy squeezed his grandma's arm. "It's okay. It's like the alarm in the kitchen when we burn the toast."

"Get the tea towel, Billy," Evelyn said to the ceiling.

Billy yelled, "You expect her to live here?"

The noise was deafening. An ambulance, siren blazing, parked outside the door.

The racket stopped as suddenly as it started. There was a knock, and a woman poked her head in. Pretty, thirty-ish, with striking red curls. Nick hadn't noticed her when he'd hauled in furniture a few days ago.

"Hello. You're here," she said cheerily. "We've been expecting you. My name is Sarah." She walked up to Evelyn and rested her fingers on her arm. "And you're Evelyn. Is that what you like to be called, Evelyn?"

Evelyn smiled. "My mother calls me Evie. I suppose everyone calls me Evie. Evie, now don't you go near that thing. It was a wild cat you know, under the porch boards."

"Well, it's lovely to meet you, Evie." Sarah turned to Nick. "And you're the son-in-law?"

Nick leaned in and shook Sarah's hand. "It's complicated," he said. "Nick Ackerman."

Sarah turned to Billy and smiled. "Well, I know I've got this right. You're Evie's grandson, Billy. I hear you're moving to Rigsbee too?"

He shrugged.

"It's not as dead as it looks. Rigsbee has a new skate park." She looked around the small room. "I just got back from a few days off. Evie's room looks nice."

"None of this is Grandma's." Billy slumped rudely against the wall. "Her stuff is outside."

"He's right," Nick said. "It's strewn all over the sidewalk. Lewis Clifton is not impressed."

Sarah laughed. "Well, why don't you two bring it in? I'll stay with Evie, and we'll boss you around. You've got a fob?"

Nick nodded, patting his pocket.

"Good. You can't get in or out without it. And you have to watch before you open the door. If residents are too close, just give them a minute to move away. And don't let anyone out when you leave, even if they have sunhats and purses and tell you a perfectly rational story about forgetting their key or needing a bag from their car."

He and Billy made three trips to the truck and back, hauling in the ratty old armchair and Evie's clothes and bags filled with knick-knacks and old copies of art magazines and God knows what else. Her room looked like a junk closet.

Evie sat in her armchair as soon as they had it wedged between the couch and the window wall. A woman marched in while he and Sarah were hanging Evie's clothes.

"Dorothy Daine, head nurse," she said, eyes sweeping the room critically. She had her grey hair pulled back in a tight bun and remarkably big feet.

"Sarah, you're needed down the hall. Clement has had another accident."

After Sarah left, Dorothy Daine recited a litany of rules and observations without making eye contact. No glass containers. No scissors. Nothing loose on the floor. (That braided rug would have to go.) Showers twice a week. A locked bathroom cupboard for toiletries. Breakfast at eight. Supper at five. Residents were to keep their doors open and their windows closed.

Evie seemed like she was half-listening to a weather report for a place she would never go. "Thank you for the tea," she said, which Dorothy Daine ignored.

Billy crossed his arms and stared at the floor, brows furrowed, his expression getting sourer by the minute. "It's horrible," he said when she finally left. "That nurse is horrible."

Nick agreed but knew enough to not say it.

"You'll drive us home?" Evie asked politely. "My purse is here somewhere."

"I'm not going to leave her here," Billy said.

Evie's arms flew up, eyes wide. "My purse. I've lost my purse." She jerked her head from side to side, scanning the room in panic. Nick was shocked how quickly she could fall apart.

"Your purse is right here, Grandma." Billy grabbed it off the floor and handed it to her. He turned to Nick, eyes narrowed. "I'm not leaving her."

To keep the peace, Nick agreed to let Billy stay with Evelyn while he drove home to wait an appropriate length of time before he could turn his truck around, retrace his route, and drag the kid out. This was his new life.

He owned the last lot on the south side of town. If Rigsbee were a boxing ring, Nick's dilapidated bungalow and Prairie View's five stories stood in opposite corners. The house stuck out on a point at the back of the lot like it was trying to start a fight with the overgrown thicket. He had a half-acre in total, no neighbours to contend with.

Nick stepped through his door and surveyed his work. He'd reluctantly booked off two weeks—middle of their busy season and he got paid by inspection—and already he'd gobbled up two days trying to make the place less awful.

He'd emptied ashtrays and picked up Candace's stray butts between the driveway and the front door. Washed dishes, boxed up the empties for recycling. Gutted the second bedroom, ridding it of boxes and the old mattress leaning against the wall. The small room now had a new bed, a dresser, a smoke detector, and a window that opened in case Billy chose to leave, which Nick could only hope for.

He'd bought the house four years ago, sight unseen. The original owner had expired in the backyard while holding an axe. By the time he was noticed missing, his body had started to decay, and his right hand had disappeared. "A handyman's fixer-upper," the ad had said. If a home inspection had been done, the house would have flunked spectacularly. It was an 800-square-foot safety violation, a dystopia of bad wiring, leaking shingles, failing beams, creaky flooring, makeshift plumbing. He'd found a certain satisfaction in squalor. It comforted him to come home to tangible proof that he could live with things broken.

He wasn't much into decorating. Nothing on the walls but a torn horse calendar and the town's wrinkled garbage schedule. The opposite of Billy and Evelyn's place. When Nick first walked through their door, he felt like he'd stepped into a Grimms' fairy tale. She'd been an artist who had given up on canvases and turned to the walls instead. Her hallway had become a vegetable garden, the living room a lakeshore. A vine had climbed up the fridge, along the cupboard and across the ceiling. Painted postcard-sized pieces were tacked everywhere—above the toilet paper roll, along the window frames.

He imagined his crumbling house with Billy in it. What would the kid do all day while Nick was at work? What would they do with each other at night?

Nick opened the freezer and peered in. He'd bought enough frozen meals to get them through a week. He took out the weighty lasagne package, peeled off the plastic wrap, and threw it in the cantankerous oven, waiting to see if there'd be heat.

The screen door slammed.

"Niiick."

Candace Philips waltzed in, a new layer of pink in her thick blonde hair. He'd met her when she'd started at the Ploughman Tavern over a year ago. She was singularly focused on owning the dive (changing the name, the menu, the bar stools), a dream he admired in large part because it didn't involve him. For now, she was his bar buddy, good 'til last call, and convincingly undemanding. She was the only person he'd ever let in his house, and even that was not on purpose. That first time, she'd grabbed his keys at closing time—*you're totally merked*—and drove him home, then half pushed, half dragged him to the front door, where they both fell through the screen. She didn't leave for two days.

Candace sidled up to him now and ran her finger down his cheek. She had new leaves and vines on the inside of her tattooed arm.

"That's gotta hurt."

She held her arm in front of his lips and waited until he kissed the fresh ink.

"I thought you might call."

He didn't know why she always said this. He made a point of not calling.

Candace pushed him against the fridge and kissed him hard on the mouth. She was remarkably fit considering she never worked out.

It often started this way. She would show up unannounced, waltz through his door, rip apart snaps and yank down zippers. They'd wound up in closets, the rusted shower, and behind the couch, seldom bothering to get all the way undressed.

Today it was the table, which until now had been too cluttered to consider. The wood squealed like a boiling lobster. When they were done, Nick slumped on top of her, her face smushed into the sticky grain of the beat-up pine. Candace squirmed underneath him, so he pushed away. They yanked up the tangle of underwear and jeans pooling at their knees and smoothed down T-shirts. She wrenched a Players package from her back pocket, but his hand stopped hers from bringing a cigarette to her lips.

"Sorry. No smoking."

She tossed her head back, about to laugh, but he wouldn't let go of her wrist.

"You kidding?" She threw the Players package onto the table. "Since when?"

"Since today." He shrugged. "Haven't even got the sign yet."

"Oh gawd. Of course. Because of the boy."

He wished he hadn't mentioned Billy to her. "Figured I should go that far."

He could hear fizzing noises behind him, cheese breaking away from the lasagne and splatting to the oven floor.

"You must be nervous. A daddy now. Your place is looking great, by the way."

He shrugged. They never could hold much of a conversation.

"So when do you pick him up?" she asked irritably. She needed a cigarette after sex.

"He's already here."

"Here?" Her eyebrows shot up like they'd just done the dirty with Billy pressed against his bedroom door.

Nick couldn't blame her for thinking so little of him. "No, he's not here. He's with his grandma. At Prairie View Manor. I have to pick him up now."

"Why don't I go with you. I'd love to meet your boy. I'll help ease you into daddyhood. My shift doesn't start until seven."

"Nah," he said casually. He'd never intended an invitation. "Let's go slow. Give Billy a few weeks." Or never.

Chapter 2

B illy hated this place. The fake plants and fake smiling woman at the front desk. He hated Nick most of all.

Her room felt like a prison cell. A stupid blue couch, too small to lie out on. The paint a pukey green, same as her hospital room. There were a few ugly prints on the walls, pictures of puppies wearing hats and kittens in a basket, nothing his grandma or anyone with taste could stand to look at. The bathroom had no bathtub, just a shower-head and a drain like you'd find at a dog wash.

He wished they were still in Chetville, except there'd be no house to go back to. The Got Junk truck pulled up as they pulled away, swooping in to empty out the last traces of them. Their pail of striped rocks they had collected for no reason. His grandma's ceramic mixing bowl. The broken cuckoo clock that never cuckooed. All of it to be thrown out like trash.

They'd have done okay in that house if people had left them alone. His grandma still had good days where she joked and laughed. Every morning he'd divvied out her pills and made her tea, hiding the old kettle under his bed so she wouldn't let it run dry and start the house on fire. He reminded her to brush her hair and teeth and helped set up her paints, then hurried to and from school, which wasn't a problem since he had nowhere else to go. He shovelled sidewalks and mowed grass and planted potatoes and dug up potatoes and did grocery runs and stood in pharmacy lines. Their system worked. She could still make great pies if he measured the ingredients, still make him laugh so hard he nearly peed himself. But when she wound up in the hospital everyone poked their nose in their business. Early onset Alzheimer's, they called it. Captain Bananas taking charge. The social worker said they both suffered from neglect. *This will be a fresh start.* Right. It felt like the end.

It's not like Nick wanted him, or his grandma, who he was only too happy to lock up and forget. Billy couldn't remember his mother, but his feelings about her went down a notch when Nick showed up at the hospital. She chose this guy? Nick was accompanied by the social worker, who propped him up and pushed him through the door. He scowled and pumped his hand, mumbling incoherently about how great it was to meet. He looked scared of Evie, who was half his weight and wouldn't hurt a bug.

Billy yanked the ugly purple blanket off her bed and stuffed it in the closet, replacing it with her comforter from the box.

"Billy, it's time to go home now," his grandma said.

He had no way to fix it. All he could do was tell her what she wanted. Yes, they'd go in a minute. Sure, he would water the garden. The beans would be up soon. They'd put the chicken in the oven. He'd learned to lie when she got scared. The first time was in the middle of the night when she woke crying for her mamma. He was so rattled he almost cried too. She died, like a long time ago, he told her, which made her sob louder. He finally figured out that she needed to believe her mamma was coming back. So that's what he told her. *She'll be here for breakfast, and we'll have pancakes. She says you're supposed to sleep now.* Which she did. He'd gotten better at telling stories since then.

He tore down Nick's lame prints and stacked them by the door to dump in the garbage. Then he ripped open the artwork he'd brought from home.

"Check this out, Grandma." He held up a still life of red poppies in a field of green and hung it on a leftover nail over her bed.

"How about these?" He spread out the set of four miniature garden scenes, which she wanted next to her armchair.

Most were summer paintings, brilliant purple and yellow flowers tucked against wood fences or along curved pathways. She'd used oil on canvas back then, teaching him to sketch first with charcoal, then paint in layers, fat over lean. By the time Billy was in school, she'd switched to watercolours, so their mistakes could not be easily brushed over.

There wasn't enough wall space.

"Grandma, I'm gonna look for a hammer and nails."

He headed down the corridor with its horrible walls, peering through open doors. Old men shrivelled in wheelchairs, on beds. Old women slumped sideways in chairs. Some milled about in the hallway. One carried a baby doll by its feet, its plastic pink toes thumping against her chest. No one acknowledged him, or each other, as they moved past him like zombies.

Sarah came out of a bad-smelling room with a mop and a bucket, her face shiny with sweat.

"Billy, how are you making out with Evie?"

"I need something to hang her paintings. They're not framed, so they don't weigh much."

"Then goop should do. Come on. I'll find you some."

She took his arm and guided him into a cramped room with washers and dryers and a row of baskets with names taped to each.

"I know it's here somewhere." She stood on her toes and peered into the highest cupboard. "There. Can you reach to the back?"

Billy stretched and brought down a package of mounting poster putty.

"Pull off a piece for each corner. Mush it in your fingers, then use your fist like a hammer and give it a good whack." She demonstrated by banging her fist hard against the cupboard door.

Billy could hear a sharp scream down the hallway. He gripped the package tightly, unable to move.

Sarah smiled. "That's Edith. She makes those noises sometimes. But she's not afraid or upset. It's how she says hello to the world." Her face softened. "It's a lot to take in, isn't it? You okay?"

"Grandma's not like these people."

"No, she's not. She's her own person. She has a sparkle in her eye."

"She shouldn't be here. She's only sixty-five. Everybody else looks like they're at least a hundred. They're way worse than her. Grandma would never scream for no reason."

"I know it's hard." Sarah leaned closer and rested her hand on his shoulder. "But I bet it's been hard for you too, especially watching over Evie all by yourself. Now she's got a whole team supporting her."

"This place is going to kill her," he muttered, sure it was true. "She won't understand why she's here."

"That's our job, isn't it? To help her every day. And every day, it will get a little easier for her. And for you."

While he didn't believe her, his chest filled with new air. The unwanted relief made him feel guilty, like he was to blame. He fled the laundry room and barrelled down the hallway, sidestepping walkers and wheelchairs. His grandma slept while he hung her paintings, oblivious to his banging. By the time he was done, the walls from floor to ceiling were covered with Evie's colours, his fist swollen and stinging, a bruise of bright red.

When Sarah pulled into the parking lot of her apartment building, she turned the car too sharply and bumped the steel post. It was a ridiculous spot for a bicycle rack; she'd never once seen a bike parked there.

"You hit it again," Carter shouted from the back seat.

"Thank you, Carter," she said. "You're very helpful."

She backed up, swinging wide this time, and eased into her spot, thankful the truck in number eight was not yet there. He always parked over the line, leaving her barely enough room to open her door and slide sideways.

"Should we call the police?" Carter had become enamoured with the police since the officer's visit to his kindergarten class.

"It was just a little bump. Police don't come for bumps."

"Yes, they do. Police always come if you call."

"That's only for emergencies. Come on, buddy. Let's go."

Carter tumbled out of the car, wearing his helmet and rain boots, dragging his backpack behind him. "Like if you crashed into a cat and it got hurt really bad, then the police would come."

Carter had exceptional verbal skills. That's what Miss Pam had told her at their first meet-the-teacher meeting. Teachers' code for *your child won't shut up.*

He prattled on. "Or if you were playing with matches and started a box on fire, and then the box started a different box on fire, and then all the boxes started on fire, then the police would come and so would the fire truck and they would use their water hose."

"That's why you definitely don't play with matches."

He'd stopped by their complex's main door, bending over to check out a beetle. "Can I play outside?"

He asked this every time, even though there was no good place to play and no one to play with.

"It's supper time. Aren't you starving?"

He slumped his shoulders forward and sat in the dirt. Sarah tugged on his arm, scooped up his backpack, and dragged him inside.

Their apartment was on the second of three grungy floors, wedged between old Mr. McGreary, who they'd glimpsed only twice in the seven months since they'd moved in, and a twenty-something goth boy who came and went without nodding in their direction. It was the yahoos above them that caused the real grief. She'd asked the landlord to deal with their loud music, which he'd assured her he'd do, but his smirk said otherwise. *What do you expect, lady? This is a dump.*

It was a pathetic place for a boy, but the only rental in Rigsbee that Sarah could afford. When she and Carter moved here last December, she had just enough money to cover the deposit and pay for her winter classes, draining her rainy-day jar to buy a few gifts from Santa. She couldn't afford the Hot Wheels Colossal Crash Tracks he wanted most. She'd been putting away extra every paycheque, determined to make Christmas more special this year.

"How about spaghetti?" she asked. "And you cannot wear your helmet in the house, so put it away, please."

"No sauce," he yelled, his head in the closet.

Carter didn't want his food groups to overlap. "Just a little sauce. Now go to the bathroom and wash your hands. With soap. And I'm going to check."

As Sarah sliced tomatoes and mushrooms, she reminded herself that she could do this. It was a mantra she repeated a hundred times a day. She would finish her nursing classes, move up in the ranks, get out of housekeeping. She could earn enough money to move Carter into a real house. He'd have his own room stuffed with toys, a fenced backyard with a swing set. Proper before and after school care. The best daycare each summer.

At supper, she tried not to rush him as he twirled his noodles into a fat blob at the end of his fork.

"Did you have a good day at Mrs. Brandon's?"

He shrugged, noodles dangling from his mouth. He'd been with Mrs. Brandon since the school year ended, a week now, and had little good to say about her or his days. Sarah wished she could have put him in the daycare in Willowridge, with its jungle gym and cartoon-character walls and smiling teachers and his best buddy, Ryan, from kindergarten, but Mrs. Brandon was half the price. She took in two other kids, a pair of dull sisters with stringy hair and bags under their eyes, both younger than Carter. He had little good to say about them either.

"Well, what did you do?"

"Nothing."

She hoped Mrs. Brandon hadn't sat them in front of the TV all day. She was in her late fifties and not spry, her children long grown. "That's impossible. Unless you're a statue. Wait a minute. You're not a statue, are you?"

Carter yanked up his arms and froze. They both laughed.

"I found two earthworms," he announced.

"That's cool. You were outside playing?"

"I wanted to do the Earthworm Shuffle, but Kelly and Carly don't know how."

"The Earthworm Shuffle! That's your favourite." Carter had shown her plenty of times by wriggling on his belly. As far as Sarah could tell, Miss Pam had turned the classroom into an obstacle course and the kids into earthworms.

"No, it's not my favourite. Frog on the Dog is. We do Frog on the Dog on Thursdays. But that's only at school. Mrs. Brandon doesn't know how."

"Maybe next time you find an earthworm you could teach Kelly and Carly how to do the shuffle. Over, under, in, on. Right?"

"You forgot *beside*. Earthworms go beside too. They're very strong." Carter dropped his fork and flexed his muscles like a wrestler. "They make slime that makes the gardens grow. Kelly and Carly hate worms. And frogs. And dogs. I can make slime. Want me to show you?"

"I want you to eat your tomatoes. Three more bites."

"Earthworms dig way down deep where they can be slimiest. But they have to come out if it rains so that they don't drown and then they get stepped on, bam, which is worser than getting drowned, so they're caught between a rock and a hard place."

Sarah laughed. Between a rock and a hard place was her most worn-out expression.

"Okay, buddy, drink some milk. It's your turn to ask me about my day."

Carter made a moustache of white around his tomato lips. "Did you have a good day, Mommy?"

"Well, yes, I did, Carter. Thanks for asking."

A day like any other. Washing, wiping, scouring, dusting. A series of re-dos. Ruth had watered her plastic flowers again, creating a puddle in her drawer that drenched her just-laundered panties. Clement had another explosive accident, his third this week, a river of brown trailing down his leg and following him into the hall. In the dining room, lunchtime usually a hushed affair, Edith refused to swallow her pills and flung them out of her hand and into Mazie's soup. Later, when Mazie refused to leave Edith's room, claiming it was hers, their angry voices carried into the hall. Sarah squeezed in on the couch between them and talked about the weather—*wasn't it such a warm summer, wouldn't the farmers be happy*—until the three of them were discussing blue skies, and how there had never been a better year for the saskatoons. They sat like that until Dorothy stopped at the doorway and glared, as if to imply that Sarah had better things to do. She didn't. Helping her residents find a little joy was worth more than clean socks.

"We had a new grandma move in today," Sarah told Carter, who was slapping his rubber boots together under the table. "Her name's Evie and her grandson is fourteen years old, and his name is Billy. They're very nice."

"Is Billy going to live in her room?"

Carter had been to Prairie View once for the Mother's Day tea. He was captivated by all the doors, wanting to poke his head in every room.

"Billy's going to live with his dad and come visit his grandma." She hoped Billy would visit. So many families dropped off their person and forgot about them.

"I don't have a grandma."

"No, you don't, Carter."

"Ryan has three grandmas. He brought one for show and share."

"Well, he's very lucky, isn't he?"

At bedtime, Carter stalled by grilling her about the solar system. The sun was a star, and the moon was not. There were eight planets, and Jupiter was the hugest with a whole bunch of moons. By the time he finally settled, she wanted to crawl into bed herself.

She sat at the kitchen table, her textbook opened to the "Overmedicating of the Elderly" chapter. She was concentrating on benzodiazepines, lost in the world of pharmaceutical side effects, barely registering the slam of the door above her, the stomping of feet. Then it started. The pounding of drums, the shrieking bass, shaking her walls, hurting her bones. She looked in on Carter, arms above his head, his sheet a tangle at his feet, mouth ajar and blowing out small puffs of air.

She went back to her textbook and stared at the page, the words blurring to a sea of black. It was eleven o'clock, hours yet before the pounding would stop. She wanted to scream, *Shut up you morons!* but knew it would be pointless, her voice drowned inside the wretched drumbeat. A tune her mother used to sing floated back to her. *If I had a hammer, I'd hammer in the evening.* She did in fact have a hammer. She wished she could use it to crack open their flat, empty skulls.

Chapter 3

B illy fought with Nick on the drive to the loony bin that morning.
You're coming home for lunch.

No thanks.

Non-negotiable.

I'm having lunch with Grandma.

Not today. You're coming home. You don't live there, Billy, you live with me.

Like I have a choice.

My point. You don't. You're coming home.

They sniped like that the whole way. Billy won when he threatened to run away with Evie. He couldn't stand Prairie View, but Nick's place was worse. Except now Dorothy told him that the dining room was too crowded, and his grandma's fees didn't include feeding him lunch too.

He slumped in her rocker, feet dangling over the armrest, waiting for her to be done. Their morning had been miserable. Mostly he'd kept his mouth shut while he'd tried to hold his shit together. His grandma had kept Nick a secret for a really long time. Billy wanted to know why she didn't tell either one of them about the other—like years ago—only now it was too late to ask. And he couldn't let on he was pissed either. It wouldn't be fair, and she wouldn't understand, and if for one second she remembered why she'd done what she'd done, the thought would fly right out of her head. So instead of bringing it up, he'd spent a lot of time staring at a tiny spider on the ceiling. The spider never moved so it might have been a smudge. He was so hungry he could eat a cow.

"Hello!" A large woman sauntered into the room. "You're here all alone?"

He stood quickly, feeling as if he'd been caught. "Grandma's in the dining room. I'm just waiting for her to come back."

She looked about, eyes veiled by subtle creases and hints of sapphire blue shadow, eyebrows sculpted with precise arcs. A cascade of vibrant feathers suspended from her ears.

"Mom's sleeping. Her name's Victoria. Like the queen." She snorted when she said that. "We're right next door."

Billy had peeked into that room with the old woman in a bed. "Oh," he said like a dork, as if this was his first conversation.

"I'm Rachel." She strode towards him. "Rachel Moss."

"Billy." He extended his hand, which she ignored.

"And your grandma's name is Evie. I asked the staff. I'm nosy like that." She cleared her throat as if something had stuck, some kind of respiratory problem, a rosiness under her overblown nose.

"I'm going for a Teen Burger at the A&W drive-through. I try to order food that I don't like. That helps me keep my figure."

His stomach griped in multiple syllables. What was wrong with Teen Burgers? He could eat five.

"Want to come?" she asked, eyebrows jumping.

Really? She seemed harmless, with her feather earrings and soft wrinkly neck, but still. And he didn't have money.

"Thanks, no, but thanks."

"My treat," she said, ignoring him. "We can be there and back before your grandma is finished in the dining room. It will do us both good to get out of here."

So he followed her to the parking lot like a starved dog. Her Volkswagen had dents and scrapes, and the engine sizzled and hissed before finally starting up. Inside was a collection of pet stuff: chew toys, a leash and collar, dog biscuits, everything still in packaging. He found a spot for his feet on the cluttered floorboard and scrunched his legs, buckled his seat belt, and hoped for the best.

They jolted along.

"I can't remember the last time I had a passenger." She tapped the steering wheel with her sapphire blue fingernail. On top of the blue, she'd painted flowers on each nail, tiny strokes of pastel to form petals. Impressive. "Never actually," she continued. "No one's been in here besides me. You don't get carsick, do you?"

She seemed to have trouble staying on the right side of the road. "How many dogs do you have?" he asked, braking with his foot as she swerved for no reason.

She laughed. "None. I'm allergic. But the neighbours are friendly. Sebastian lives next door—a bouncy Great Dane, and Velcro beside him, probably a rescue by the looks of his Rottweiler backside and lab snout. Honey is my favourite, the bichon frise across the street. She loves watching the bunnies through the screen door."

"You have bunnies?"

She laughed again. "Not mine exactly. They're wild. But they like hanging out with me. I feed them greens every day and built them a hutch for when the weather is crappy."

She took a wild turn without using her signal and the car rumbled past a row of matchbox houses. His stomach roared, no A&W in sight. It occurred to him this might be a kidnapping.

"Here!" She slammed on the brakes in the middle of the road and pointed to a tiny house nearly as bad as Nick's. It had a saggy roof and chipped paint and a large piece of plywood nailed crooked over the side window. "Home sweet home. I'm looking after it until it sells. I sure as hell don't want it; spent enough time in this shitbox as a kid. Moved halfway across the country a few months ago. That's when my dad died. He croaked the day before I got back, which was just as well. His whole life he didn't even try to not be his worst. Mom's close to the end now too. She's easier to get along with than she used to be." Billy held his thumbs inside his fists and studied the For Sale sign tamped into the dirt. Rachel surveyed the yard, the street, looking this way and that. "See them?"

"Sorry?" Hay bales scattered along her dead brown grass.

"The bunnies."

The only wildlife were a few tiny birds poking around the cracks in the sidewalk. No sign of Sebastian or Velcro either.

"The lettuce is gone. And the carrots." She stared off into space, lips drawn down, as if she were seeing a bunny murder. They sat like that in the middle of the road, not going anywhere. He thought about inching open his door and making a run for it, but then she laughed and said, "They'll be back!" Her foot slammed on the gas, and they bounced down the road again.

No car parts fell off on the way to the A&W, which was squeezed between a car wash and a used bookstore at the far end of town. One truck idled ahead of them in the drive-through. She pulled up to the microphone, rolled down her window, and barked out their order without asking what he wanted. Three Teen Burgers, two chocolate shakes, and a large onion rings. Good choices for a lady her age. He hoped the extra burger was for him.

"So how are you and your grandma getting along?" she asked.

He shrugged, not having the words for it.

"What brought you both here, anyway?"

"Nick." The name tasted bitter in his mouth.

"Your dad?"

"Apparently. That's what the papers say. We haven't known each other long."

"Oh," she nodded. "I get it. Your dad's new to the business of fatherhood. He'll eventually figure out that a boy needs lunch."

He snorted. It wasn't all true but close enough.

"Big adjustment for you," she said.

He watched while she dug into her purse, pulled out a wad of Kleenex, and blew her nose ferociously.

"Allergies," she said. "So you've got a new town. New house. New school in the fall."

He felt like they'd been dropped into a rat-infested refugee camp. "I hate it here."

"Perfectly reasonable." She seemed unfazed as she popped the glove compartment and scooped up scattered bills and change. "Although it sounds like despair, and I don't believe in it. You can be desperate. Miserable, sure. But despair is a dead end. It means no hope and there's always that."

What hope? "Grandma doesn't fit in here," he said, irked to hear his voice crack. "There's nothing for her to do."

"My mother gags and drools and snores and farts. She can't sit unless she's propped up with pillows. Doesn't know who I am or why I'm there."

He couldn't stand to think of his grandma winding down like that.

"I tell her my secrets, and she's never been a better listener." She didn't sound sorry as she counted toonies. "And she doesn't judge me at all anymore. Does your grandma still know who you are?"

"Yeah."

"And you can still have a conversation?"

"Yeah, if we keep it simple."

"Her legs work. I've seen her clipping down the hallway."

"Yeah."

"Then when it gets hard, you can take her for a walk. There's a bench to sit on by the spruce tree at the end of the parking lot."

Maybe he really could just walk away with her.

The truck ahead drove off and she rammed the Volkswagen up to the window. A life-saving waft of salt and oil and dripping meat washed over him. She scrunched her nose in disgust as she passed him the bag.

"If you want something and can't have it, you need to want something else. Now eat."

He tore open the bag. He could think of nothing new to want in this horrible place.

He bit into his burger; he'd never tasted anything so good. Rachel Moss might be the world's worst driver, but he'd say yes to a road trip if she asked him again.

Nick pointed the truck towards the highway, Billy sullen beside him. It was less than ten miles to the county office, located halfway between Rigsbee and the lake. The county was responsible for a thousand square miles of land surrounding Rigsbee and a few dozen hamlets, with departments for agriculture, environment, and enforcement. They did a piss-poor job at all three.

The boy made it clear that he was doing a piss-poor job at this father thing too. The kid spent all day every day at Prairie View. When Nick picked him up at night, they could find nothing to say to each other. *How's your grandma doing?* Rolled eyes. *What did you do all day?* No comment. *Think we should get Evie a TV?* which at least forced Billy to speak. *She doesn't watch TV*, the mumbled response, like Nick was an idiot.

For what little time they'd spent together, each minute dragged on. At one point, Nick banged on the old wall clock, thinking it must have quit moving forward. They sat through silent suppers, concentrating on their food's journey from plates to mouths. When they were done, Billy carried his dishes to the sink and disappeared to his room. Nick wondered why he cared what Billy was doing in there, as he paced back and forth, driving himself crazy. Billy would stay locked away until the next morning when they would do it all again.

Nick's parents would have known what to do. They were naturals with kids Billy's age, with kids any age. He didn't have a clue, but even idiots knew that fourteen-year-olds couldn't hide indefinitely in a place like Prairie View. Leaving him there every day would be like clubbing a baby seal. Too easy. Wrong.

Billy had grumbled about joining him on this road trip. It was a dreary day, matching their moods, low clouds dulling their view of the yellow fields.

"What kind of music do you like?" Nick clicked through the truck's radio stations. When Billy shrugged, he settled for an old Stones song.

"The county office is just a few miles up." Nick sped along the empty road. "I've got some unfinished business that won't take long."

"I got unfinished business too." Billy stared out his window.

"Yeah? And what's that?"

Billy wouldn't look over. "I don't need babysitting."

"And you don't have to babysit your grandma either. She's being well cared for."

Billy snorted. "Like you'd know."

He didn't. He knew dick about either of them. "Well, tell me then? Tell me about your grandma. What did you guys used to do? Before this."

Nothing.

Nick would just as soon dump Billy where he'd found him. But he kept his mouth shut and cranked the radio, Mick belting out the words to "You Can't Always Get What You Want," an appropriate tribute to the pair of them.

By the time he pulled into the county office, Nick was bristling with pent-up frustration and spoiling for a fight. He cut the engine and he and Billy sat, staring at the showy building with floor-to-ceiling windows, a large Canadian flag flapping in the wind.

"We're here," Nick said, stating the obvious. "Our tax dollars at work." He'd been dealing with the county for years with nothing to show for it. The situation had gotten worse since a new developer had proposed taking over the northeast side of the lake. Nick unbuckled his seat belt and opened his door. "Come on, let's go."

"No thanks," Billy said, unmoving.

"This won't take long. Then we can head to the lake and check things out if you want."

"No thanks," Billy said again, looking straight ahead.

Nick didn't need the kid beside him, but he didn't want to lose this fight. He slammed his door, marched around the truck, and yanked open Billy's.

"Get out of the truck."

"Jesus," Billy hurled himself out of his seat, nearly falling on his way down.

Nick marched his son into the county office and up to the receptionist's desk. Marjorie Cohen, a fifty-something woman with big glasses and bigger hair, looked up from her computer. She scrunched her nose like a bad smell had just wafted into the room.

"Hi, Marjorie. Is Peter in?"

"Hello, Nick." She looked from Nick to Billy but didn't ask about the awkward, sullen boy standing beside him. "Do you have an appointment?"

"Peter's expecting me." Nick smiled widely.

"Oh, I'm sure he is." Marjorie heaved herself up off her chair. "I'll see if I can find him." She shuffled through the glass door leading to the maze of cubicles. Nick had been back there many times, but after his last few yelling matches, those invitations stopped. Now he wasn't allowed past the reception area beside the exit door.

"We might as well take a seat." Nick pointed to the chairs in front of the glass wall.

Billy flopped down like a limp cabbage leaf. The kid was too long for his stick frame, big feet attached to skinny legs, not yet grown into himself. "She looked real happy to see you," he said.

Nick laughed. "We're the best of friends." He sat beside Billy and leaned forward, elbows on knees, ignoring Billy's squirming. He'd given Peter the flash drive last week. Fifty-seven photos of the land's hot mess between the cottages and the shoreline. He could have shot a hundred more: deep trenches of muck; mudholes the size of swimming pools; broken branches and destroyed marsh. The county was doing nothing to stop the damage to these wetlands.

Billy blew air out of his cheeks. "You said this wouldn't take long. I don't think that lady's coming back."

"You got somewhere else you'd rather be?"

"Um. Yeah."

Marjorie came back through the glass door. "He'll be with you shortly." She placed her fingers on the keyboard, lifting her eyes over the top of her glasses to focus in on Nick. Peter followed a few minutes later, a short balding man with plenty of nose hair and yellowed teeth. He kept his head down as he marched over to where Nick and Billy were sitting.

"Nick. I'm heading into a meeting. It would be great if you could call first, save you any inconvenience."

Nick stood, extending his hand, which Peter shook limply. "I was in the area."

Peter turned to Billy, who straightened himself out.

"My son, Billy," Nick said.

Peter looked genuinely surprised as he stared at the boy. "Oh, you didn't mention you—"

"Did you get a chance to look through the photos?"

Peter took a second to readjust and switch his gaze from son to father. "Yes, I've seen them. I'm sorry, but I can't deal with this now. I'm heading into a meeting."

As Peter stepped back, Nick stepped forward, staying close to the man. "You can't keep ignoring this. Those wetlands are fragile. And now the ATVers are driving through the bush to avoid the pits they made last year. You've seen the damage. Well, not up close. I guess county development officers don't do site visits to see the shit soup brewing under their noses. But the photos prove the point. The impacts are gonna last for decades. For your kids and your kids' kids. And you're letting it happen."

"Look, Nick, we realize there are issues at Goose Lake. And we're dealing with them. We have an information pamphlet going out next week. We've put up the No Motorized Vehicle signs, like we told you."

Nick raised his hand and pointed two fingers in Peter's face. "Two. Two signs for a thirty square mile area. And one's down already. Tossed in the bush. You knew that, right?"

Peter pursed his lips. "No. No, I didn't. But like I've told you, we've got a lot of stakeholders here. It's going to take the will of the cottagers to make the lakeshore an ATV-free zone."

"Oh right, the cottagers. City folk. In for the weekend with their fancy toys, tearing up the land."

"They're good people, just using their ATVs to get their kids to the beach and back. We don't have the manpower to patrol the shoreline, handing out tickets."

"Except now you're allowing this new development to do the same, only bigger scale."

"That's a totally different situation. Overdale Developments will generate a lot of revenue for our county. Yes, they will have designated ATV trails, but they will be stewards of the environment too. We've gone over this."

Nick's jaw tightened. "Give me a break. You think their ATVs will stick to their paths? They'll be up and down the shoreline, just more of them."

"There's been plenty of consultation. Focus groups, open sessions."

"Right. With the developer and his cronies. Promising paradise to the city folk. You're condoning an environmental catastrophe."

Peter sighed wearily. "What do you want me to say? Whatever issues you got going on, you need to deal with them. I've got a meeting to get to, and we're finished here."

Nick brought out his last card. "I've sent the photos to all the councillors too." He'd mailed a set of photos, along with a terse two-page letter, to all twelve county councillors. "What do you think their response will be?"

Peter smirked. "Yeah, I've had some calls. I know exactly what their response will be. The councillors are pro-progress, Nick. You're not even a constituent. Your parents owned land at the lake, but they don't anymore, and neither do you. This is not your concern. This development's going through, and you need to get on with your life."

Peter disappeared through the glass door. Nick glanced at the smug Marjorie. When he turned to collect his boy, he found him already heading for the exit.

They buckled up in the truck without saying a word. He couldn't take Billy's lip right now, but the kid just said, "Can I see the photos?" with no sign of snark.

He handed Billy his phone and watched him scroll through the photos, taking his time, enlarging some, furrowing his brow.

Billy said nothing as he handed back the phone.

"We could go take a look if you want." Nick started the engine. There were not many people he showed himself to, but if Billy wanted in, he could open that door a crack. "The lake's just a few miles west of here. There's still some pretty parts. I grew up there. My family ran a campground."

"You giving me a choice?" Billy asked.

Nick didn't know the right way to answer. What would a father say? Before he could respond, Billy added, "Cuz I'd rather go to Prairie View."

Right. That door would stay closed.

Chapter 4

They didn't speak on the drive back from the county office to Prairie View. Billy could almost feel sorry for Nick—the photos were gross—except that Nick was rude and unlikeable and too full of himself. A loser.

His grandma was not in her room, which was weird. Where else would she be? He poked his head next door. Rachel Moss sat in the chair beside her comatose mother, thumbing through a magazine. She wore a psychedelic blazer of crazy shapes and swirls, the only burst of colour in that ugly room.

"Have you seen Grandma?" he asked.

"Don't think so." She lifted her magazine and scanned under it. "Not here."

He laughed. She had an odd sense of humour.

"Keep looking," she said. "She can't have escaped. Check closets and under beds."

He wandered down the hall, peering in open doors. He was starting to recognize some of their faces, even talked to a few people, the same conversation each time, *I've got potatoes to peel,* or *I just love the birds,* or *Where do you come from?* or *Have you seen my Caroline?*

He found Evie in the dining room with a handful of others. They were at the big table wearing plastic bibs, small paint pots scattered about. They each had a wooden tulip in front of them on a piece of cardboard. The woman handing out paintbrushes turned and stared.

"Can I help you?" she asked, as if he had wandered in off the street.

"Evie is my grandma."

"Oh." She looked from one blank face to another. "Which one is Evie?"

Billy pointed to his grandma, whose eyes lit up. She blew him a kiss.

The woman said, "I'm only in once a week, and they come and go so fast, I haven't got their names straight. I think this is Evie's first time."

"She just moved here."

"Well, take a seat beside your grandma. You can help her use her brush. We're painting tulips this morning. I'm Jennifer. The rec aide. I'll get you one."

It reminded him of a kindergarten class, minus one iota of enthusiasm. No one spoke except Jennifer, who barked out orders cheerfully—*hold it like a pencil, that's it, a little more paint, no, no, no, dear, not near your mouth.* They kept their heads down, hunched over their tulips, swiping tiny dabs of paint on the same spot over and over.

His grandma had put hers aside. She fixated on her cardboard piece, as good a canvas as any. While she only had one brush and a few colours, she went straight to work, her face scrunched in concentration, which made him feel both hopeful and sad. She used long bold brush strokes, sweeping down and curving back up again.

"She's supposed to paint the tulip, not the cardboard," Jennifer told him. "Why don't you show her how it's done?"

Billy ignored her, and dipping his brush into red, zigzagged across his cardboard until the paint petered out. He'd work out a frame for the graphic novel he'd been fiddling with all year. Fig standing on top of his planet, a rocky orb not much bigger than him, shouting at the universe to stop spinning.

They continued their projects wordlessly. One of the men painted his tulip black, leaves and all, the tips of his fingers sticky with paint. The tiny woman held onto her doll while she painted orange freckles on her piece of wood, which smeared onto her elbow. Another woman asked if she could go back to her room, which caused Jennifer to sigh before nodding.

His grandma worked quickly, the blues now a shoreline of rounded rocks, an ocean lapping against them, the sky splashes of red blended into milky white. He admired how she used colour to create depth and movement, the world she imagined when she held a brush. She had tried to teach him to trust in the process, but he'd never have a fraction of her talent.

Jennifer circled the room, asking people their names, printing them with felt pen on the backs of their art pieces before setting them on the window ledge to dry. She helped each with their bibs, telling them they could go, reminding them she'd be back next week to make kites to hang in their windows.

When Jennifer got around to his grandma, she stared at their painted cardboard without saying a word. Evie's painting could go straight into some fancy art gallery. Billy didn't mind his either. He'd gotten Fig's mad terror just right, a look he usually had trouble with.

"My grandma's an artist," he said, stating the obvious. "She doesn't need our help."

"Well, I can see that. Your work is good too." Jennifer's cheeks flushed. They'd disrupted her chain of command, which seemed to upset her. "But finish up now. The table needs to be set for lunch."

As the black-tulip man shuffled out the door, she yelled, "Stop right there. You have to take off your paint smock. And you use a walker, don't you?" She marched out after him, dragging a walker, leaving Billy and his grandma alone.

"I like your painting, Grandma." He put his hand over hers.

She put down her brush and turned to him, "Oh, hello, Billy," she said. She stared at her seascape. "Did you paint this?"

"No. You did. Just now. You just finished."

"Really." She scrutinized the work more closely. "There's not enough reflection. Here and here." She reached for the orange pot, but Billy put his hand on her shoulder.

"Sorry. We have to call it quits. They need this table for lunch. Are you hungry?"

She looked about the room, the strange fridge and sink, clearly not her own. "What have we got, Billy? Is there leftover chicken?"

"We don't have to cook today," he said. As he helped Evie to her feet, Sarah pushed in a cart stacked with dishes and cutlery and jugs full of water.

"Evie went to art class. That's so great," Sarah said, leaving her cart and coming close. "So which of these flowers is yours." She peered down at their work, eyes wide, hand over her heart. "You painted these? In this class?"

"We disobeyed the teacher," Billy laughed. "No tulips for us."

"A+ for the pair of you. Let me guess. This one is Evie's. And this one's yours."

"Yep."

"It makes me want to know the whole story, Billy. Like who is this guy standing on this rock in the middle of space, and what's he yelling, and who is he yelling at? It's really something, and Evie, your work is extraordinary. It needs a frame and your signature. I'm blown away. I wish you could paint every wall in this place in these bright, bold colours."

"Really?" Billy stared at Sarah as she gathered paint pots.

"Of course, really," she said.

"You think we should paint the walls?"

She pointed to the wall with a handful of brushes. "It looks like it's been dunked in pea soup. They all do."

"We could, you know," Billy said. "Paint the walls."

Sarah laughed. "Good. And while you're at it, do something with the door at the end of the hallway. Make it look like something else so our residents quit bashing into it, trying to get out. No offence, Evie. I know *you* don't bash into doors."

"Like paint a scene, you mean? Like a flowerbed or hillside or something?"

"Why not?" Sarah scrubbed off the table's paint splotches with lightning efficiency. "A barnyard of chickens. Pigs, even."

"I could do that." Billy felt lighter than he had in weeks. "Grandma will help."

"Well, take it up with the big cheese," Sarah said. "Whoever that is this month. Lewis Clifton, if I'm not mistaken."

"Maybe I will." Billy waved as he ushered Evie out, his mind swirling with colour, the designs they might choose.

Sarah sat beside Edith, sneaking a minute between chores to help her sort through photos. A man's shouts boomed down the hall. That would be Harvey; someone must have taken his chair again.

Sarah sprinted towards the racket. Ruth had planted herself in the middle chair in front of the dining room, Harvey spread-legged in front of her. Ruth must have pulled her hearing aids out again, which was just as well. Head down, she was oblivious to Harvey's building rage as she pulled Kleenexes from her purse, building a mountain range of craggy white peaks on her lap.

Sarah put a hand on Harvey's arm, which caused him to yell in her face, "That woman is in my seat. She's not supposed to be there. I bought a ticket."

Harvey had been a train conductor his entire career. Always waiting for a train, always worried he'd miss it. Sarah smiled. "We can get a cup of coffee before the train pulls up. Let's go find one, shall we? You have lots of time."

As she manoeuvred Harvey away from Ruth, Dorothy lumbered down the hall, the type of woman who could stay upright in a hurricane, hands on hips, trees and cars hurling about.

"Good again, Harvey?" Dorothy asked, though his upset had evaporated the second both the chair, and the woman on it, were out of his view. "Really, I could hear you bellowing all the way from my office."

"These encounters can be like runaway trains," Sarah whispered, hoping for a smile that never materialized. "I thought Harvey and I could grab a coffee."

Dorothy scowled. "I'll deal with Harvey. You're needed in the Moss room. Rachel is on the warpath again. Her mother's sheets are wet."

Sarah knew only a little. The care aids liked to gossip, and those who grew up in these parts said the Mosses were a family to be avoided. Mr. Moss was known to sit in a burnt-out armchair in his front yard, case of beer at his feet, a tub of Stoker's snuff on his lap, pellet gun under his arm, pointed at the trees. He had a distrust of birds. And dogs and kids and anything that made noise. Whenever he clipped a magpie or a crow, he'd hang it upside down from a tree branch, a family of cadavers swinging in the breeze. Mrs. Moss had been seldom seen around town, but on summer nights, her screaming at her husband carried through children's open windows and into their nightmares.

Rachel was the Mosses' only child, surprising the whole town with her recent return. She'd fled Rigsbee decades ago, when she was not yet sixteen and well before she graduated from school. To where, no one could say. Mary, one of the kitchen staff, remembered her from elementary school. She was a ghost, invisible, skin and bone. She got caught sleeping in the janitor's closet when she should have been at recess. Caught stealing sandwich scraps and half-eaten apples from the lunchroom's garbage. The child never uttered a word, never showed a hint of enthusiasm for field trips or sports days or school dances. Her singular claim to fame involved an incident in Mrs. Mitchell's grade two class when she was called to the blackboard to print the day's secret story word. She stood there rigid, her back to her classmates, hands squeezed by her side. Everyone fidgeted, waiting for Rachel to lift the chalk, until finally someone yelled, *Teacher! Look!* They gasped and tittered. A river of yellow snaked down Rachel's stick leg and puddled on the floor, and yet there she stayed, a melting ice sculpture, until Mrs. Mitchell gingerly pulled her away. They called her Piddle Pants after that.

Sarah hated the gleeful pettiness in the retelling of these stories, and she turned away whenever the gossipers got going. But she couldn't unhear the snippets or get the pictures out of her head. That skeleton of a child, an outcast, no little girls' hands to hold, no shoulder to bury into, no homemade cookies or orange wedges in her lunch bag. People must have guessed what had been going on in that home. And no one stepped forward.

She knocked before entering the deathly quiet room. "Morning, Rachel. How's your mom today?"

Rachel leaned over the bed, dabbing rouge over her mother's milky cheeks. Victoria Moss had mere days left, weeks at most.

"Never any sense in letting yourself go." Rachel snapped shut the compact as she surveyed her artistry. Victoria, motionless, lay like a soul lost in the morgue. Rachel herself seemed rosy and robust, everything about her an explosion of eye-popping colour.

"I wish I could do her hair." She'd arranged her own hair into a sleek upstyle, wisps framing her face, a touch of softness to the polished look.

An ache squeezed Sarah's chest. Despite the tales of Rachel's dismal childhood, here she was. She'd been coming to the unit for weeks. Occasionally she took breaks, wandering the halls or stretching in the lunchroom. Mostly, she stood vigil in this sad, lonely room, hour after endless hour.

"I'm a hairdresser," Rachel said.

Sarah grinned. "Well, that explains it. You always look like you've stepped out of a beauty salon."

"I would have loved to give Mom a perm."

Sarah shuddered to think of it. Victoria's perm days were long over, her thinning hair matted to her scalp like wood ash.

"Her sheet is wet again," Rachel said. "And she stinks. I told Dorothy. If looks could kill! Just because the government subsidizes her bed doesn't mean she deserves a wet diaper."

Sarah nodded; families' finances were none of her business.

"God knows, I couldn't spring for this 5-star resort." Rachel scrutinized the oppressive room, forcing air through her nose, a rough harsh sound. "All my father left her was a shitbox house, mine to get rid of."

Sarah hoped the house sale would give her enough to start over.

"Dorothy must think since it's not our money, I demand too much."

"You're not demanding at all. And we'll fix her right up. It's hard to get the diapers snug when she's so tiny." Sarah looked between the hearty daughter and the skin-and-bone mother with the sunken rouged cheeks. A karmic reversal had unfolded across the years.

She slipped on disposable gloves and changed the wet diaper. Then she gently rolled the woman to one side of the bed, her body weightless, like turning a page in an ancient book.

"If it's any consolation, wet is a good sign," Sarah said. "It means your mother is not dehydrated." Rachel stood with her arms crossed. Four hands might have been better than two, but she could not blame her for staying on the sidelines.

Sarah removed the wet sheet and laid out the fresh one on the exposed part of the mattress. With Victoria rolled back again onto a waterproof pad, she pulled the sheet taunt and tucked in the edges with hospital corners.

"There we go. Good as new." Sarah bundled up the dirty linen, pulled her gloves off, and scrubbed her hands. Neither mother nor daughter moved. Neither made a sound. She came back to the bed and rested her palm on Rachel's back. "She seems comfortable now," she whispered. "Her breathing is steady, and she's not in any pain."

"We weren't close," Rachel stated matter of factly. "We hadn't spoken in decades."

Sarah was taken aback by her unblinking disclosure. It was as if she believed she didn't deserve more.

"I'm so sor—"

"Maybe she knows I'm here."

"Of course she does."

"How much longer?"

Sarah shook her head helplessly. She wanted to lead Rachel away, feed her warm cookies and milk.

"Will you be doing hair here in Rigsbee, Rachel?"

"Oh," she said, as if she hadn't considered it. No wonder, stuck like she was in this wilderness.

"Well, the town would be lucky to have you. You should have your own salon."

Rachel squinted and pursed her lips, as though imagining her name in lights. *Moss Locks. Rachel's Renewals.*

"And you could do makeup too."

Rachel nodded. "It can be a slippery slope. Stop with the mascara and eyeliner and the next thing you know you're prancing down the street in sweatpants and no bra."

"Exactly. We need your flair around here."

Rachel smiled. A hint of light shone through her, as if a crack in the obstinate wall of death might acknowledge a fresh start.

Sarah had three rooms to finish before lunch. She hadn't done much for this woman, just a moment of tenderness between them. Sometimes a moment was enough.

Chapter 5

Nick turned left instead of right at the stop sign. If Billy noticed they were going the wrong way, he didn't comment.

Nick was driving him to the new skate park before supper. He hadn't seen it yet himself. Given the objections splashed across the pages of the *Rigsbee Globe*—*too dangerous, too noisy, spawning grounds for drug deals*—the town consigned it to the far side of the tracks, away from Rigsbee's toddlers and toddling seniors.

Nick hoped they'd find kids Billy's age doing jumps and flips, yelling and laughing. He hoped Billy might show some spark when he saw it. But when Nick pulled into the lot, the park sat empty, and Billy sat unmoved, head tilted back on the headrest. Nick cut the engine.

"This is the new skate park," he said. It wasn't as impressive as he'd hoped. "You can come here whenever. Want to get out and take a look?"

"Nope."

"Just thought you'd like to see it. You like skateboarding?"

"Nope."

"Have you tried it?"

"Nope."

Nick tried to keep calm. "Then you don't know, do you? It's pretty cool." Did kids even say cool anymore? "They've got a skateboard section at Home Hardware. Knee pads. Elbow pads. Everything you need. We can check it out."

Billy sneered. "I'll pass. Why don't you take a look. You seem pretty worked up about it."

Nick imagined smacking the kid on the side of his head. He started the engine and slammed the gear into reverse.

"I've got other plans." Billy clasped his fingers and stretched his arms.

Nick pressed on the brake hard, his ribs jamming against his seatbelt. "What plans?" He'd hoped the kid had found a long-lost uncle to go to. But it wasn't that. He was going to paint the walls in Evelyn's hallway.

"You're going to paint walls?"

"Not just one colour. Scenes and stuff. Murals. And the door by Grandma's room too. To make it less obvious it's a way out."

"When did you come up with this . . ." Nick wanted to say *asinine idea* but didn't.

"Sarah says you should talk to Lewis Clifton. That guy with the clipboard. I need his permission."

"You talked to Sarah about this?" She'd seemed like a woman with her head on straight.

"It was her idea. She thinks Grandma's a good artist. She thinks I'm okay too."

"I'm not questioning your artistic skills, Billy. I'm sure you're great. I know you are. I've seen your paintings in Evie's room." The framed prints he'd bought had long since disappeared.

"Those are Grandma's, not mine."

"Maybe you could paint our walls. At home. Spruce the place up a bit."

"No thanks."

Nick backed the truck up slowly. He'd get them home. Put hamburgers on the barbeque. Kids liked burgers. Billy could watch TV, get caught up in a cop show, and forget this stupid idea.

"So when'll you talk to Lewis Clifton?" Billy wanted to know.

"It's an institution. They have standards and protocols for what goes on their walls. You'll find other things to do, Billy."

"Like what? Skateboard?" He shook his head in disgust. "Painting the walls is better than staring at them."

A train was coming, a long pull of its horn. Nick sped up, his tires rumbling over the tracks as the arm started to descend.

"You don't have to spend all your time there. Let Evie settle in. And you too. There's stuff to do in this town. You can make new friends before school starts up." Nick looked up and down the empty sidewalks, searching for gangs to throw his boy at. He'd pay bribe money to get him onto the streets.

Billy said, "Lewis Clifton's office is by the front entrance. He never leaves it, so he's easy to find."

He was worse than a hound with a bone. "So let's say Clifton agrees. Who's going to pay for the paint? How are you going to know what to get? What colours?"

"I'll work up some designs. Grandma will help. She knows her way around a paint store."

Nick blew air out his lips. "Take Evie to the paint store?"

"Why not? She hasn't broken any laws. I'm sure we can spring her on a day pass."

Nick pulled up to the house. It had been the longest five-minute drive of his life. "This is a big project you're talking about. You can't get halfway through and quit. School will be starting in a couple months, and then you'll be into other things."

Billy opened his door before Nick cut the engine. "I'm not you. I finish what I start." The door slammed behind him.

Nick stayed where he was, locked behind his seatbelt. It was not yet even five o'clock. He had supper to get through, then the whole long evening, then all the rest, one long night after another, just the two of them.

Billy and Nick ate burgers, the only noise to break the silence their pounding on the ketchup bottle. After they cleared the dishes, Billy shut himself in his room. He sat cross-legged on the bed, fiddling with ideas for murals, but when nothing came, he took out his graphic novel. His original concept was that Fig didn't fit in, so he built a planet for himself where he could be who he wanted without anyone telling him otherwise. He half-heartedly added details to Fig's expression of defiance. But the more he tried to draw, the more he questioned the storyline. Maybe he had imagined it all wrong. Maybe Fig didn't build a planet, he got dumped on a planet. Maybe a supervillain stole him in the night. He looked up disgustedly and studied his surroundings, the barren walls, the curtainless window, this place as foreign and far from home as Fig's desolate rock.

He hurled his sketchpad, the loud thunk reverberating against the door. Ten seconds later, Nick poked his head in.

"You could knock," Billy yelled, jumping up. He grabbed his sketchpad and burrowed it under his pillow.

"Sorry," Nick said. "You okay in here?"

Billy nodded.

"I thought you might want to use the computer. Google wall murals or something. I've set it up for you in the kitchen." He walked away before Billy could answer.

Billy didn't want Nick breathing down his neck, but he wasn't getting anywhere with his sketches. He needed stuff to look at other than what lived in his head. So he left his room and sat at the table in front of Nick's laptop. Nick stayed on the couch, watching a baseball game, the TV on low. After a while, Billy forgot he was there.

Nick's laptop was rocket-fast. Billy's old one had chugged along, whirring and wheezing, taking an eternity to load even the simplest of web pages. A few weeks before Nick showed up in Chetville, the screen blared a system failure message, like an omen of bad things to come, before conking out for good.

Now he scrolled through image after image—walls made to look like forests and oceans and vineyards and downtown Manhattan. It frustrated rather than inspired him. The images were too complex, too commercial, photographs enlarged and stuck to the walls on pre-pasted wallpaper. They were more than Billy could draw.

He googled walls in old folks' homes, where he found shop front windows—candy stores, bookstores—nothing that grabbed him.

Nick pulled a beer from the fridge and stood over his shoulder. "Is that what you're thinking?" He peered down at the painted umbrella stand beside a coat rack. "It looks kinda cartoonish to me."

Billy wanted to slam the computer lid shut. He didn't need advice from this guy.

Nick said, "Maybe you want to think about local scenes, close-to-home stuff that the old people around here would relate to. Prairies and cows."

Billy closed Google; he'd call it a night. But there it was, the background on the computer screen. A wooden bridge on logs rising out of the water, yellow grasses and cattails, a winding path and bushes off in the distance. The colours were right. He could paint this.

"That's the boardwalk from Goose Lake," Nick said, pointing to the screen. "One of the few spots not torn to shreds."

"This is your photograph?"

"Yeah."

Billy didn't want to admit it, but that's the one he wanted.

Billy and Evelyn sat in the chairs at the end of the hallway, Harvey between them, waiting for his train. Harvey kept looking at his large watch, but it was upside down, time frozen at twenty after eleven. Time stood still in this place, dragging on and on and on.

One of the staff had dropped a basket of wool in front of them. She winked at Billy and said she could use their help. If they could just roll the wool into balls—*like this*, she demonstrated, pulling a wool string from the basket and wrapping it round and round her fingers, then sliding it off her hand, scrunching it in half, wrapping the other way.

"Keep going round from different angles until it's as big as a baseball. I want to see great big, beautiful balls," she said before trotting off.

So the three of them sat there, doing what they were told, making great big beautiful balls. His grandma chose blue, wrapping meticulously, turning the wool this way and that. He and Harvey had trouble with theirs. Billy picked orange, but kept losing focus, the lump on his lap more carrot-shaped than round. Harvey's, a mess of tangles, kept dropping to the floor and Billy kept bending down and picking it up. Harvey said he could not abide a late train, there was no excuse for it, to which Billy agreed. Beyond that, there was not much to talk about.

Billy was thinking about the painting project. He'd hardly slept last night, his brains on fire as he visualized every wall. He would break it into sections. Down Grandma's hall, cattails and yellow grass coming up from the floor to the chair rail. Clouds and birds in the sky. Train tracks and a grain elevator farther down. Harvey would like that.

It was stupid to dwell on it. Lewis Clifton said definitely not, painting was out of budget and out of schedule and the independents needed new flooring, but when Nick pressed him about customer satisfaction and quality of life and family involvement bullshit, Clifton hemmed and hawed and said he'd take it up with Toronto. What a dipshit.

Billy was surprised by Nick, the way he crossed his arms and stood his ground and did all the talking, like he was pitching a brilliant idea. When they left Clifton's office, Nick said, "We gave it our best shot." Fight over, case settled. He told Billy he would pick him up for lunch today, no arguing, and he should be at the front door at noon.

Harvey had fallen asleep in his chair, his head tilting towards his grandma. She'd already moved onto yellow, her ball of sun growing fatter by the minute.

Rachel came towards them from down the hall. Today's earrings were mind-blowing, a mesmerizing tangle of translucent flowers and leaves dangling from beaded vines in clusters as big as fists. They were the most interesting things he'd seen in this place. Any place.

"I see they've got you doing the wool. Busy hands make happy hearts and all that." She laughed and so did his grandma, but when he shrugged, she crunched her eyes and studied him more closely. "Although you look rather glum. Not despair, I hope."

Billy stared at her ears and asked her what she thought of the walls.

"The walls?" She looked about, frowning. "Bloody awful puke green."

Billy spilled the details of his painting idea. She walked down the hall with him, pointing to each wall, asking what kind of scene he envisioned, what kind of paint he'd need, whether he'd work from drawings or photographs. He talked fast, his voice cracking. When they got to the end, he kicked his runner against the door, and said, "But it's no good talking about it. Lewis Clifton says no."

Rachel snorted. "Figures. So you talked to him already?"

"We went to his office this morning. He says they don't have the money."

"Who went? You and your father?"

He nodded.

"See. He's getting the hang of this daddy stuff. He supports the project?"

"Totally," Billy lied. "And so does Sarah. It was her idea."

Rachel pulled a Kleenex from her sleeve and blew her nose violently, earring flowers swaying from the storm. "And this is really what you want? To spend your summer holed up in here with this lot?"

He did.

She stared at him like he'd gone bonkers.

In defence, he stammered, "I could have done it."

"Giving up so soon?"

"Lewis Clifton said if they did have the money they'd hire professionals, not a kid. It's not like I was asking to be paid or anything. And Grandma would have helped. She's a real artist."

"Don't worry about Lewis Clifton," she said dismissively. "He's a pencil pusher and his job is to say no."

"But he's the one who gets to make the rules."

"And who says you can't break them? I'll deal with Clifton. In fact, I'll go find him now."

With a swift swipe of her fob, she opened the door and strode off, leaving Billy standing there with his mouth open, trying to make sense of her words. It didn't have to be hopeless. If Rachel could pull off those earrings, maybe she could pull this off too.

Chapter 6

B illy put his dishes in the sink. The meatballs tasted like sawdust and the rice was burned. He missed his grandma's oven chicken.

"You're kidding?" Nick repeated. "They're letting you paint wall murals?"

Billy wished he'd kept his mouth shut. He headed towards his bedroom, a knot in his stomach. He had a lot to work out.

"Wait a minute," Nick grabbed him by the shoulder. Billy furiously shook him off.

"Sorry. Sit. We need to talk."

Billy slumped back down at the kitchen table. He could too easily be talked out of his stupid idea right now. He didn't need Nick's grilling.

Nick sat across from him. "So what changed Clifton's mind? He seemed pretty adamant the painting project was a no-go."

"Rachel."

"Who's Rachel?"

"Rachel's mom is next door to Grandma."

Nick leaned back and laughed. "She must be a ball-buster."

Nick had nothing good to say about anybody.

"She thinks it's a good idea," Billy said defensively. "And she's going to pay for everything." Although not exactly. Rachel told him she didn't have two cents to rub together before she showed up in Rigsbee. She said she nearly died when she found the stash of cash in the shitbox house. Her mother's escape money, Rachel called it. She didn't say what her mom was escaping from, just that she'd never gotten around to it, the crumbled pile growing fatter and mouldier with each passing year. *My mother's life stayed stuffed inside that rotting mattress*, were her exact words.

He turned to Nick and stared. "So can you drive us to the paint store or not?"

"Hold on, okay." Nick touched his arm lightly. "Look, I think murals are a good idea too. Bloody brilliant. They'll make it more . . . livable. So yeah, I'll drive you to the paint store."

Billy crossed his arms, eying Nick sideways. If Nick had his way, Billy would play in the sandbox all day.

"So why don't we just go over the plan," Nick said. "You're the painter. How do you paint a mural?"

Billy rolled his eyes. "With paint. And brushes."

"I get that part, smartass. But it's a big surface. A whole wall. You're going to need ladders, maybe scaffolding. The right light. How do you even start something like that?"

Billy felt his stomach flip. How was he going to start? And yeah, he would need a ladder. What if he couldn't lay in the shapes right? What if he got the sizing all wrong?"

"So, do you know what you're going to paint? What scenes?"

"Yeah."

"So?"

"Cattails. A wooden bridge. Trees. That kind of stuff."

Nick pulled over his laptop and flipped the lid. There they were. Cattails. "You mean something like this?" he asked.

Billy nodded. They both stared at the computer screen.

"Well, let's find it then." Nick moved his chair close to Billy and clicked on his photos folder. He found the original in the Goose Lake batch. "Why don't you take a look through? See if there's anything else you like."

Billy took over the mouse, scrolling slowly. Folder after folder, one photo at a time. It was hard to choose. Big skies and rolled hay bales, yellow fields, red grain elevators. Nick might be lousy at seeing things in real life, but he had a good eye for photography.

"Do you have any trains?" Billy asked.

"Yeah, maybe. Try Big Valley."

Billy found the one he wanted. Big red train cars battered with graffiti in the foreground, getting smaller as they snaked along the tracks and towards the hills, the sky a pool of crimson, spilling light over the white clouds and golden fields. Paintable. He'd skip the graffiti. Harvey would love it.

"Choose the ones you like, and we'll put them on a flash drive so they're all in one place. We can get them printed. Enlarged, if you want."

As Billy clicked on photos, saving them to the flash drive, Nick asked, "Are you going to sketch out the scenes first? On paper? You could make a grid. Do the math, transfer the grid to the wall, blow it up. You get what I mean?"

He'd already thought about a grid. He'd used one for the Garbage Bin Paint-Off in grade six, winning the competition with his carousel horses. The problem was Evie. She could paint anything from a photo. From a drawing. But a grid might confuse her, the scale too big for her to wrap her brains around. And if he was going to do this, he needed her beside him.

Nick had a dumb way of staring.

"A grid's not gonna work." Billy stood, itching to be alone where he could think.

"Stay here," Nick said. He rummaged through the closet by the front door and came back with what looked like an old video player, only with a camera lens. It was covered in dust. He set the thing on the table, plugged it in, and pressed the button, which started with a low hum. "Good. It still works."

"What is it?" Billy asked.

"A digital projector. Short throw, which means you don't need a lot of room. It takes a minute to warm up." He plugged the flash drive into the box and turned on the lamp. "There, look on the wall."

There it was. The cattails photo. The full deal, floor to ceiling. Extraordinary. Nick fiddled with the zoom and brought the picture into sharper focus.

They both looked hard at the scene draped over the TV and the messy bookshelf and spreading across the cracks in the wall.

"Do you think this will work?" Nick said.

Billy tried to see it through his grandma's eyes, imagining her in front of it, bringing the wall to life, the wall bringing her to life. "It might," he said. It would. "Thanks," he added after a pause.

"Good. I'll rent you the projector. Plus $500 per photo."

Billy looked closely at Nick for the first time. He seemed earnest, pleased, as though he'd been waiting for this moment. They stood like that, staring at each other until Billy's neck started to heat and he had to turn away.

Nick was amazed at how Evelyn took charge in the hardware store, the only place in town that carried paint supplies. She lost all frailty, so at ease, her breathing low and steady as she pushed her cart, the set of photographs lined up along the child seat. He couldn't fathom why her hand went for certain brushes, rejected others. How she chose the paint swatches, dozens of them, colour after colour he'd not thought of, talking to herself as she laid them on the table. *We need a titch more purple. Blue as blue can be, are we.* She and Billy worked together, like they had their own language, and he was missing a translator.

Nick stood at the cash register and watched each item being scanned. Rachel had given Billy a wad of cash a day earlier. She'd made a point of emphasizing that price was no object. For some baffling reason, the boy needed this, not skateboards or baseball games. Nick figured Billy would sour on the project before the week was out, but that was Rachel's problem, not his.

It took two trips to get the supplies from the truck to the dementia door. Paint cans and tubes, brushes and rollers, tarps and tape. Billy took Evelyn to the bathroom, while Nick stacked the works on the shelves in the laundry room.

Sarah marched in with a heaping basket of clothes, nearly crashing into him. "Oh goodness," she said. "We have to stop meeting like this."

Nick laughed.

"You've taken over my laundry room." She heaved her basket onto a dryer and swiped the back of her hand across her forehead. She had bags under her eyes like she hadn't slept in a week.

"Busy day?" he asked.

"Busy night. Neighbours, not me."

"Ah, neighbour problems. Mine are the four-legged variety. Coyotes like a good serenade. So, yours? Which neighbours are creating the ruckus?"

"It's the yahoos in the apartment above us. They stomp all night, music blaring."

"There should be a law against stupid. And lousy construction. I'll bet the contractors skimped on the insulation. It's unnatural, sticking people on top of each other."

Sarah sighed and turned to inspect the labels on the paint cans, reading down the line. "Spring Sky, Jewelled Peach, Violet Blush. I can't believe they went for it. And Rachel's paid for the whole thing! Which is supposed to be a secret, by the way. It's so lovely."

"I wouldn't get too excited. Billy could give up before he starts."

"He seems pretty determined." She pressed buttons on the commercial-sized washer and measured detergent.

"Don't you think it's weird?" he said. "He seems so out of step. Like he's missing all the teenage markers. Shouldn't he be at the football field or sneaking smokes in the back alley?"

"You haven't met my five-year-old. Carter wears rain boots and a helmet wherever he goes, including the bathroom."

"Okay, that's weird."

Sarah laughed as she sorted through old lady underwear and slopped bibs and tossed them into the barrel.

He shifted his weight from one foot to the other, hands fidgeting with the edges of his shirt. He wasn't ready to let the subject go. "One minute Billy acts like a little kid in need of a bedtime story, but then the next, he's an old man, fussing over the room temperature and the state of Evelyn's wardrobe. I don't know if I should be giving him playdough or a briefcase. Now he's engineering this massive project. God help us all. What am I supposed to do with him?"

Sarah fanned out her arms and shrugged.

"Come on," he said. "You got nothing?"

She curled her lips in a playful grin. "How about playdough in a briefcase?"

"So helpful."

She fixed him with a serious gaze. "Billy had to give up a bunch of his childhood to start caregiving. If he seems out of step, it's because he's missed out on a lot. But he's had to grow up quickly too. Wouldn't it make sense that he seems both young for his age and mature? He's a wise old soul still growing into his boots, trying to find his footing."

She was right, of course. This woman was a wise soul too. He wondered if she had a partner or if she was raising her kid alone. "Is it just you and Carter then?"

She sang her answer from the song, "Just the two of us," which made it seem easy.

He eyed the laundry baskets with names taped to the sides. "How do you know whose are whose?"

"I have X-ray vision. Plus, I help people get dressed. Plus, everything's labelled. You've labelled Evie's stuff, right?"

"I have to label her stuff?" The thought of going through Evelyn's personal things made his stomach lurch.

"Yep. It's all there in the orientation brochure. Page one. You obviously haven't done your homework. D-minus for you."

"How are you supposed to label underpants?"

"You embroider her name on rose-coloured labels and sew them to the back of all her panties. And to everything else."

Nick stood there dumbly. Maybe he could get Billy to do it.

Sarah burst out laughing. "You can use a permanent felt marker. And I've done it already. Even her panties. Saved you, yet again."

He could have hugged her. Instead, he blurted, "I don't have a clue what I'm doing. With Billy. Or Evelyn."

Sarah sighed. "Who does? We all just muddle through."

"But you've had Carter from the beginning. You've had a hand in shaping him. I don't get Billy at all."

"But you will. And don't you dare blame me for Carter's helmet and rainboots."

"I'm not sure I want this." There, he'd said it out loud. To another person. To someone good.

It didn't seem to unsettle her. "You will," she said. "And for what it's worth, half the time I'm not sure I want my life either. Muddle, muddle, muddle. That's how you do it." She slammed the machine lid closed. "That will be two hundred dollars, please. Twenty-five for the laundry lesson. One-seventy-five for the wise words."

Dorothy marched through the doorway, towering over Sarah. "Who gave you permission to put this paint in our laundry room?"

"That would be Lewis Clifton," Nick piped up cheerily.

"We'll see about that," Dorothy muttered. "If an auditor shows up, we'll be cited for safety concerns. This area is for laundry, not storage. It's designated staff only." She glared at Sarah. "And those cans are too heavy. If that shelf breaks, someone could lose an eye. Or worse."

Dorothy reached up and pushed the paint cans further back on their shelves. Nick rolled his eyes, which made Sarah press her lips and stare at her shoes.

Dorothy crossed her arms and examined Sarah. "Shouldn't the tables be set by now?"

Nick wanted to stuff the woman in the washing machine. Sarah blushed, the skin around her freckles turning a brilliant pink. "Sorry. Heading to the dining room now."

He stepped in front of Sarah, facing Dorothy. "Entirely my fault," he said. "I've held her up. She's been helping me learn the rules. Excellent customer service. That's the whole point in these places, right? Keeping the paying customers happy."

Sarah sidestepped through the door and disappeared.

Dorothy sneered. "This is health care, Mr. Ackerman. Not an amusement park. Not rainbow colours and finger painting. You have no idea what it takes to run this place."

Nick gave her his best smile. "But it doesn't have to be nasty, does it? Health care, I mean. It could be pleasant too." He flicked off the light switch as he exited, leaving mad Dorothy alone in the dark where she belonged.

Chapter 7

July 10th. Nick had to go back to work on Monday. Some vacation. Three weeks of Billy felt like ten years hard time with no chance of parole.

He wondered why the kid wanted the damn murals so badly, the project a manifesto—*this place sucks, my father sucks, life sucks*—the walls the proof, needing to be covered over. Billy seemed both excited and terrified at what he'd taken on. Nick would catch him chewing on his lip as he hunched over his drawings, his eyes lighting up when he got something right. With Nick, he was as sullen as ever, turning away from his questions with a stone-cold look.

Nick picked him up at Prairie View before supper each day. Billy dragged his feet, paint splats in his hair, blobs of colour on his T-shirt and jeans. It was obvious he hadn't given up, but the particulars were scarce. Nick could have gone inside to see for himself, and while he was tempted to see Sarah again, the place gave him the creeps, so he stayed in the truck.

"How's the project going?" Nick asked every time Billy slammed the truck door. He'd drum his fingers on the steering wheel, refusing to take his foot off the brake until Billy gave him an answer. "Good," he'd finally mumble. Every time.

He'd dropped Billy off first thing that morning, then headed west. He wasn't sure what sick compulsion kept bringing him back to the place where he started. He pulled the truck into the ditch along the county road and hopped the new gate with the No Trespassing sign. There was a stack of Overdale Developments' permits stapled to the wooden post. The grand plan included rows of upscale country cottages weaving around spring-fed canals, a boat dock and playground, a scenic walking bridge built high above the water, ATV trails. The house and its wrap-around veranda, the tree and its tire swing, the vast and pristine acres on all sides—all of it to be bulldozed.

He'd failed miserably in slowing any of it. After the last dead-end trip to the county office, he'd couriered a thick package of Goose Lake photos to Ducks Unlimited, with a cover page that read DO SOMETHING scrawled in fat black letters. He'd let his membership lapse years ago, along with everything else that required a scintilla of commitment. He did not expect to hear back.

He walked along the private road that wound through the trees, ignoring the diggers waiting to tear through it all. Back when his parents ran the campground, he'd spent his childhood on this land. He stared at the rambling old house on top of the hill, its shingles and peeling paint, his bedroom window beneath the gable. Behind it was the black pit that used to be Campers Hall, the heartbeat of the place, now a smattering of foundation stones and jagged charred posts. He forced himself to turn away from its gravitational pull.

The old campground sites were nothing like their former selves, overrun by thistle and weeds, bushes spilling over the spots where the tents were once pitched. It was hard to tell where one site ended and the next began.

He sat on top of a rotted picnic table. This had been the Robsons' site. Number thirty-seven. Mrs. Robson came with the twins, Randy and Zak, at the end of each June. When they were little, Nick had run alongside them barefoot in the sand, darting behind trees for games of hide-and-seek, lighting firecrackers inside Coke cans. The Robsons had a two-room tent with rows of dingle balls on the outside canopy. They'd move the picnic table, the one he sat on now, into the screened veranda, away from the mosquitoes. Mrs. Robson and the boys stayed until late August each year, her husband joining them from the city on weekends.

If you cut through site forty-two, where the gravel road stopped and the deer path started, you would enter the wild, zigzagging through untouched wetlands, wild bushes and sedges, cattails exploding in the quiet shallows.

It would be torn away soon, the earth, the shoreline, even the stars, the bright lights of progress obliterating what once shone in this place.

Nick could walk through the overgrown sites and name the regulars who'd camped there. He could still see the pup tents and tent trailers and tarps strung on trees. Kerosene lamps, coolers in trunks, mismatched lawn chairs around fires, tins of tobacco and packages of rolling paper, beach toys scattered about. Nothing fancy. The big motor homes went to the other side of the lake, paying five times as much to take forty-minute showers and run TVs and air conditioners day and night.

In the mornings, you could smell bacon sizzling, coffee perking. At night, fires roared beneath black starry skies. Flashes of lightning. Bats swooping above.

Down at the beach, you'd see water volleyball games and horse-shoes tournaments. Babies crawling in the wet sand; teenage girls slathered in oil and lying on towels; teenage boys playing frisbee in the water, trying to impress the girls; parents with a beer and a book in their hands; dogs galore given free run.

Squeals of laughter echoed off the lake all summer long. The smell of wood smoke permeated everything. During a downpour, campers would cover their heads with garbage bags and run with go-cups filled with brandy to Campers Hall, the central gathering place and his family's pride and joy.

Campers Hall had been an intergenerational Ackerman project. His father designed and built the large two-storey structure with the help of his own father when Nick was still in diapers. Campers could come and go as they pleased. On rainy days, they pulled games out of the cupboard, shuffling decks at the wooden tables scattered about. Women sank into the deep couch to knit and visit in front of the massive stone fireplace. Readers borrowed books from the antique bookcase passed down through the Ackerman generations. Rain or shine, kids came in herds to buy chips and candy from the Tuck Shop, a room no bigger than a closet, dropping change their parents had given them into the honour system bucket. Photos of campers' growing families plastered the walls; trophies for the annual competitions shone through the glass door cabinet that Nick had built with his dad. It was more than a building. Laughter and memories echoed through the rafters.

Nick turned away from those thoughts, wandered down to the beach, and sat on a washed-up log. He kicked off his runners and buried his toes in the sand. A cool breeze came off the water, and the waves frothed lazily at the shoreline. He'd sat in this very spot a thousand times, ten thousand times.

How lucky he'd been. He'd lived for those summers.

That last one ended when he was seventeen. He worked at the campground, same as every other summer since he was eleven. The stakes felt higher that year; he'd be leaving in the fall for engineering school, and he needed to save enough to keep his student loans down. There were no free rides in the Ackerman family.

His parents were demanding, but fair, and paid him overtime for extra. They expected a lot of their only son; in return, they let him set his own schedule and work as he chose. It was his call when to mow the grass or weed the garden or scrub the outhouses. His job to clear the drains of the communal shower rooms. When new arrivals showed, he manoeuvred their tent trailers into the tight spots. He helped set up tents and tarps, chopped and hauled wood, emptied garbage bins, bandaged the scabbed knees of the kids that followed him constantly. He scrambled up tree trunks and hacked off the broken branches after a hailstorm. Captured the raccoons that holed up under the deck, drove them east, opened the cage's trap door, and watched them waddle away.

Something always needed fixing. An outhouse roof. The chainsaw blade or kitchen chimney flue. A leaking tap or tire. He fixed more by feel than by book learning. His mother told him that when he was four, he'd disassembled the stereo with his miniature electrical set, tubes and wires scattered across the floor.

He liked taking stuff apart. Back then, he had a knack for putting things together again too.

Each summer since puberty he'd choose a new campground girl, sometimes two or three, depending on how long they stayed. He avoided the loyalists, the ones whose families would come back. There were plenty of options. Plenty of pretty girls in skimpy bikinis, clear-skinned and freckle-faced; girls too timid to look him in the eye; girls who had their tongues down his throat before he could ask their name. He didn't want love or commitment; the conquest was the prize.

That summer was Miranda. Miranda Peat. He'd not thought of her in years, not until Billy.

She showed up in a rusted red Buick near the middle of July. Miranda and another young woman, who had registered for a two-week stay under the name Simone de Beauvoir. He'd never heard the name before, so his mother explained. *"One is not born, but rather becomes a woman,"* Simone de Beauvoir—author, feminist, thinker—one of his mother's heroes from her college days. They discussed her at length at the dinner table. *C'est bien. Let her pretend to be Simone,* his mother had joked. *Those girls will spice things up around here.*

Both Miranda and Simone wore tie-dyed skirts and Birkenstocks and had long yellow hair—old hippies in young bodies. They pitched their tent in less than five minutes. After that, they kept to themselves, reading fat books in front of the fire pit. Sometimes they disappeared into the wetlands and didn't return for hours.

Nick gleaned a little about them from the other campers. Calvin Pond, in the next site over, swore they ate nothing but fruits and nuts, like squirrels, brewing their own teas from forest forages, reading the tea leaves for all he knew. Teresa White, while trying to quiet her cranky baby at sunrise, stumbled upon Miranda heading back from a swim. *At that ridiculous hour? She didn't even have a towel with her.* The campers' dogs loved her, even Spoof, an irritable and standoffish old hound. He trailed after her every step, settled in front of her camp chair as if she were his new master.

Nick had his first up-close encounter with Miranda early on her second morning. He came upon her bent upside down in front of the water pump, a chill still in the air, hair flowing nearly down to the ground. She had a bottle of shampoo in her hand.

"Whoa, whoa," Nick said, or something like that. "You sure you want to do that."

She poked her head up and pushed hair from her face. She had the most startling green eyes.

"Why not?" she asked. "It's biodegradable."

"That water's cold. Really cold. You'll get brain freeze. There's a shower house at the end of Row 1."

"I like cold." She raised her hand to the pump.

"Okay, well, I'll work it for you."

He expected her to scream but she merely moved her head into the flow, adjusting the angle of her neck to take the cold full on. Nick pumped the metal arm, again and again, until every strand was soaked.

He watched while she lathered her mass of blonde into foam and worked the pump for her until all traces were gone. When she came up, hair plastered to her goose-bumped skin, he was startled by her enormous eyes and long wet eyelash clumps. It was as if he could see more of her than he had just the moment before.

"You must be frozen." Her T-shirt was soaked, and she hadn't even brought a towel. He felt overdressed, cowardly, looming in front of this fearless girl.

She laughed. "Well, that got rid of the cobwebs." She gathered up her hair to one side and twisted and squeezed, water pouring out of her into puddles on the ground. "Thanks for your help."

"Helping campers, that's what I do." He cringed as soon as he said it, but he gave a thumbs-up, which made her smile. "I'm Nick. This is my parents' place."

"I know. I've heard the kids calling your name. I'm Miranda." She extended her hand formally, and he took it. He chose her for his summer girl in that moment, her small hand inside his.

Except she wasn't. Not like the others.

Nick never saw her at Campers Hall or at the beach or wearing a bathing suit. He stopped by their campsite often, failing to get her attention. *Can I bring you more firewood? Move your table into the shade?* Miranda waved him away with a smile, like he was an annoying yet harmless bug.

Mrs. Robson, a persistent interrogator, managed to coax Miranda to her campsite for an afternoon iced tea. She shared the findings with Nick's mom, who relayed the details over supper. Miranda had been raised in Vancouver and French-schooled since kindergarten. Her father died in a dreadful accident on the Coquihalla just as she was about to graduate. She and her mother packed up their lives and moved to small-town Alberta. As Mrs. Robson told it, the girl had been wandering ever since. She planned to backpack through Australia in the fall. *On her own and so young! All those snakes in the grass. What is her mother thinking?*

"You know the funniest thing," Nick's mom added as they were drying the dishes. "I assumed Simone and Miranda were lifelong buddies. Forever best girlfriends. But it seems they just met on the road. They've only known each other a few weeks. Imagine that. Isn't it amazing how people find each other?"

Nick tried his best to make his own connection. He invited her to beach volleyball games and bonfire nights, but she gracefully declined, which made him feel small. By day six, he was ready to give up and move on. A fiery redhead from Saskatchewan had arrived. She had a mean pitching arm and manhandled her little brothers with ease while they climbed her legs and clung to her every word.

But then Miranda came out of the water, and everything changed. When he first saw her, naked and glistening, he panicked, as if he'd been caught at something. It was after midnight, all the campers were asleep; he'd been nearly asleep too, but he remembered he'd left the chainsaw in the bushes, so he'd snuck out of the house to retrieve it.

She was a mirage, nothing a person could prepare for. She waded out of the lake and towards him. Her towel hung on a tree branch, so close he could have reached out and pulled it down. She smiled as she came closer, not the least bit embarrassed.

"Are you a good person?" she asked. She stood before him naked under the stars, not waiting for him to deny it. "Of course you are."

That's all it took. She wanted none of the smooth talk he'd mastered with the others. She leaned into him, her wet skin smelling like lake, her lips shiny as ice, her breasts fitting perfectly in his cupped palms. He yanked his hoodie over his head, fumbled with his zipper, laid down with her in the cool sand. She clung to him as he thrust into her with everything he had. He was spent in all of ten seconds. Never even got his socks off.

He rolled away and lay on his back. He didn't know how to explain his pathetic performance.

She stretched out in the sand and stared at the stars. "Let's say you've been dropped from a plane. You'll be rescued in a week. You can only bring one thing. What would it be?"

He felt immensely relieved. And bewildered. What had just happened? Who was this girl?

"Am I wearing clothes?" he said.

Miranda laughed. "Yes, of course. Why wouldn't you be?" She threw her leg over his. Her skin felt warm, even though it was chilly, and she was still damp from her swim.

"Is it summer or winter?"

"Fall. You're in the wilderness. The ground is coated with decaying leaves."

She seemed impervious to cold.

"I'd bring you. In a waterproof bag."

She sighed. "You have to do this on your own, Nick. That's the whole point."

"But they're coming back to get me? The plane people. You're sure?"

"I promise. In seven days."

"Alright, I'd bring my *Watchmen* comics, also in a waterproof bag."

She laughed. They lay side by side. She covered his hand with her fingers and rubbed his palm with her thumb. He leaned on his arm, memorizing the shape of her thigh, the line of her shoulder.

"Your turn. You get dropped from a plane. What do you bring?"

She lay silent for a long time.

"You can't say *Watchmen* comics in a waterproof bag," he prompted, hoping to hear her laugh. After an awkward wait, he changed the subject. "I heard you're dropping from a plane into Australia this fall."

"News travels fast in these woods," she said, slipping her hand from his.

He laughed. "True. But Australia's cool. I've been thinking about travel too." The thought hadn't popped into his head until that moment. Seeing the world. No parents to rescue him from travel disasters. "Europe, maybe."

"Then go," she said, as though it were simple. Her self-assurance was astonishing.

She stood and reached for her towel. "I need to get back."

"Wait a minute." He scrabbled up out of the sand, embarrassed by his shrivelled nakedness and the hole in his sock. "Just let me get dressed, and I'll walk you to your campsite."

She wrapped the towel around her while he frantically pulled up his underwear.

"I know the way. Au revoir, mon doux Nick." With that she turned and walked out of his life, while he stood there dumbly, jeans puddling around his feet.

She was truly gone the next morning. She and Simone pulled out before dawn, a full week still to go on their reservation. Their site remained camperless with their early departure. Nick sat at their empty table, tossing pine cones into their fire pit.

He looked down the shoreline to where he'd been with Miranda some fifteen years before. The overgrown shrubs had inched up to the water's edge, leaving no sandy beach, erasing the place where it had happened. He didn't know what to call it. Miranda had given him more than Billy. It's not like he'd lost his heart that night. He didn't love her or dream of her or spend much time pining over her sudden disappearance. His seventeen-year-old brain was mostly stupefied and a little pissed. She'd taken him by surprise, left without saying goodbye. Yes, he'd committed similar crimes with a dozen girls or more, but he didn't dwell on that. Not back then. Miranda had started a longing in him, a new and persistent grinding in his gut, a dogged feeling of everything drawing closer but too far to reach. Her dreams had seeped into his, his predetermined life not as enticing as it once was.

The summer turned to shit after that. He ignored the redhead and the ones who came after. His games of polite flirting felt awkward and childish, so he dug into work instead, painting the shower house under the blaring sun, repairing the rotted boardwalk posts he'd long been putting off.

He fell into bed each night, sunburnt and restless. Until Miranda, he'd had his life figured out. Engineering, a non-bullshit degree. Interesting problems to work on, like Ironman. Good money. Home for the holidays and noisy reunions. But now, doubts lingered like shadows, the certainty of his future gnawing at him. He questioned what problems needed solving, what regrets might crop up. When sleep finally overtook him, he dreamt wild dreams where he was a tiny speck in a big world, scrambling along steep cliffs, a pack strapped to his back.

His parents told him to ease up, enjoy some time off before university, but that only made him work harder. He didn't want to think of school. He became sloppy. While up on the roof, he absentmindedly stared at a circling gull, lost his footing, and tumbled to the ground, requiring a tetanus shot and eleven stitches along his thigh. When he went to town for two-by-fours, he didn't cinch them down properly in the back of the truck. The top board flew onto the highway, nearly creating a collision.

After Miranda, everything once effortless seemed fraught with complications. He still untangled the kids' kite strings and patched their tire tubes, still joked with the parents and fetched their wood, but he second-guessed himself often. He questioned what lives these people lived when they weren't holed up in tents. He questioned what life he could live if he opened himself up.

The day of the fire started like any other. It was the last Friday in August, and the campground was packed, campers cramming in the last bit of fun before school. The twins, Randy and Zak, joined their parents for the weekend. Now six-foot-three and U.S.-bound on basketball scholarships, they were jumping out of their skin to set off firecrackers at the bonfire that night. Nick was happy enough to reunite with them, high-fives and slaps on the back. But he couldn't find that easy banter they once had. When Randy suggested they race to the floating dock for old times' sake, Nick backed away and said he had chores.

Every camper, from the grandparents to the babies, headed down to the beach after supper that night. As the sun dropped under the horizon, the temperature dropped with it, the air tinged with an early autumn crispness. The fire pit was six feet wide. Nick had the logs crisscrossed so high that sparks flew and danced over the water. Campers circled close for warmth, most perched on sawed-off log stools, strollers parked nearby.

His dad always gave a memorized speech at these things, while his mother clasped his hand and looked out reverently at the crowd. *We welcome you all to this sacred space. As we share fellowship here tonight—with you our beloved camp family—we boldly carry on the long tradition of sacrificing one of you to the gods of the lake—*at which point there would be confused shuffles from the newcomers and winks and horselaughs from those who had memorized the shtick too.

This sacrifice keeps us safe from the monsters beneath the depths. The blood suckers and lake sharks. The sand dragons and sea snakes. The fifth wheels and gas-guzzling motor homes upon yonder shore. Who among us tonight is willing to be our sacrifice? Who is willing to take the plunge?

Bedlam ensued. Campers jostled, yelling out names, even the newbies, who hadn't a clue what came next. Randy, the loudest, became the chosen one, much to Zak's disappointment. Four of the men, old hands at this ritual, stripped out of their runners and socks and rolled up their pant legs. Randy yelled melodramatically, *I do this for you*, as they wrestled him to the ground, each grabbing a hand or foot. They waded into the water with Randy splayed between them, onlookers chanting *Randy, Randy, Randy.* They swung him once, twice, three times, getting as much lift as they could before letting go. Randy sailed through the air and made a resounding splash. He came up sputtering to loud cheers, arms stretched high like the champion he was.

Nick laughed with the others. Randy duck-walked to the fire's edge in squishing runners. He bowed low as Nick's dad placed the Soggy Sacrifice medal around his dripping neck.

Nick left the fire soon after, his mom catching his arm as he walked away. When he told her he was packing it in, she smiled and said, *No wonder, you've been working so hard.*

But it wasn't that. He fixed things, rescued campers, plucked summer girls like saskatoons off a bush, yet he'd never once let himself be chosen for all those sacrificial dunkings. Why was that? Until Miranda, he had no questions. Now he questioned it all.

He left the roar of the bonfire crowd echoing off the water and headed to Campers Hall. Inside, he unlocked the door to the large storage room, the only area of the building off-limits to campers. This was where they stored tools and supplies, spare parts and equipment, odd bits of lumber, different-sized propane tanks and gas cans, and a large fridge stocked with items for purchase. He grabbed a six-pack, something his parents would vehemently disapprove of, and climbed the adjacent steep stairs to where the teens sometimes hung out.

The loft was a mess, kids' paintings spread on newspapers littering the floor. Nick lit the candles he kept hidden in the wall shelf, their wicks jumping and crackling before settling into teardrops of yellow white. He dragged a chair to the window and opened it, letting in the cool breeze, cracked a beer, and stared into the blackness. He could hear the distant *pop pop pop* of the twins' firecrackers, the random shouts of teenagers, a baby's cry. He guzzled, stewing.

By beer two, a stunning new reasoning began to burble inside him. It wouldn't be the end of the world to take time off. A year. Maybe more. Figure himself out. He didn't have to go to school in the fall.

It was not too late to unwind the steps. No one was holding a gun to his head. He could use his savings to live a little, take some risks.

Around beer four, he was dreaming about mustering cattle in the outback, building a well in Africa. By the time the beer was gone, he had talked himself into a different life.

At the loft window, he mulled over his pitch to his parents, his brain turned to mush. Campers' noises faded until all he could hear was the rustling of the poplar leaves down by the tree line. Then something more. Scratching and scampering noises, too loud for mice, coming from beneath him.

Nick stumbled drunkenly down the steep stairs. He poked around, lifting blankets, peering under tables, kicking a stack of wooden crates—anywhere a critter might hide. He found none.

He left Campers Hall and staggered into his sleeping house. The bonfire had long since been extinguished with buckets of lake water, the campers zipped into their tents. He could hear faint splashing and high-pitched girl screams and boy shouts from farther down the beach. He kicked off his runners, felt his way up the dark stairs, passed his parents' closed door, and fell into bed, drunk but still innocent. He remembered nothing more before he tipped into sleep.

The fire smouldered for some time before the first explosion, which everyone said woke them at a quarter to four. Charlie Carr, taking a timely leak beside his tent, was the only one to see the wall blow out, which he later described as *the mother of all firestorms, boards jumping into the air and raining down like matchsticks*. Teresa White, nursing her baby in her sleeping bag, said the boom made her shriek so loud her baby bit her hard, then howled.

A few minutes later came a second blast. Scrambling out of tents, campers imagined earthquakes or ungodly thunder or some other horrible and unnamed freak of nature. Glenda Hill, seven years old and missing both front teeth, swore she saw a fire-breathing sand dragon streak across the sky.

Nick's parents tore out in their pyjamas and gathered with the campers by the hall. Larry Pond joined the crowd in his skivvies, his wife eventually catching up and wrapping her sweater around his middle. The air filled with a heat-haze of dust, black smoke billowing, chunks of soot floating. A sizzling crackle drowning out all else.

Nick's dad ran back to the house to call the fire department and fetch the hose and shovels, while the men stomped on sparks in the wild grass. Nick's mom wove among her charges, touching them as she queried in a hoarse voice, *Is everyone alright? Is everyone accounted for? Is anyone hurt?* Some of the children cried. Everyone coughed.

Nick, for his part, was the last to arrive at the scene, where he stood on the sidelines in shock. At a moment during the chaos, his mom pulled his dad aside. He watched as they clung to each other, their look of loss so palpable he felt as if he was swallowing their sorrow along with the soot. It nearly knocked him to the ground to see them like that. They had questions for him in the hours that followed. After the campers packed up and moved out, and the wreckage of the burnt building had been roped off, the police chief and the fire inspector had questions for him too.

Yes, he'd heard the teenagers from his bedroom window sometime in the night. No, he didn't get out of bed to look. No, he saw no one by the hall. His mother vouched for his scanty accounting. Her son had packed it in before the fireworks. She'd seen him head towards the house.

No one could disprove it. The inspector surmised that the fire started in the loft, cause unknown, a tossed cigarette being the top theory. The fire spread across the loft, crept down the stairs, jumped to the wood shavings in the storage room, and snaked towards the gas cans, two of which exploded simultaneously like a detonated bomb. A propane tank burst next.

The police chief concluded that a pack of rowdy teenagers, names still undetermined, had been roaming unsupervised until the early hours of the morning. Melted beer cans were found in the rubble. Campers Hall was unlocked, easily accessible. Beyond that, they had nothing.

With the smell of smoke still in the air, the campground closed for the season. Through tears, Nick's mother baked him a double-layer chocolate cake to mark the beginning of his new life. His parents were so proud of all he had done, of all he would do with his engineering degree. Nick's father handed him a bonus of five hundred dollars alongside his last paycheque. *You'll be eighteen and legal soon. This could buy a few beers.* He had no choice but to take it, though he couldn't look his father in the eye. Hadn't looked his father in the eye since.

That fall he went off to engineering school as planned. But he didn't last long, failing out before Christmas his first semester. Despite all his musings about finding himself, of choosing another path, he couldn't bear to think of his future, any future. He didn't feel he deserved one. Those stupid drunk dreams burned them to ashes, destroying everything his parents held dear.

In the end, there could be no restoration. His parents sold, and now Overdale Developments would erase the last traces of the Ackerman Campground. He'd kept his mouth shut, through those first smoke-filled days, then smouldering months and years, his silence a ringing in his ears that never went away. Carelessness might be forgiven, but a body crumbles without a spine.

Nick threw on his runners and turned away from the shoreline, willing himself to stop looking back. All that was left from that time was Billy, and if he couldn't make it work, Billy might go up in flames too.

Chapter 8

TO: All Dementia Unit Staff
RE: Staff Meeting
WHEN: Tuesday, July 10, 3:00 PM
WHERE: Downstairs Rec Room

Attendance required. No exceptions!

T he day shift was told the meeting would be short so they could
expect to leave on time. The evening shift was told they had
to start a half hour early. The night shift, who clocked in at eleven,
was told to show up from wherever they were and that a half hour's
regular pay would be added to their next paycheque. Assisted living
aides, plus a few kitchen helpers, would keep an eye on the dementia
unit until their business concluded.

Staff clustered in the lunchroom, where complaints and rumours
multiplied like rabbits. A few surmised that it might be the murals
project, which they would champion in solidarity. Yes, it had caused a
few spills, and yes, they had to keep a close eye on the residents around

Billy, but it was worth the trouble, and they liked the distraction. Who didn't want something other than drab walls?

They speculated if it might be another change in management. A new directive from Toronto. The night staff, many of whom worked two jobs, grumbled about being forced to attend during their off time.

On the day of the meeting, the old pipe under Mazie's sink sprung a leak, and Sarah had to remove the soggy towels from the cabinet so that maintenance could do the repair. By the time she flew down the stairs to the rec room, it was one minute to three. She'd explained to Carter that she might be late picking him up. He asked if it would be dark by then and if he should bring his night goggles to Mrs. Brandon's.

Sarah scanned the room with its impressive array of sour faces. Nearly every chair was taken, many by night people she didn't recognize. She squeezed into the second row between two of the cleaning staff just as Lewis Clifton approached the podium.

"Thank you for coming today," he yelled into the microphone, jumping back when it screeched. He coughed into his hand and started again without yelling this time. "Thank you for coming today. We appreciate the fine work you're doing in our dementia unit. We know you all work so hard, and we are proud of your dedication to best-of-class service. But—"

"Here it comes," whispered a woman down from Sarah.

". . . serious concerns we want staff to be aware of. A number of items have gone missing. Items of importance to our clients and families."

Sarah had been well aware. They all were. Stuffed animals and knick-knacks were often found behind couch cushions or in garbage cans or on top of lamps. Staff would simply return them to residents' rooms while doing their rounds. But recently, things seemed to have vanished altogether, and even a thorough search in Ruth's room, who was a notorious hoarder, proved fruitless.

Clifton continued. "As you know, you work in a locked unit. Nothing, and no one, can enter or leave without the use of a fob. Which means there is simply no place for items to go unless they're walked off the unit."

There was a shuffling among the crowd; Sarah could not make out the words mumbled behind her.

"We have received several complaints from families over the past weeks."

Sarah knew at least two of the families in question. Edith's patch-work quilt had disappeared. Worn and faded, it had been in the family for over a century, passed on from one mother to another and on down the line. Edith's daughter was frantic to get it back where it belonged, on Edith's bed, her family's history covering her like a security blanket. And Harvey's pocket watch, his retirement gift when he left CP Rail, the watch he relied upon as he waited for his train. Harvey's son, an arrogant, infrequent visitor, had roared to the staff that the watch was gold plated and he wanted it back.

Clifton droned on. "Now, I know that the orientation manual states that costly items—jewellery and cash for instance—should not be brought into the unit. But value is subjective, and one man's trash can be another's treasure." Finished, finally, Clifton smiled at the stone-faced audience and asked Dorothy to come join him.

Dorothy marched to the front and adjusted the microphone. She towered beside Clifton, who stood off to the side and examined his shoes. She read from the paper with her clipped, determined voice, pausing and looking out at the group between each item: "Room 9A, heirloom quilt, honeycomb pattern; Room 9B, silver brush and mirror set; Room 11A, single-string pearl necklace; Room 14B, gold mechanical pocket watch, engraved; and most recently Room 16A, baby doll, pink bonnet."

Not Violet's doll? Sarah hadn't heard this yet. Her dolly had been pressed against Violet's heart for years. And Mazie always wore her pearls; they were strung around her neck each morning before her teeth went in and her bra was clasped. And why did Dorothy have to be so clinical, calling out room numbers instead of names, as if these losses had no feelings attached?

"Dorothy looks awfully pleased with herself," the woman beside Sarah whispered. "She loves making management look bad."

Dorothy folded the paper, placed it in her pocket, and strode back to her seat.

Clifton stepped into her place at the microphone. "These are the missing items we've been made aware of. In light of these concerns, we are installing security cameras in the common areas. Six cameras in the hallway. Two in the resident dining room. One in the staff room and one in the laundry area."

The room let out a collective sigh. Heads shook. Arms crossed. Eyes narrowed.

"The cameras go in tomorrow and the contractors ensure us there will be little disruption." Clifton braced his hands on the podium and raised his chin, as if trying to make himself appear larger. "I see we have a question." He pointed to the back of the room. "Yes, please, go ahead."

Sarah turned to see Angelica stand, an afternoon care aide who liked to share knock-knock jokes with the residents. Angelica asked, "Why the staff room?" Others nodded.

Clifton cleared his throat. "Cameras are going in all common areas, staff room included. Safety first. It's best practice in care facilities. We're merely catching up."

Someone piped up from a few rows back. "So, what you're saying is that there's a thief among us?"

And from the front row, "You're accusing us of stealing Edith's quilt?"

To which another yelled, "That's right."

"Well, no, obviously not." Clifton raised both hands, which did nothing to quiet the swell of murmuring. "No one is accusing anyone here. One of the families, which shall remain unnamed, is threatening to go to the police. We want to nip that in the bud. The new security system will show that we take these concerns seriously."

The room had become rowdy, and Clifton moved closer to the mic and spoke slowly, enunciating each word. "We value your input." Many tittered and several laughed outright. "We see you as part of the solution. All we're asking is that you stay vigilant. Keep your eyes open. Stay alert."

"Spy on each other?" someone yelled.

One woman stormed out, slamming the door behind her. Everyone talked over each other, craning their heads to catch the words down their rows.

Sarah whispered to the woman beside her, "Well, this is a mess."

"A frigging shit show," the woman replied. "Prairie View at its finest."

Clifton crossed his arms and squeezed his chin with one hand, contorting his face into fish lips and puffed cheeks. He stepped away from the podium and stared pleadingly at Dorothy, who once again rose from her seat and stood behind the mic.

"Quiet," Dorothy yelled, which shut down the room instantly. "We must act like the professionals we are. Together we will sort through this problem. I want you to do your jobs to the best of your ability. To be on the lookout. Cleaning staff, you must be especially alert. Leave no stone unturned, no corner untucked. When these missing items turn up—and I most assuredly believe they will—I want you to report directly to me. That will be all."

Sarah hurried out of the building, not wanting to linger with the disgruntled group that had assembled in the parking lot. She needed a shower to wash off the meeting's stain.

When she got to Mrs. Brandon's, she found Carter on the floor, helmet on, staring at the blaring TV. The two little girls slouched side by side on the couch, zombie-eyed, limp. They didn't so much as turn their heads when Carter jumped up and grabbed her hand and tugged her towards the exit.

Mrs. Brandon shuffled out from one of the back rooms, hair flattened on one side, cheek dented. She smelled like a package of stale cigarettes. "I thought you said you had a meeting?"

"It didn't last long." Surely, she hadn't been sleeping. "How was your day?"

Mrs. Brandon smiled. "Oh, we had a fine day, didn't we Carter? The kids played outside all morning. Then we did crafts after lunch. I was just letting them watch a little telly to unwind a bit."

The girls were comatose, clearly unwound. Sarah kept a hold of Carter, who was pulling away, ready to bolt.

"Well, thanks for everything," Sarah said. "Say goodbye and thank you, Carter. Nicely."

"Goodbye and thank you," Carter repeated nicely.

Sarah couldn't face going back to their apartment, so she drove past their building. She would take them to the fancy park on the other side of town.

She stole a quick glance at Carter in her rear-view mirror. He was swinging his legs, smacking his rainboots into the front seat.

"How was *Paw Patrol*?" she asked. He'd long outgrown the *Paw Patrol* gang, preferring *Transformers* instead. "Stop swinging your legs, Carter. So how many *Paw Patrol*s did you watch?"

"All of them."

Good lord. No wonder he was so wired. "So, what was your craft today?"

"Nothing." Carter had replaced foot swinging with arm swinging, now poking his finger up, trying to reach the roof. "We didn't do a craft."

"Mrs. Brandon said you did."

"No, we didn't. She gave us crayons and paper. That's it."

"Well, that's something. What did you draw? A Spinosaurus? Or a Triceratops?"

"Crayons are too fuzzy and don't make spikes. I hate crayons."

"We don't say hate in this house."

"We're in the car, Mom!"

"We don't say hate in the car either. Tomorrow we'll bring markers from home."

"Mrs. Brandon said markers are too messy and the lids get lost. And I'm supposed to shush when she's on the phone."

The ear-splitting TV and a package of broken crayons. Mrs. Brandon yacking on the phone all day, taking naps, blowing smoke rings out her window. What kind of a mother sends her kid to such a place? Carly and Kelly's mother, whose girls never seemed to get their hair washed. She couldn't be that mother. She had to find something better before Carter lost his shine too.

He was shineless now, pouting, his helmet head slammed against the back of his car seat. "Hey, guess what. There's a mystery at Prairie View. A real mystery. That's what my meeting was about. Some things have gone missing. Vanished into thin air."

Carter leaned forward. "Really? People?"

"No, not people. A watch and a blanket and a necklace."

He was all attention, straining against his buckle. "Did you call the police?"

"Not yet. We're going to do our own search first."

"I bet I could find them."

"I bet you could too."

He stuck up his arm and pointed his finger. "I found Peppa, remember."

"You sure did. Under the bed, right where you left her. You are an excellent finder. Detective Carter, on the case. Look, we're here."

"Where?"

They had the park to themselves. "I bet I beat you to the swings."

Carter scrambled to get unbuckled, flying out of the car, shiny as ever.

Billy had never tackled a project this big. He flopped in bed each night, stewing about whether he'd get the colours right. Whether he'd remember to treat the positive and negative space as equal. Whether Mazie would tip over a paint can. Whether Harvey would leave his palm prints on the wall. Whether Evie would find it too much. Whether the projector would quit. Whether the whole thing would blow up.

Nick dropped him off after breakfast each day. He never came in, thankfully; Billy didn't need him hanging around pretending to be a father. But still, Nick had surprised him with his helpfulness. At home, Nick made him practice setting up the projector and watched as he fiddled with the zoom until the image lost its blur. He lent him a ladder and an extension cord and demonstrated how to attach the work light in the cage to the ladder's ledge. He'd carted the works to Prairie View, giving explicit directions to lock up his stuff in the laundry room at night, which Billy did every time.

Each morning, Billy set up their workspace. Each morning, he'd help Evie with her paint smock and lead her into the hall. Once there, her brush magically did what she asked it to, Billy trying to keep up. A fan club had developed among the residents—watching paint go on a wall was even better than TV—so the nurses set up chairs along the hall where they could have an up-close view. Time flew between breakfast and lunch, lunch and supper. He would have happily kept going if Nick didn't force him home each night.

It was a little after nine, day six. The regulars had taken their seats, Mazie and Edith in the middle, Ted and Ruth on the ends. Every now and then Ruth would clap. He liked having them there, where they seemed content, as if it were their choice.

Billy perched high on the ladder. He'd worked on the blue sky in the days before and was adding in trails of grey as wispy as fading smoke. Evie stayed in the bulrushes, painting long, firm leaves in seaweed green and yellows, three-sided stems with drooping clusters of small, brownish spikelets. She wasn't so much copying the projected image as bringing to life a brilliant marsh of her own. She talked to herself like she used to when she sat at her easel. *Come on, my beauty* and, *Let's see what we can do here*. Billy leaned on his ladder to listen and watch, her arm dancing over her canvas. When she was like this, back in her body, her mind lit up, he could almost be happy too.

Rachel fobbed in through the escape doors, a riot of colour in her floral shirt and shimmering purple pearls. He'd like to try painting her one day.

"Late start," she said breathlessly, as though she'd run from the parking lot. "Wish I could say I had a bit of a lie in, but it's the bunnies."

"What's wrong with the bunnies?" he asked.

"The babies are out of their nest now and on their own. I had to dash into Peavey Mart for more alfalfa pellets."

"Wow. How many?"

"Four, I think. Or five. I'm worried sick that Sebastian or Velcro might try to take a chomp. They're tiny as chipmunks."

She studied the wall and clapped her hands. Ted and the women lined up in the chairs clapped too.

"Bloody brilliant," she gushed. "Have you thought of hairdressing? It's another art form, you know."

He could feel his cheeks heat under the glow of the trouble light. "Grandma's the real artist. I'm just following her lead."

"You're every bit as talented. And I have a very good eye. Your painting looks so real I can feel its breeze wash over me."

He didn't want credit, especially with his grandma right there, her brush flying over the wall in bold strokes, but he felt proud just the same. Even so early along, less than one wall painted, he could feel the difference. They had cut out a little piece of the outside, a slice of pie, and given it to Harvey and Mazie and Ruth and the others to chew on whenever they wanted. It wasn't such a dumb-assed idea.

"The world needs more colour, Billy. A little excitement. And that's what you're giving them."

Billy laughed. She was so overblown and intense, adding plenty of colour herself. "You bought the paint. This wouldn't have happened without you."

Evie kept talking to the wall, coaxing her brush to do what she asked.

Rachel smiled. "I made a little deal. If you want something from someone, you need to zero in on what they want more and dangle it in front of them. We get the murals, they get new flooring. As soon as the walls are done, they're going to tear up this old carpet and lay down vinyl plank, which will be easier for the wheelchairs."

"Oh," he said.

"When I was little, the neighbours had a scruffy old dog. He hated getting clipped. But he loved cheese more. They lined up four pieces of cheese in front of him. One paw. One piece of cheese. He sat like an angel, drooling, transfixed, while they lifted each foot. I watched the whole thing through a hole in the fence."

If he'd had a dog, he'd have tried hot dog pieces instead. He stepped down the rungs carefully, needing to move his ladder. He would mix purple into white, create a softer contrast in the cloud trails. Rachel stared at the camera mounted across from Ruth's room.

"Smile for the camera," Billy said. The staff hated being spied on. Sarah had talked with him about the missing stuff and how if Evie had special treasures, she'd have to put them in a locked cupboard.

"Rachel?"

She kept staring into the lens. Her frozen expression caught him off guard. "It's not right," she said, before turning away.

He watched as she disappeared into her mother's room. When he turned back to the residents, Mazie had fallen asleep, shoulders slumped, her chin resting on her breakfast bib. He wanted to right her head so she wouldn't get a kink, but his fingers were sticky with paint. Ruth clapped when she caught his eye, which made him laugh. Ted yelled, *The clouds need more purple.* Evie hummed.

Rachel had just said, *It's not right*, but he didn't agree. This did feel right—right here, right now. He might as well hang on to that feeling and forget the rest.

Chapter 9

It was a muggy Sunday afternoon, July half gone, mosquitoes swarming Nick's boots after the early morning rain. The yard was a mess of overgrown shrubs and towering poplars with half-dead branches and roots bulging and snaking towards the house. The sagging garage was little more than a shed, filled with rusted rakes and an old lawn mower seldom used.

Nick set up a couple old lawn chairs beside the fire pit and lit the kindling. He watched as the flames burst then fizzled around the half-burned log. It was smoke, not heat, he was after, to dissuade the bugs.

Tomorrow he'd be back to work, back to his normal routine, except there was this kid in his house that belonged to him, and nothing would be like it was before. He'd been planning this father-son talk for days.

He'd set everything up on the wooden picnic table, the one he'd stolen from the campground after his parents had moved on. Cokes packed on ice in the cooler, chips and dip, a package of Red Hot beef jerky. The only thing missing was the boy, and Nick had run out of reasons to keep stalling.

He walked slowly to his back door, opened the screen, and yelled inside. "Billy, can you come out here for a minute. We need to talk." He let the screen slam, went back to the lawn chair, and waited. It took forever, but Billy finally came to the landing and yelled, "Yeah?"

"No, come here," Nick said, leaving no room for hesitation. "We need to talk."

Billy walked painfully slow and slumped in the chair beside Nick. "Yeah?" he said again.

"You want a Coke? I got chips too."

"No thanks. Is that it?" Billy pressed his hands into the armrests and leaned forward, ready to take off again. Nick knew he was pissed at getting picked up early from Prairie View and not being allowed to go back. He'd been locked in his room since.

"Hold on, Billy. I just got some things to say." Nick's mind went blank, his rehearsed words evaporating into the smoke. "I went to Prairie View last night. Kinda late. You'd already gone into your room, and I figured you might be asleep, so I didn't want to bug you. Plus, I figured you'd been there all day, so you probably needed a break from that place. Anyway, someone had called. Not Sarah, somebody else, a Rose or Ruby, it doesn't matter, but she left a message and said Evelyn needed . . . well, supplies, so I stopped at the drugstore and headed over." Why was he babbling like a running toilet? Billy didn't need to know all this.

But the boy had been listening. He sounded indignant when he demanded to know what supplies, like no one had a right to get into their business. "Grandma has toilet paper," he added. "And paper towels too. I check every day."

"I know. I sorta overdid it in the toilet paper department. They just asked me to pick up some other personal stuff."

The kid wouldn't let it go. What stuff, he wanted to know.

"Depends. Like pull-ups, only for adults."

"Pullups!" Billy spat out the word. "You mean diapers." He looked horrified. "Grandma doesn't need those."

"I guess they think she does. She's been having little accidents."

Billy clamped his mouth shut and stared at the ground. "I didn't know," he finally said.

"It's not your job to know, Billy. That's what the staff are for. To help with those things. Anyway, Evelyn's all squared away. She was asleep, so I left the package in the staff room. What I wanted to say is that your mural is amazing. I can't believe how much you've done. It's really something."

Nick was astonished by what the boy had accomplished. His boy. The unit had been quiet when he'd used his fob to open the locked door. Colour splashed across the wall. He had to sit in one of the chairs across the hall just to take it in. One of the night staff sat beside him, and they stared together for a few minutes before she put her hand on Nick's knee and whispered, *We all love it. The staff. The residents. The families. Ruthie's daughter blubbered when she came by last night. That's some special kid of yours.* Her words made him feel foolish, like he'd been the only one not let in on the secret. He couldn't move for nearly half an hour.

"It's going faster than I thought it would," Billy was saying. "The projector works good."

"It hasn't given you any trouble?"

"Nope. Starts up quick. Doesn't take much to get the zoom to fit."

"The trouble light? And ladder? You got all you need?"

"Yep."

"You and Evelyn. You make a great team. I really like the bulrushes. And the sky. It's so real, like the photograph, but not like the photograph." He wanted to tell Billy that the painting made him feel like he was standing on a boardwalk in some better world, but he couldn't get his mouth to work.

Billy stayed quiet. Nick thought maybe he should move on and get to the main reason for this meeting, but then Billy asked tentatively, not more than a mumble, "So you like it?" The question felt precious to him, breakable.

"Yeah. I do." Nick placed a hand on Billy's arm and held it there.

"Yeah, okay." Billy squirmed away. "Maybe I'll have a Coke."

"Behind ya. In the cooler. Toss me one. There's chips too."

Billy rummaged through the cooler on the picnic table. Smoke billowed in their faces, so Nick dragged the lawn chairs to the other side of the pit. Billy came back with two Cokes and chips, tripping on the uneven ground. When he tore the bag open, chips scattered everywhere. When he popped the Coke tab, fizz bubbled up and onto his T-shirt. The kid was a disaster without a paintbrush in his hand.

They took turns reaching into the bag, chomping on chips, tipping their heads back and guzzling their Cokes.

"The boardwalk isn't quite right," Billy said. He had chip pieces all down his shirt. "The railing is fatter on one end than the other."

"That didn't jump out at me. The proportions looked right. And I stared at that boardwalk a long while. What does your grandma think?"

"About the boardwalk?"

"About the mural." Nick wished he hadn't asked it. How could Billy know what was in Evelyn's head? She didn't know herself.

"She's foggy when she starts out. Yesterday, after breakfast, when she came down the hall and stood close to the wall, her eyes got really wide. She ran her finger over each brush stroke, turning her head one way and another, taking it all in from different angles. I tell her, *You painted this, Grandma*, and she says, *No, I didn't. I did not*, like she can't remember holding a brush. But once we get her set up her brain clicks in. She gets sharper the more she works and that blank film in her eyes goes away. After lunch she said, *Billy, you've grown two inches since breakfast. We'll have to buy you some new jeans before school.*"

94

Billy kicked at the half-buried root. "That's good, right? Her telling a joke? Her remembering I'm supposed to go to school?"

It was a lot of words. And more coherent than anything Nick could drum up. Billy had been caring for his grandma for God knows how long. All that time, he'd deserved boyish hopes, careless days. Instead, he had to worry about whether Evie would remember to turn off the stove, pay the light bills. Nick couldn't imagine all he'd lost out on.

"That's good, right?" Billy repeated.

It was Nick's turn to say something. "Yeah. That's good. Really good." It's not like he had much better to offer the kid.

The smoke shifted again, drifting across their shirts, into their eyes. They sat without speaking for a while. Nick grabbed more Cokes and the package of beef jerky. Billy kept swigging and chomping.

"I gotta start work again. Tomorrow morning," Nick said.

"Yeah? Okay," Billy said, like it had nothing to do with him.

"So that means you're on your own during the day."

"Yeah. Okay."

"You gonna keep on painting?"

"Yep. We're gonna do the train wall next. Close to the dining room."

"Good."

Nick felt nervous. "I got something for you." He ducked inside the dilapidated garage and came out wheeling the new BMX street bike. He'd picked it up at Pedal Pros in Red Deer, where he was assured it was the most popular brand for teenage boys. When he was asked his boy's weight and height, Nick shrugged like a dipshit absent father.

"I won't be able to drive you to Prairie View on my workdays." He avoided Billy's eyes as he wheeled the bike to the fire pit. He might think himself too old for a bike. He might think his father dumber than a box of rocks. "It's a long walk across town. Figured this would be faster."

Billy stood. "I can borrow this?"

"No. I mean yes. I mean, it's yours. I didn't notice a bike at your old place. Thought you could use one." A mad thought ran through him. This couldn't be the kid's first bike? Did Billy know how to ride a bike?

"It's been a while." Billy pressed his thumb to the seat and watched it spring back. "Can I take it for a spin?"

Nick stopped holding his breath. "Yeah, sure. Go for it."

Billy rested one foot on the pedal and coasted through the yard, then swung his leg over the bar and took off. He looked like a normal kid, rocketing away on a Sunday afternoon.

Nick sipped on his Coke. The log had quit smoking, and the bugs were taking over. He used the metal poker to stir up the embers. He didn't trust the easiness of it, all that giving and receiving. What pieces was he missing?

By the time Nick had polished off the last of the chips, Billy was gliding back up the gravel driveway. He braked hard, skidding, cheeks red, hair wind-whipped.

"Did you try all the speeds?" Nick asked.

"Yep. They work."

"There's a bike lock on the kitchen counter. You can set your own combination. Keep the bike in the garage when you're home, and lock it when you take it out, okay? Even at Prairie View. You don't want a grandpa using it as his escape vehicle."

Billy didn't laugh, but he didn't scowl either. He walked the bike into the open garage, came out, and pulled down the door. Nick tossed him the jerky bag, which Billy easily caught with his left hand.

"You're left-handed," Nick remarked, already knowing this, but saying it out loud.

"Yep." Billy plunked down on top of the picnic table and ripped off a piece of jerky with his teeth.

Until now, Nick had been the only one in his family to sign his name with his left hand. "I'm left-handed too," he said.

"I know. What about a helmet?"

Nick had never worn one except for football and hockey. "I'll pick one up." He'd tell Sarah about Billy's helmet request, ask if Carter had any suggestions. But he should have thought of it on his own. Kids were expected to protect their brains; parents were expected to know that. "You'll probably live until tomorrow if you follow the road rules. You know your signals, right?"

Billy rolled his eyes.

"Good. I bought lunch meat for sandwiches and apples and bananas and cookies. There's baggies and brown bags in the drawer under the cutlery. Make yourself a lunch before you head out in the morning. Since Dorothy doesn't want you in the dining room, I guess you'll have to eat in Evelyn's room. Or come home for lunch. That would be good too."

"What kind of cookies?"

"Oreos."

"Okay." Billy held out the jerky bag to Nick, but he shook his head. Red Hots made Nick's throat burn and eyes water. Billy was snarfing them down like candy.

"And there's a backpack in the closet," Nick added.

Billy crinkled up the empty bag and stuck it in his pocket. He leaned forward on the table, hands on knees, and looked down at the ground. "Thanks for the bike."

Nick waited for him to look up, which he didn't. "You're welcome."

"I didn't think you had a job," Billy said.

"Yeah, I do," he answered too sharply. "I work five days a week. All year long." It riled him that Billy hadn't registered he'd taken time off work to help him get settled. But then why would he? They hadn't spent time together. Hadn't talked about what came before, what might come next.

Nick surveyed the overgrown yard, the decrepit house, the tilting garage. They had a roof over their heads but not much more. All the colour at his grandma's house; art plastered on every wall. Window planters filled with petunias. The mushroom-shaped cookie jar. The straight rows of carrot tops and lettuce leaves waiting to grow. All gone for this.

"I'm a home inspector," he said, trying to create some legitimacy. "I pick up inspection requests every morning, usually four or five renos and new builds. I check structural stuff mostly. Joists and beams, firewalls, railings, foundations, that kind of stuff. Then I write a report—pass, fail, what needs to be done. I go all around the county."

He couldn't tell Billy how he spent the rest of his time. Stopping in at the bar at the end of each shift, guzzling every beer Candace brought to his table, passing out in a drunken sleep so he could do it again the next day. That routine had to change now anyway. Now he'd be required to come home, dig out something decent to feed the kid, find the adult diaper aisle in the drugstore, hit the milk aisle at the Foodmart. It made his head spin to think of what would now be expected of him.

Billy made a big deal of choking as he stepped off the picnic table and into the black smoke. He dragged the largest log from the back of the wood pile and chucked it onto the fire pit, sending sparks and flecks of char flying.

Like that would work. Nick wondered if the kid had ever built a fire. He found a couple dry logs and split them in three with the axe. He dumped the stack of wood beside the firepit, along with kindling sticks scattered around the chopping block. With the poker, he pushed Billy's log to the side of the pit, throwing kindling into the centre.

"Take these pieces of wood and stand them up, like a teepee, let the air get under."

Billy got down on his knees and did what he was told.

"Now slide this kindling between the wood chunks. It'll catch from the embers."

Billy wedged the sticks into the teepee's holes, meticulously slow, stopping between each to see what would happen.

"You might want to blow?" Nick said.

"Blow?"

Definitely the kid's first fire. "Get your head down, level with the base, nice long blows, help it get started."

Billy got on all fours, puffed his cheeks out, and gave it everything he had. They heard the crackle before the first burst, one tiny flame, then another, then all the kindling ablaze and spreading up the sides of the splintered wood.

Billy sat on his knees, and rubbed his hands together, brushing away the pebbles and dirt clumps. He had a smug look, one side of his mouth curled up.

"Good looking fire." Nick pulled the lawn chairs up close to the fire's edge and they sat side by side, staring into the flames. He handed Billy the poker. "I'd let it be for a bit before you stir it around. You built it, you tend it. That's the rule."

There should be other rules too—curfew, laundry, chores—but Nick didn't want to break from this moment. It was a Sunday afternoon, and he was sitting by a fire with his son.

Billy piped up, "Would you give Grandma's house a pass or fail?"

"You mean as a home inspector?"

"Yeah."

"I wasn't wearing my inspector hat when I picked you guys up. It looked pretty sound to me. Your bathtub wasn't filled with kitty litter. No pigeons in the attic." He could have filled the kid with horror stories. "Mostly, I just thought how interesting your house was. An artists' house. Exciting. Like what you're making Prairie View."

One of the logs tumbled over, and Billy carefully turned it over with the poker. "What about your house? Pass or fail?"

"This house? Fail. Definitely. It's tilting like a ship in bad weather. In case of emergency, crawl out your bedroom window. And don't stay in the garage too long. That roof's hanging by a rusty nail."

"Maybe I should keep my bike in my bedroom."

They both laughed at the same time, a first, which made Nick wish he'd caught it on video. "That reminds me." He pulled the cellphone from his back pocket and handed it to Billy. "This is for you."

Billy looked dumbstruck, like the phone was radioactive and he was afraid to touch it. He turned it over, examined it from every angle.

"I put my cell number in there already. And the Prairie View desk. Your birthday is the password, month and date. Zero four, twenty-seven. There's not much data, so use the computer to surf, not your phone, okay? No porn. No sexting. It's more a *can you pick me up, we need cereal* sort of device."

It took a few minutes, but Billy finally punched in the password and stared at the icons.

Nick didn't know what to make of him. "Earth to Billy. What did I just say?"

"No surfing," Billy said distractedly, clicking on the Contacts icon. Nick cell. Prairie View, just like he'd told him.

"You can fill that up with all your friends' numbers once you start school." Nick was at a loss as to why Billy was acting so weird. "Or add your old friends' numbers in there. Texting is free so you don't have to worry about long distance."

Billy got out of Contacts, put the phone on his lap, and stared at the screen. A spark soared up, a loud popping sound. Billy's hands flew over the phone to protect it, then he leaned forward and tucked it in his back pocket.

"So we all good here?" Nick couldn't tell.

Billy kept his head down and poked at the fire. Then he mumbled, "I've never had one of these."

Seriously? The kid was fourteen years old. "You've never had a cellphone?"

Billy looked up indignantly. "Of course I've had a cellphone. I had a stupid old piece-of-shit phone. It got busted when Grandma was in the hospital. I just meant I've never had one of these."

"Oh," Nick said, imagining what made his son hurl his piece-of-shit phone against the hospital wall. "So you're an iPhone virgin. No big deal. Give it a day and it'll be an extension of your arm. You won't leave home without it. You might forget pants, but you'll have your phone."

Billy turned and stared at him. "How do you know my birthday?"

Nick wanted to get this right. It took a full minute to figure out the words. "I don't know much, but I want to." When Billy still looked dubious, he added, "Your birthday was in the paperwork they FedExed up here. If I'd known about you before, I would have been there for every one of your birthdays." He felt bitter and sounded it. God knows if he'd have shown up, but he should have been given the chance. "Now I know Evelyn's birthday too. End of September, right? Maybe they'll throw a party at Prairie View."

"Or we could have one here," Billy said.

Nick didn't bother to respond to the absurd idea.

"Do I have another grandma?"

"Yep. You have another grandma. And a grandpa." Nick hadn't spoken to his parents in months. The last time he saw them was two years ago, for his mom's sixtieth birthday. They met at a diner along the highway, a sorry and stilted affair that filled him with guilt.

"Do they know about me?"

"Not yet. But they will." The kid would figure out soon enough that they were on their own. "My mom loves art. And artists."

"And camping. You guys had a campground, right?"

"Yep. That's where I met your mom."

Billy nodded, like he'd heard the story already. Mommy and Daddy on a warm summer's night, moonlight shimmering off the water, love in the air.

Nick didn't know what the boy knew, other than their DNA was a supposed match, the gods amused as they knocked their heads together. "She was really pretty," Nick added, to make her sound real.

"I don't remember her." Billy sounded flat, emotionless. "She died when I was little. I always lived with Grandma."

"I know," Nick said. The paperwork included a copy of Miranda's death certificate and a few scattered facts. Miranda Peat. Age twenty-two. Ovarian cancer. (He'd since googled the chances: incredibly rare.) Billy would have been in diapers.

The big log had caught fire and Billy banged it with the poker, scraping off the outer black chunks. The sky darkened, and a cool breeze swept in.

"I've got hot dogs and buns," Nick announced. "Wanna roast some wieners?"

"Sure," Billy said. "Did you live in a tent or what? At the campground?"

Nick laughed. "No. We lived in a house up the hill from the campground. The campground was only open May through September. The rest of the year, I went to school, did my homework, played hockey, had a few scrapes along the way like every other kid." He instantly regretted describing what he thought every kid did. Billy had probably never scored a goal, never got into a brawl.

"Do you know how to play crib?" Nick thought to ask. He'd played crib with his father on Sunday afternoons. An ancient crib set, the wood scarred and chipped, toothpicks for missing pegs.

"Sure." Billy sounded like he thought the question stupid. Like do you know how to brush your teeth.

Nick and his father kept a journal of wins and losses, each score accompanied by Nick's childish declarations. Happy faces, mad faces, *LOSER*, *He scores AGAIN*. He could search through the boxes in the basement. Find the crib set. Buy a new journal.

"So how come your family got rid of the campground?" Billy wanted to know.

The answer was straightforward. He'd started a fire and burned it all down. "It stopped being fun," was what he said to the boy. "We just decided to move on."

"To here?" Billy scrunched his eyes. He had a right to be skeptical. Why this dump?

"Yeah." Nick looked around, disgusted. He'd been living here four years and hadn't so much as pulled a dandelion. "We got some fixing to do. You're in charge of design. I'll try and be more handy."

"You should start in the bathroom," Billy said. "That shower. Be easier to use a squirt bottle."

Nick nodded. "Yeah. It's pathetic. You should start in the living room. Get some of your art on the walls. Or Evie's. Rearrange the furniture."

"Or blow it up and start over."

Nick laughed. "No explosives. House rule."

"Get decent dishes," Billy said.

Nick whistled through his teeth. "You mean matching forks?"

Billy seemed to consider it. "Why not. All the plates are chipped."

"Listen to us. Yacking about home decor like a couple of ladies."

Billy rolled his eyes. "That's sexist."

"Like a couple of old cowboys, then."

"That's stupid."

They were laughing when the rusted red Ford churned into the driveway. Nick stood, knocking his chair over, as Candace sauntered towards them. She was busting out of her skimpy sundress, hotter than a jalapeño on a summer grill.

"Nick Ackerman," she yelled. "Where have you been?"

"What are you doing here?" His hands balled into fists as he marched to her. She kissed his lips and wrapped around him. He pulled her off more roughly than he intended.

"I came to meet Billy." She wove around him and waved at his son. "Hello, sweetie. I brought you a present." She held up the bag and stepped forward.

Billy was standing by this point. Backing up, getting dangerously close to the fire. It was too late now, Nick's life presenting itself as a spectacle of sorry detours.

"Billy. This is Candace."

She threw her arms around Billy. He stood stock still, arms planted firmly at his side, eyes huge. He spread his legs to keep from tipping backwards into the flames.

Nick grabbed her waist and pulled her off him. She pushed the bag into Billy's chest, laughing.

"It's comics and stuff. And a drag racing magazine. And Tootsie Rolls."

"Thanks," Billy said.

She sat in the chair Billy had just stepped out of. Billy backed all the way to the picnic table and climbed up.

"I met your daddy at Ploughman Tavern. It's going to be mine one day, you wait and see. Candy's Bar and Grill. I'll give you your own special table. You play pool, right?"

Billy shook his head.

Candace laughed, throwing up her arms. "What, no pool? You're a shark, Nick. Why haven't you been teaching your son?" Then to Billy, leaning forward and winking conspiratorially, breasts spilling out. "Don't worry, sweetie, we can fix that. We can sneak you into the tav during off-hours. By the time we're done, you won't just be sinking balls, you'll be whispering sweet nothings to them."

Nick panicked. She was talking about we. *We.* The word a threat, teetering on the edge of disclosure, like going back meant no going forward, no getting out.

She continued happily. "So what do you think of our little town? Quaint, right? Not exactly postcard material. But football's a big deal here if you're into that kind of thing. And there's a skate park. Best advice. Avoid the diner, especially the blueberry pie."

Clouds were rolling in fast, a chill in the air as the wind picked up.

Nick stood. "It's time for you to go, Candace. We've got plans."

She cast him a withering look. "Well, that's rude. Billy and I are in the middle of a conversation."

"Thanks for dropping by."

She ignored him and tilted towards Billy. "So tell me. Is Nick being good to you? He's a good daddy, right. It must be a big change for you coming here. Have you met some new friends?"

Nick glanced at his bewildered son, who kept his eyes on her as he chewed on his lip, bounced his knees.

"Look at you, sweetie. You got Nick's mouth. The way it turns up on one side. So sweet. The first time your dad came into the Ploughman, he had that exact same deer-in-the-headlights look. You remember that night, don't you Nick?" She ran her fingers along Nick's thigh.

That was enough. He clamped his hand on hers and hauled her up.

"What's this now, baby?" she said, suddenly serious, eyes narrowing.

"It's time for you to go."

Candace stood her ground, flinging his arm away as he tried to push her into leaving. "I just got here. You got something to say, then bloody well say it."

"Go," he yelled. Billy jumped. She stared defiantly, before finally turning to leave.

As she stormed towards the car, he turned to Billy, whose pasty face spoke volumes. The kid had caught a glimpse of his real father. Mean. Thoughtless.

Shame washed over Nick. "Sorry, Billy."

They both turned to see Candace yank on the car door, step inside, bang it shut.

"Give me a minute," Nick said, desperate.

"Whatever," Billy turned away and hunched over the dying fire.

Nick bolted down the driveway and jumped into the passenger seat as the car roared to life. He needed just a minute. To explain, to say sorry. But Candace slammed hard on the pedal, the car hurling backwards, spitting gravel, the momentum slamming Nick's door, shutting him in with a resounding thud.

She drove at a crazy speed and braked hard when she pulled in front of her place. More slamming doors. Their houses were six blocks apart, hers as crumbling as his own.

"What the hell, Nick," she hissed, as soon as they were inside. "You're an asshole. What did I do that was so wrong? I just wanted to meet the kid. Is there a reason Billy and I can't be friends?"

"I know. I know." They faced off in front of the open door. He had trouble looking her in the eye. "I'm sorry."

"What the hell is wrong with you?"

"I don't know." He studied the toes of his work boots. "It's, it's hard to explain."

"Well try, moron."

He swallowed hard before speaking. "This afternoon, I was having a moment with my son, okay. I haven't had too many of those. None, if I'm honest. I didn't want it to end."

"And then I showed up and the moment went to shit." Her voice cracked with hurt. "Is that what you're saying?"

"The spell broke. That's all."

"You could have told me nicely."

"I tried. You didn't take the hint."

She pushed his shoulder, knocking him against the wall beside the door. "You embarrassed me."

"I know. I'm sorry."

Her expression softened. She rubbed her shoulder like a weary mine worker. "I sprang a double shift yesterday. Frigging inventory.

I'm the only one in the bunch knows how to do any of that. Up all night. I ache all over. My feet are killing me. And now this. You and your shit. Keep it together, asshole."

Nick nodded. "I will. I'm sorry. I should get back."

"Stay here." Candace stomped down the hallway and out of sight.

He ignored the voice in his head, his feet glued to the floor. The rain had started, pressing down like a heavy hand. This was the first time he'd stepped through her door. Her house was remarkably tidy. The beat-up coffee table wiped clean. A blanket folded across the battered chair arm. Worn hardwood gleaming. No butts floating in stale beer. No sign of the roommates. Candace split the rent with two long-haul drivers and a greasy-haired dishwasher from the Ploughman. *Every penny counts for a businesswoman with dreams.* The neatness of the place would have been Candace's doing. She ran her shifts at the Ploughman with the same military rigour.

She sauntered back with a fattie wedged between her lips, lit the paper, sucked a long, wet toke, and passed it over. Nick leaned into the wall and inhaled deeply. He needed to be less present, less acutely aware of how screwed up he was. They passed the joint back and forth until there was nothing left.

"That's better," Candace said, her voice smoky and far away. "Wanna beer?"

"I gotta get back." He didn't move.

He held her beside the open door, tasting spits of rain, loud as drumbeats, bits of leaf at the back of his throat, bits of Candace on his tongue.

Her fingers spidered across him, under his shirt, sliding their way down. She got his pants bunched down around his knees. She got on her knees too. Nick didn't stop her. He tilted his head back, closed his eyes, and drifted off until he was floating in a wet dark void.

She stayed on him until he came with a wretched shudder. He pulled up his pants looking down on her.

"Candace, why do you do this?"

She smiled wearily. "Well, that's new. You've never seemed to question the way I do you. You got a problem with that?"

He reached down and pulled her up and held tight.

"I didn't think so," she mumbled into his sleeve. "I'm so done. I gotta get some sleep."

He half carried her down the hallway to her bedroom. She curled into a ball on top of her crisply made bed. He slid a pillow under her head.

"I need water," she said, eyes closed.

He found a glass in the kitchen. When he got back, she was out. He placed the glass on her nightstand, adjusted the pillow, and covered her with a purple blanket he found on a chair. He kissed her damp forehead and left her there.

He walked home slowly, the rain doing nothing to wash away his shame. He thought about this woman he'd left, and the boy too, needing for him to be someone different. Needing for him to be more.

By the time he got back, the rain had extinguished the fire. The cooler had disappeared, and the lawn chairs were folded under the garage awning. The bike was gone. No trace of Billy, no trace of their afternoon. No way for Nick to explain what he'd made of his life.

Chapter 10

Sarah was having a bad day. She'd fallen asleep early for once, but then woke with a start just before two, the thumping so loud that her water glass nearly danced off her night table. She gave up at three, and though the blaring had stopped, her mind kept racing. She'd sat sullenly at the kitchen table in front of her opened textbook, the words swimming in and out of view.

Then just after breakfast, Clement had the runs again, and no sooner did she clean up one explosion than another erupted. She was sure he was not sick. His cheeks had colour and his spirits were good despite her continual fussing to get him in and out of pants. She'd told Dorothy as much.

"I'm sure there's no need for quarantine," Sarah had insisted. She didn't want him locked in his room again, which he hated as much as the dark. "Clement's body just does this. Every fourth day like clockwork, then he's back to normal."

Dorothy had looked like she wanted to smack her in the face. "You do your job, and I'll do mine." Clement was to stay in his room until he was symptom-free.

These battles with Dorothy were nothing new. Sarah's real angst was with Carter, who was getting sulkier each day. This morning he'd locked himself in the bathroom and had refused to come out. She'd succumbed to bribery, promising him an after-breakfast ice cream in the car. He hated going to Mrs. Brandon's, and she hated herself for taking him there. Mrs. Brandon's home was as lifeless as a morgue, no place for a curious and bright boy with energy to burn. Sarah had checked everywhere for a better daycare arrangement: the community board at the Red Apple; the ads page in the *Rigsbee Globe*; the staff hotline for Shop & Share. There was little to choose from and nothing she could afford. Maybe money can't buy happiness, but it sure as hell could have bought Carter a decent summer.

Her morning's only bright spot had been witnessing Rachel hand Billy a new helmet. She'd caught the pair of them in the staff room after the breakfast rush, Billy tearing open the box, so full of enthusiasm, his smile as wide as the world.

"It better be the right colour," Rachel had said, "'cause I can't take it back."

Billy seemed smitten. "It's great. Thank you."

Sarah had seen Billy fly down the road, jacket flapping, hair whipping pell-mell on his helmetless head. That Rachel had seen this too made Sarah's heart swell. The woman had surprised her more than once with these out-of-the-blue kindnesses. Mostly, Rachel kept to herself, standing vigil over her mother's crumbling body, but she'd formed a closeness with Billy that seemed to do them both good.

The day's fourth laundry load had finally dried. Sarah slammed the dryer door shut and hip-carried Evie's basket to her room. Billy, alone, stared out the window. He swiped his cheeks with the back of his hands before turning towards her, red-faced. It was obvious he'd been crying.

"Oh Billy, I'm sorry. I didn't mean to barge in like this. I'm here with Evie's laundry, but I can come back."

"That's okay," Billy said hoarsely. He slumped into Evie's old chair.

Sarah didn't want to pry, or fill the space with drivel, so she worked silently as she folded socks and panties and hung blouses. She could feel Billy's eyes on her, though she didn't turn to look. The boy had seemed happy these past weeks with Evie beside him and a brush in his hand. But what could she know about how he felt? Maybe Billy too was having an indecently bad summer.

"Well, that's it then." Sarah closed the last of the drawers.

"She didn't even know who I was," Billy said, without looking up. "She yelled, *Who are you?* and pulled her hand away when I tried to walk her to the dining room."

Sarah sat across from him on the edge of Evie's bed.

"Like she'd never see me before." He practically spat out the words. "Like we hadn't been standing side by side for the last two hours painting the damn train."

"Oh Billy, I'm sorry."

Billy propped his elbows on his knees and stared at his runners. "I thought she was getting better. But she's not. Maybe all this is too much for her."

"It's unfair, isn't it."

"At least in Chetville she always knew who I was."

Sarah stood. "Look, I'm on break now. Why don't you have your lunch outside with me?" She grabbed Billy's lunch bag from the counter and dangled it in front of him. "We can sit at the picnic table, swap cookies. It's a beautiful day."

Billy followed her unenthusiastically. She was grateful for the shade of the aspen tree towering over them as she brushed the twigs off the picnic table and sat across from Billy. She didn't know what to say. Losing someone in pieces was difficult, especially for a fourteen-year-old boy who'd been ripped from his home. At least he still had his appetite. She watched him wolf down his first sandwich in three rapid bites.

"Lucidity comes and goes for people with dementia. Some days, actually some moments, are harder for them to grab hold of than others. But that doesn't mean your grandma doesn't know who you are. You're her Billy. You're special to her and you always will be."

Billy scowled with his mouth full. "What's the point. I thought the murals would help."

"And they have! All this painting has been so good for her. For all of us. She comes alive with a brush in her hand. She's got you by her side, and even if she sometimes gets mixed up, you don't. You remember she loves you, and she's worth fighting for, just like she's always fought for you."

Billy frowned. "You sound like my old school nurse."

Sarah pointed her finger and narrowed her eyes. "Do you mean old or former? Because I'll have you know I ain't old, Buster. I'm still in the bloom of youth. Still blooming, damn it."

Billy shook his head, laughing. "No. I just meant she sounded like a cheerleader, sorta like you."

"I can break out into a cheer right now if you like."

"Please don't."

They traded small talk and cookies after that, one of Billy's Oreos for two of her chocolate chips.

As they sauntered back to the unit, he seemed less grim. Sarah dropped Billy at Evie's door, willing her to smile at her grandson and call out his name, which she mercifully did.

She got on the computer in the staff room and looked up Nick's contact information. It was against the rules, she was only in housekeeping, but she would call Nick anyway and replay her conversation. If it were her son, she would want to be told of the hurt, even if there was no way to fix it.

112

Nick couldn't believe how much the kid ate. The cupboards were bare, again, even the Costco-sized cereal box, so he shoved Billy into the truck to take him to a restaurant. Things between them had been off since Candace had shown up, Billy keeping his distance and his words to a minimum, heading into his room after supper, coming out only to forage for snacks and milk swigs every half hour.

Nick hadn't imagined that easiness between them when they poked at the fire. Now they were scraping through a new layer of grudges and disappointments.

"Thought we could try Full Moon Pizza," Nick suggested in the truck.

"Whatever," Billy said.

Nick cranked the music and stayed silent the rest of the way. Sarah had called the day before last. She'd told him Billy had been upset when Evelyn hadn't recognized him, crying even. He had no clue how to help, imagining himself trying. *Hey Billy, I hear your grandma didn't know who you were today. That sucks.*

Country music blared in the crowded restaurant. Friday night families filled the large booths, waitresses jogging past carrying trays the size of tabletops. A line of people milled around the front door. Nick felt a wave of heat rise in him. He'd be damned if he'd stand in line beside his mute son with all the other dumb schmucks chatting amiably to theirs. They could head to the Chinese place beside the tracks, the one caught with mice in the walls. There'd be no line up there. He was about to turn them around when Billy waved and bounce-stepped away. It was Sarah waving back from the far side of the restaurant, Sarah and her little boy, her mop of red hair the only bright spot in the whole damn place. He followed Billy, a slight bounce in his step too.

"Well of course you'll join us," Sarah insisted after introducing Carter. "We haven't even ordered yet, and we could use the company."

Billy plunked himself into a seat, so Nick sat too.

"Do you like worms?" Carter asked Billy.

"Not for breakfast," Billy said. "But after that, they're okay. Do you like snakes?"

Carter scrunched his eyes, thinking. "I haven't met one. But probably I like them. Unless it's poison. Then you call the police."

Sarah shrugged for Billy's sake. "Well, now that we have that out of the way, Carter and I thought we'd share a pizza."

"Sounds good," Nick said. "Billy, want to share a pizza too?"

"Sure." Billy sounded more agreeable than he'd been for days.

Nick felt the kink in his neck let go. It was easy to be with Sarah and his boy, the four of them at the table, Carter yipping a mile a minute. He didn't have to worry about his side of the conversation. Carter was a cute kid, full of questions and reflections on his world. He never stopped talking, not even as the waitress took their order. When she tried to slip away, Carter had to know if she too liked worms, and whether she had a bicycle or a car. Before the pizza arrived, he had bounced through a myriad of topics including a preview of the solar system and the importance of road safety rules.

"I have to go to the bathroom," Carter announced loudly.

"I'll take him," Billy said.

"Wash your hands, okay," Sarah said.

"I will," Billy replied solemnly.

As the pair clomped off holding hands, Sarah leaned towards him and whispered, "My Carter is smitten with your Billy. Me too, by the way."

Nick was momentarily confused. Who was smitten with whom? Surely, he couldn't be that transparent, his eyes glued to the shape of her face and the way her cheeks creased when she laughed. But no, it was Carter she was talking about, Carter being smitten with Billy, Sarah being smitten with Billy.

Nick took a swig of Coke. "They're good kids," was all he came up with after a too-long pause.

Sarah seemed unruffled. "He's done such an amazing job with the murals. Have you seen the train? Harvey is beside himself. And Evie, oh my gosh, she's right there with him."

He knew he shouldn't ask, but he had to know. "How can you stand it? Working there. With those people?"

"Those people?" She stared at him for an uncomfortably long time. "Those people could be you or me one day." She folded her napkin and placed it on her lap, so Nick did too, afraid to look her in the eye.

"Ruth thinks her stuffed cat is real. She's concerned about every little thing—is the cat warm enough, fed enough, held enough. She leaves little dishes of water on her floor. Made a bed for it in her sweater drawer. She pours out more love in a day for a stuffed cat than some folks give in a lifetime. Whose world is better? Or more real? Sometimes I get a glimpse of what their lives used to be. A leaked hope or want in their eyes, the way they tilt their head and laugh at their own private joke. It gives me goosebumps. I love Ruth. And Evie. And all of them. So yeah, I can stand it."

Nick held his self-loathing tongue and stared out the window. She was too good for him. When he finally looked back, breathing heavily, Sarah was starting to blush. It was remarkable to watch, a sunset of colour spreading from the tips of her ears to the bottom of her neck.

He'd embarrassed her, first with his question and then with his silence. If there was shit to step in, he'd smear it over everything.

He scrambled to put together some right words, but she jumped in first. "Sorry," she said, as if the problem were hers. "I get carried away."

"No, it's me who should be sorry. I have the emotional intelligence of a rock."

Sarah smiled. "A rock wouldn't make that assessment. It would just lay there and say, 'I am a rock.'"

"What I mean . . . I mean it's a . . . it's nice to meet someone so passionate about her work."

Sarah snorted. "Housekeeping? Not so passionate. But I'm studying for nursing and will get there one day. Maybe. Hopefully. Some day. If I can manage to get enough studying done."

"You will," he told her. "And my offer still stands."

"Pardon me?"

"The contract on your neighbours. The yahoos upstairs that make all the racket."

She pressed praying hands in front of her mouth. "You remembered."

"Of course, I remembered." It was true. He had remembered all the words she'd said to him—in Evie's room, the hallway, in front of the washing machines.

The frazzled waitress arrived with the pizzas, and as he and Sarah pushed glasses and menus aside, his fingers accidentally brushed against hers. He wanted to cover her hand with his and hold it like a ball of light. It was a yearning so different from his usual cravings that he felt both sheepish and bewildered.

"The troops are arriving." He pointed to the boys marching towards them, thankful for the distraction.

Sarah turned and watched until they noisily plopped into their seats. "Eat up, boys, before it gets cold."

"Where's your mom?" Carter asked Billy once he'd crammed his mouth with pizza.

"Don't have one. Where's your dad?"

"Don't have one neither. Or a grandma. Don't have one of those. How many you got?"

"One," Billy looked at Nick. "No, two, I guess."

"You're lucky," Carter said.

"You can borrow mine sometime if you need one."

Carter turned quickly to Sarah. "Can I, Mom?" She smiled and dug into her pizza like a man. Billy too. He was an eating machine. Nick wondered if he'd have to order more.

"Are you going to the Family Council meeting next week?" Sarah asked between bites.

"Family Council?"

"The Council meets once a quarter. Next Monday's meeting is at seven. We're in a bit of a pickle. Some residents' items have gone missing, and families are upset—understandably. Staff are invited so we can hash things out."

"It's a mystery," Carter chimed in. "I'm a detective. I get to go to the meeting. And then no bed story 'cause it's past my bedtime."

"I'm going too," Billy added. "Guess I won't get a bed story either."

"The Council was explained in the orientation package," Sarah said, one side of her mouth slightly curled. "And you should have gotten an email."

Nick had not heard of the Council. Not opened his email for days. But he didn't want to confess this—even Carter was in on the meeting—so he said, "Oh right, yeah, I was thinking of going. Monday at seven."

Billy narrowed his eyes suspiciously.

Nick needed to change the subject, so he looked at Carter and asked, "Do you drive a car or a bicycle?"

"I'm five," Carter replied disgustedly.

Nick tried not to laugh. "So that would be bicycle?"

"Uh-huh."

Sarah dipped the tip of her napkin in her water glass and wiped the pizza sauce off Carter's chin. "Billy has a new helmet," she said.

"Where is it?" Carter wanted to know.

"In the truck." Chunks of pizza crust spewed out of Billy's mouth with his barely decipherable words.

Nick had picked up a helmet for Billy. The most expensive in the store. He placed the box on Billy's pillow, planning to let him make the discovery himself. But when Billy pedalled up to the garage, shiny helmet on head, Nick shoved it into the back of his closet. Nick just nodded when Billy grudgingly doled out the story. Rachel was nice. Liked to give away things. Brought in baking. Wasn't she the best?

"Mom won't let me wear my helmet in the restaurant," Carter was saying. "Your dad won't neither?"

"Nope, he's mean like that." Billy winked, no residue of grudge.

Carter shook his head, as if to say *parents are a sorry lot*. Nick felt his chest expand. He was part of a lot, sorry or not, mean like Sarah.

"So, should we talk about our days?" Sarah asked their ragtag group.

"Do we have to, Mom," Carter grumbled. "I'm busy."

"Well, you can listen then, while you keep eating. So, Nick, Billy, this is how we do it." She leaned in and looked from one to the other conspiratorially. "Every night at supper we share our favourite part of our day."

Carter pouted.

"So why don't I start. Today at work, Rachel brought really fancy cupcakes with lemon filling and chocolate icing. And I got to have two. They were delicious."

"Easy," Billy scoffed. "I had three cupcakes in the morning and three more in the afternoon. Rachel said I could have another one, but by then I felt kinda pukey. My day was . . ." he closed one eye, calculating, "three times more favourite than yours."

Sarah shook her head. "Cheating. The cupcakes were mine. Technically, that requires you to come up with a different favourite."

Billy leaned back and thought. "Okay, so I guess maybe when we got the tracks done for the train mural. I was worried we'd get the perspective wrong as they got more distant. But I think they work. I'm glad that part's done. Relieved, actually."

Sarah clapped. "Bravo. And they absolutely work. I think the train mural is going to be my favourite. I could break out into a cheer right now."

"Please don't," Billy said, holding up his hands. He and Sarah burst out laughing, like they shared a secret joke.

Carter didn't find it funny, whatever it was. "What's a murmal?"

Billy wiped his eyes. "A murmal is a mural. It's a great big painting, bigger than you, as big as a whole wall."

"Billy's an artist," Sarah said to Carter. "He's an excellent painter."

"Oh." Carter nodded appreciatively. "I can do mur-als. I've got paints and four brushes. I'm an excellent painter too. Can I paint my wall, Mom?"

"We'll see," Sarah said, smiling wide. "Your turn, Carter. What did you do today that you liked the best?"

"Nothing." Carter looked down at his half-eaten slice.

"You can't say *nothing*, honey, remember. Think about your day. What was the best thing?"

Carter's lip trembled. "There was no best thing."

"Did you play outside?" Sarah tried.

He shook his head.

"Not even with the hose?"

More vigorous shaking.

Nick watched as her mother brows furrowed, lips pressed into a thin white line. It was clear they'd had this same conversation before. The same worry, same regrets.

"New rule," Nick blurted. "Just for tonight." He hadn't a clue where he was going. Hadn't a clue where Carter spent his days. But he was a boy once too. He could tell when a child needed a rescue.

Billy rolled his hand. *So come on already.*

Nick looked directly at the small boy. "Okay, Carter. This is what you're going to do. You're going to use your imagination. If you could be anywhere in the world for a best day, the best day of all, where would you go and what would you do?"

Carter perked up. "Like pretend?"

"Yeah, pretend. Where would you be and what would you do?"

He squeezed his eyes shut and blurted, "The zoo. With Lucy."

Lucy the elephant, Sarah mouthed.

"So what would you do with Lucy?" Nick asked.

Carter leaned both elbows on the table, one landing on his piece of pizza. "I'd climb on top of her. She'd have to bend down first, on her knees, and we'd walk right out of there. She never runs 'cause she's wrinkly, but we'd stay on the sidewalk." Carter's words tumbled out, like he'd been waiting since diapers to share the right answer.

"When the people wave, I don't wave back 'cause I need to hold on. They get out of the way 'cause they don't want to get pooped on. Lucy's poops are big as basketballs and smoke comes off them. When we get to the lake, she walks in the water 'cause she's not afraid and me neither 'cause I have my Sunfish Badge and we swim around and see some Nemo fish but not sharks. Sharks live in the ocean."

Carter tried to stand on his chair, but Sarah made him sit back down.

"And we eat bananas that Lucy gets off the trees with her trunk, and I peel them for her 'cause I got fingers. And she sprays sand down her back with her trunk and gets it on my shirt, but I don't mind. Elephants are supposed to do that 'cause they don't have sunscreen. Nobody told them. They just know. We have to go back to the zoo when it gets dark. Our apartment says no elephants. Least I think it says no elephants. It says no elephants, right Mom? And Lucy is sad, but I tell her I'll come back tomorrow and she's happy again."

Carter blinked at the group, as if contemplating the complexity of his ending. Then he added, "Course I'd have to have my helmet."

The table erupted. Billy reached across and gave Carter a high-five, shouting, "Best day ever, bud." Carter got on his knees to high-five them all, twice each. They clinked glasses, Carter's chocolate milk dangerously close to spilling.

They were still heehawing when the waitress came to clean up their mess. "Well, you sure are one big happy family." She looked more frazzled than her last time, a sheen of sweat on her forehead. Billy grabbed Carter's leftover pizza slice and stuffed it in his mouth before she could whisk away the plate. Nick grabbed the bill too, despite Sarah's protests.

"This was fun," Nick said. "We should do this again." And he meant it. He could gladly come back every night and sit across from her.

Carter shrieked. "Can we, can we, Mom?"

Sarah smiled, looking at Billy, who chewed through the words, "Cool, yeah, very cool."

"Settled. We've got consensus." She stood with the others, then plunked herself down again. "Wait!" she yelled. Everyone slid back into chairs. Composing herself, she said, "We can't go yet. Nick, you haven't had your turn. My cupcakes. Billy's train. Carter's elephant. What was your favourite part?"

Nick didn't have to second guess himself. "Right now. This is it."

He ignored Billy's groans and Carter's babbles and focused on Sarah. She was painting herself from the inside out, her cheeks reddening, the green of her eyes catching the evening light.

Chapter 11

Nick might live through July yet. Things were smoother with Billy since their dinner with Sarah, more ribbing and clowning around. Billy had yelled from the living room, "For God sakes, do we live in a barn," when Nick left the door open between grocery loads. Nick countered with, "I'm not your Sherpa, get your ass off the couch. There's a cow in the truck. That should last you 'til breakfast."

The kid was a walking contradiction. He carried in groceries. Washed dishes without being asked. Nick caught him sweeping the floor, leaning feverishly into the broom handle like a curler. Yet he'd taken over their space, empty milk glasses on the coffee table, backpack thrown onto the kitchen chair, half-finished sketches lying about, wayward pastels and sharp-tipped charcoals. Nick now checked under couch cushions before he sat. Billy could not keep the toothpaste lid near the tube or wet towels on the rack, but picking up after him had begun to feel as routine as breathing. Sometimes he had trouble remembering his before-Billy days. With the boy in the house, it felt more like a home.

Billy seemed surprised that he wanted to go to the meeting. "What for?"

"It's Family Council," Nick shot back. He wanted to see Sarah, which he knew Billy knew, but he wasn't going to announce it.

He'd hoped they'd get a seat beside her in the dingy meeting room, but they'd arrived too late. She and Carter were wedged into a cramped row, all seats near her taken. Carter had a colouring book on his lap. She waved when she saw them, and whispered to Carter, who got on his knees and flapped his hands.

Another wave from the crowd, closer to the front, Rachel in a sparkling top and swooped back hair, huge gemstones on her fingers, beckoning them over, shifting her jacket off the empty chairs beside her to make room.

"Billy, I'm glad you're here," Rachel said, ignoring Nick. "I don't think I could sit through this without you. Half of Rigsbee is here."

He was glad Billy sat between them. He couldn't quite pinpoint how he felt about this woman. It would be plain stupid, counterproductive even, to admit to being jealous of his son's regard for her. Yet his vague unease seemed like something else. Something off. The way she fawned over his teenage boy—too intimate, too eager. He chided himself for being overly suspicious, and reached past Billy, to thank her for the helmet. She nodded curtly. "I'd do anything for your boy." He believed her.

And she wasn't Billy's only fan. The old man behind him patted Billy's shoulder, "You're doing a great job, son." And others too, bobbing heads, wanting to know where he got his talent, his can-do attitude. Nick wanted to know too, wishing he'd been some part of it. Billy squirmed in his seat, mumbling thank-yous, eyes searching for an escape route.

Lewis Clifton walked in, followed by a young guy in uniform who Nick hadn't seen around town. The police had been called? He should have opened his email.

Lewis laid it on as thick as drywall mud. A welcome to the families of the loved ones they so gratefully served. The richness of community. The power of shared values.

Then a rundown of recent improvements, which included the new murals. It was all part of some overarching and carefully executed Prairie View beautification plan. *To transport the landscape of the unit to idyllic scenes that add excitement and colour to their loved ones' everyday view.*

What a load of shit. Lewis had erected a brick wall of obstacles when they'd approached him with the idea. The man would turn down apple pie if he thought his chewing would stir the air.

The cop stood at attention as Lewis lauded their new intern, Billy Peat. (Billy their intern? They wouldn't even let him eat in the dining room.) *And his beloved grandmother Evelyn, herself a young-at-heart resident, with project funding by a generous benefactor who wishes to remain anonymous.* So Rachel hadn't outed herself? That brought his estimation of her up a notch.

Everyone stood and clapped except for Billy, who sunk further in his seat, more heart than ego. Nick heard a two-finger whistle from behind them. He smiled, sure it was Sarah.

Then on to the real reason for the meeting. The mood in the room changed perceptibly. Crossed arms, dead silence. Even Billy sat straight.

It had been determined these were thefts, not simply misplaced belongings. Lewis droned on about the new security system and the protocols in place to prevent further escalation. Two-person spot checks, video reviews, daily staff meetings.

The young cop, Constable Bob they were to call him, switched to life when it was his turn to talk. He soothingly explained the ways in which the police were involved. Communications with management, situation response plans, and the like. He assured families they were treating the matter seriously, suggesting they all complete an inventory and take items of value home with them, even temporarily. Soon they would get to the bottom of it.

When he broached the idea of families purchasing small safes to bring into rooms, the man behind them, the one who had praised Billy earlier, stood up and said in a low and measured voice, "We shouldn't have to get safes. This place should be safe."

Constable Bob nodded in agreement. His rehearsed speech given, he invited folks to call him to discuss additional concerns. He left behind a stack of business cards and a pile of Community Safety and Wellbeing brochures before striding out the door.

A small and shaken Lewis hid behind the podium. Another man stood and bellowed, "If Prairie View doesn't get this under control, I'll pull my wife out of here."

Panic was contagious, and others joined in. The lack of background checks, disgruntled staff, poor supervision. Were these possible contributors? One person wanted to know about Prairie View's insurance coverage, to which someone retorted, "You can't put a price on these things!"

Billy sat unflinching, uncharacteristically straight. Nick could hear Rachel blow her nose, surprised to see she'd been crying. Maybe her mother's room had been raided too. Even he found himself thinking the worst. Was Billy locking his bike like he promised?

The thief seemed more vindictive than criminal, snatching bits and pieces of people's pasts. Ironic. Nick had spent years trying to rid himself of his, only to find it walk up to him in size nine shoes. He could feel their sense of violation, even if for upside-down reasons.

He swivelled to catch a glimpse of Sarah. Carter flopped on her lap, as wide-eyed as she was. Nick wanted to get them out of there, take them for ice cream.

Lewis ended the meeting abruptly, dashing out before he could be mobbed.

Nick stood, yanking Billy up with him. "Let's get Sarah."

Rachel stood too. "It's all so horrible," she mumbled, her face blotched.

As he and Billy wove away, Billy was stopped by a small woman carrying walking poles, her sweater covered in cat hair. She wanted to know if Billy painted cat portraits and if he could give her his card. Billy blushed and stuttered, so Nick told her his son's schedule was booked solid.

They found Sarah outside the room, leaning against the wall as Carter ran laps up and down the hallway.

"That was dismal." She pressed her fingers to her temple like she had a headache.

She looked too pale. "Wanna go for ice cream?" Nick asked.

"Yeah," Billy jumped in. "We can take Grandma."

But it was Sarah Nick wanted, and she quickly declined.

"Sorry. Can't. Gotta get Carter to bed. He's calm and sleepy, as you can see."

Carter barrelled towards them and crashed into Billy's knees. Sarah grabbed her panting, shiny-faced son. "Let's have a quick look at the murals and then it's home to bed."

When they got into the unit, soft music piped down the hallway. A staff member pushed a cart of steaming drinks and plates of little cookies. An old man shuffled along in his housecoat, tipping his imaginary hat as he wished them the top of the morning. A tiny woman, not much bigger than Carter, came up to Sarah and hugged her around her waist. Sarah bent down and kissed the top of her head before the woman moved on, feeling along the banister with her gnarled hands, one over the other.

The place felt serene, uplifting almost, so different from Nick's first impression of vacant eyes and withered bodies. He felt strangely protective of this lot, and sheepish too for his initial cowardice. How could anyone steal from these people?

Billy's train wall was adjacent to the dining room. As they walked up to it, Sarah said. "Ta da! Meet your first mural, Carter. Billy painted it."

Carter got close and leaned forward, hands on knees, squinting at the swirls of paint. "Can I touch it?"

"Sure," Billy said nonchalantly. "Paint's dry."

Nick stood back to take it in. It was magnificent. The boy's talent. And Evie's. Nick remembered setting up the shot on the day he took the photograph. How he laid in the thistle, camera ready as the train bore down, a living thing, tracks sparking, the earth's floor rumbling.

Carter dragged his finger across the tracks. "How come the train's top isn't on?"

"It isn't finished yet," Billy said. "We'll paint the top tomorrow. And finish the smoke. And clouds. And hills."

"I know how to draw clouds." Carter made loops in the air, clutching his pretend brush.

"That's exactly right." Billy backed up beside him. He leaned against the opposite wall and studied his work, his bottom lip getting a workout. Nick wondered if his son could understand the extraordinariness of what he'd done.

Carter lay on the floor and picked at a paint chip wedged into the old carpet. Sarah bent down, struggling to get him up again.

"I'm gonna get Grandma," Billy said.

Presumably for ice cream. Too late for Nick to back out now.

"Can I go too?" Carter yelled, upright again.

Billy smiled and held out his hand. "But you can't borrow Grandma tonight. You can just look."

Carter dragged Billy along until they were out of sight. Sarah blew a loose curl from her eyes. Then she held her hands behind her back and stretched, head turned to the ceiling.

"Carter's a special kid," Nick said.

"Exhausting. But yes. Billy too."

Nick stared at his son's wall. All the paintings he'd missed.

"It just makes me so angry," she said. "It's so petty and mean. And poor Violet. She's gone completely mute. She only talked to her doll."

He could picture her spitting mad, a fast-moving tornado. Jaw clenched, face crisped red, freckles lit up like Christmas. He wanted to rest his palm on the small of her back.

She sighed. "We're all on edge, looking over our shoulders, wondering who the next target will be. It needs to stop."

Everyone's door was open as they sauntered down the hallway. A few dozed in their rocking chairs. TVs were on. They hadn't made it to Evie's room when the boys came into view.

"Did you know there's another mur-al?" Carter asked, running to meet them. "It's a bridge."

Billy caught up to the group. "Grandma's asleep." He sounded disappointed.

"Her bedtime's before mine!" Carter exclaimed, as if he couldn't imagine an adult sleeping when he wasn't. "We tiptoed. She was breathing."

Nick was relieved. He didn't have the energy to steer Evie in and out of his truck, in and out of the Dairy Queen's glass door, in and out of the plastic-backed booth. Couldn't watch as she snapped her purse open and closed, pulling coins from the zippered pouch in her wallet, dropping them on the table, shoving them back in their pouch again. Couldn't deal with the over and over and over of it.

"Too bad, Billy. Guess it's just you and me then." *I can manage just Billy.* It surprised him how quickly that thought popped into his head.

Chapter 12

B illy decided to pack it in early. There was a July Birthdays party in the other wing, and all the dementias were invited. They'd each get a carnation and eat cake and drink coffee and clap when the birthdays were announced and then listen to a guy with a banjo. Sarah said that Evie should go, that it would be good for her to be with her new friends. His grandma could care less about new friends (he didn't tell Sarah that), but he wanted her to get a flower. He was invited too, Sarah told him, but he couldn't stomach being trapped with a hundred old people and a banjo, and he wanted her beside him for the hillside—she mixed colours better than him—so he packed up the painting supplies and took off on his bike.

He rode aimlessly, looping up and down streets, imagining which house he'd live in if he had any choice. That two-storey one with the apple tree out front. His grandma could have the main floor; he'd be upstairs. But even as he imagined it, he knew she was better off where she was. That certainty had hit him hard one morning, days ago now. Billy remembered going into his grandma's room to find her in the shower, an aide by her side. He had stood with his ear pressed against the bathroom door, absorbing the soothing instructions, gentle and unhurried, their conversation light and filled with laughter. He nearly sunk to his knees to think of all the things he didn't have to worry about anymore. Yes, his grandma was in the right place. Now if only he could feel that way too.

He pedalled hard and found the school across from the pond, Thomas Berkley Junior High, the one Nick said he'd have to go to in the fall. A group of shirtless boys were shooting hoops in the school's playground. He stopped his bike at a safe distance and pretended to work on his chain while he watched.

These boys made it look easy; not the hoop shots, but the bond between them, the hollering and high-fiving. He'd lost that easiness a long time ago. During his first years of school, he and his buddy Jason were as close as blood. Jason lived with his grandparents too, which both brought them together and set them apart. They ran back and forth between houses, sharing secrets and sandwiches, bug nets and baseball cards. They worked a month of recesses digging a tunnel in the snow with their pencil tips. Spent a good chunk of a summer constructing a makeshift tree house using old bed sheets and branches. Jason was the bright sun around which his life orbited. And then he was gone, like that. Jason's grandparents moved him from their dinky town of Chetville to the other side of the world—Munich, no less—which might as well have been a different solar system. Billy started grade six without Jason beside him, Evie having one bafflingly bad day after another. Things really exploded when he brought a few classmates to his house for a science project, and Evie waltzed past them in the living room wearing nothing but a paint smock. While those eleven-year-old boys stared at her exposed backside, mouths gaping in mocking laughter, Billy understood in that moment how risky life had become. He could not bear to let others see her that way, afraid they'd make fun of her, and even more afraid of what she'd do if left on her own.

Billy now watched as the boys dogpiled and rolled on the basketball court. He'd had plenty of experience with their type in junior high. These were top baboons, he was sure of it, the ones who tossed backpacks, stole cookies from lunch bags, taunted the old ink-smeared lady who got lost in the school hallways. He wanted to douse them with black paint, splash away their creepy grins. He felt inside-out hot, hair plastered to his helmeted head, bugs gnawing on his sweaty bits. He did better on his own anyway. And he couldn't afford to get caught gawking, that would be too easy, so he turned his bike around and headed to Nick's.

As he weaved closer to home, swerving around garbage wheelies and parked cars, he tried to picture where Candace lived. Nick said her place wasn't far. He couldn't imagine a girl like her in a regular house with a fridge and a stove and a bowl of apples on her counter. She was intense, but intriguing too, like a slow-motion crash that couldn't be stopped. He could still feel the sticky heat of her round breasts crushed against his ribs. Still hear her husky drawl, *Well, look at you, sweetie*. He had tried to sketch her from memory, but Nick lurked around the corner whenever he got started, and he couldn't get the shape of her lips right. He wouldn't mind seeing her again; he'd be better prepared a second time.

Billy stripped the minute he got in the door. Helmet, runners, socks, shirt. The house was baking hot and smelled like old shoes, so he slid up the windows to let in some air. But the screens had gaping holes, which meant the flies swarmed in too, so he slammed the windows down again, hauled out the big fan from the closet, and stood in front of it with his arms stretched.

He hoped his grandma had fun at the party. Hoped she got two pieces of cake and a red flower. He was hungry. He pulled out everything he could find in the fridge. Lunch meat, tomatoes, cheese, pickles, leftover chicken. He slathered bread with mayo and ketchup, dumped everything on top, slapped on more bread and pressed, ketchup oozing onto his plate. He brought out the milk jug and cereal box next, poured himself an overflowing bowl, and sat.

He jumped in his chair, startled by the still unfamiliar ring in his pants. Nick—who else would it be—surprised to learn Billy was home already. He'd be late, a stop-work order three hours out at the Crimson Hills development. He'd pick up fish and chips, but Billy might want to grab a banana or something to tide him over 'til then.

He dug into his heaped plate and powered up Nick's computer. He googled LIPS, scrolling through the words and images. Fat lips, skinny lips, red lips, chapped lips, sugar lips, shiny lips, devil lips. None of them right.

He wolfed down the sandwich and googled BOOBS. Droopy, puckered, as flat as poached eggs. Pointing up, pointing down. Round, rounder, holy shit humongous. He choked on a spoonful of cereal.

He typed in SEX next—why shouldn't he—and scrolled down the list of videos. There was too much to choose from. He couldn't stop clicking. He couldn't look away.

He felt sweaty and light-headed, all their rushed and heavy breathing.

He was about to explode when he was snapped back with a knock at the door. Candace? He was sure he heard it. There it was again. He had barely enough wits to click out of the video. He'd willed her here. There was no way he could be alone with her. He sat frozen, trying to stop from panting. A flashy ad popped up on the screen—BUTT NAKED NASTY—but as soon as he closed it another popped up, SINGLES IN YOUR AREA, then another.

He slammed the computer shut. The knocks became heavy fist bangs. She had to have heard the racket coming from the speakers.

She would not go away.

He death-marched to the door. He would tell her he had the stomach flu, he'd been barfing all day, and she couldn't get near him.

He inched the door open and blinked several times. It took a minute for his brain to register that it did not see her standing there.

He swung the door open and stared at the couple, harmless enough, a man and woman. They stared back. They looked well put together, too good for this street. The man was tall with silver-tipped hair and a weathered face from spending time in the sun. He towered beside her. She was pretty for an older lady, white hair with floppy bangs, an oval-shaped face. Their shiny SUV had pulled into their driveway by mistake. They had the wrong house, obviously.

"We're looking for Nick," the woman said timidly, her small hands folded against her chest. "Is he here by chance?"

A magpie, not used to company, screeched from across the yard. Billy could see his long tail sweeping down from the top branch of the crab apple tree. "No, sorry. Nick's working late tonight. He won't be back for a couple hours."

"Oh." A pleading expression brushed over her face before she brightened again. "We're his parents. I'm Cathy and this is my husband, George. We took a chance, hoping we might catch him."

Nick's parents? This was a freaking disaster.

"Ni-nice to meet you," Billy stuttered. Who knows what they'd heard? At least he'd got his jeans zipped. He looked down to be sure.

George put his arm around Cathy's shoulder. "Who are *you*?" He had a deep voice, no nonsense, like he was used to getting answers.

"Billy. Billy Peat." Billy extended his sour and unwashed hand, and they shook. Then Cathy had a turn. She seemed a lot more coherent than his grandma, with her straight back and crisp collar and articulate sentences.

George cleared his throat. "I guess what I'm asking is how you know Nick."

Nick was to blame. For not telling them. For screwing his mom without a condom. For bringing him here. He probably had surprise kids holed up in small towns all across the country.

Billy wanted to hurt him, and this fancy couple too, so he took a deep breath and blurted, "I'm his son."

The magpie stopped screeching. George stared at Billy, jaw clenched as he gripped Cathy's shoulder. She dipped slightly, a pink flush high on her cheekbones and near the tip of her nose.

"How old are you?" George asked.

"Fourteen." He supposed he should say more. "He and my mom hooked up at the campground. Your campground. Back when you had one. She's dead. She died when I was little. My grandma's here too. At Prairie View. That place for old people." He flung his arm behind him. "Over at the edge of town."

That was the sum of it. There was nothing more to tell.

Cathy's eyes were watery bright, blinking. She reached out her hand to him and then took it back, letting it hang by her side. "Billy? I'm so sorry. We didn't know."

He felt ashamed he'd made her sorry. This wasn't her fault.

"That's okay. Nick didn't know either." He made it sound like it was no big deal. He didn't know what they'd expected to find at their son's house. Not him.

George extended his hand again, which Billy took, the grip studier and longer this time. "It's good to meet you, son," he pronounced decisively, although Billy was sure it was not.

"You can stay if you want until Nick gets back." Please God, no, no, no, don't let them stay.

"No, we shouldn't," Cathy said in a shaky voice, lip trembling.

George shook his head. "No, we'll get out of your hair, Billy. Please let Nick know we stopped by. Tell him to call us. Tonight. Tell him to call us tonight." It was a command, not a friendly request.

They started down the porch steps, but Cathy turned back and took his hand and kissed him on the cheek. She whispered in his ear, "We have a dog named Bear. He's going to love you."

He waited until they backed out of the driveway before closing the door. Then he ran across the room and locked himself in the bathroom. He leaned into the sink, appalled by what he saw in the mirror. Helmet hair, blown into a frenzy by the fan, sticking up every which way. A knife wound of ketchup across his left cheek. His scrawny bare chest, pimply and blotched.

I'm your grandson. Your son's huge mistake. So happy to meet you.

Sarah swooped into the staff room, fifteen minutes late for her shift, Carter on her heels, dragging his grubby backpack behind him. Mrs. Brandon had a toothache—a toothache!—and couldn't possibly be expected to mind children today. Sarah learned this thirty minutes ago when she rang the woman's bell. As she stood on Mrs. Brandon's front porch, it hit her like a stab to her heart first, then a beating on the inside of her forehead. She had no one. No aunties or sisters or girlfriends, no church ladies or gym partners. No favours to call in from a roster of happy new acquaintances. She'd orchestrated this lonely planet, this series of choices that led to her unpopulated life.

She could not afford to miss a day's pay. Carter had a dentist appointment next week, his overdue first, and with time off to get him in and out of the dentist's chair on top of the bill, she was already tapped out for the month.

She'd run back home, stuffed his backpack with everything she could think of to keep him busy, and here they were. But what had she been thinking? Bringing her little boy to work? It was bloody insane. Verging on child neglect.

She scurried about the staff room, whipping on the sturdy runners she kept in the closet, pinning her name badge to her uniform, barking orders like a haggard sergeant lost in the woods. "You have to be good, and quiet, like we talked about in the car—you've got oodles to do. I'll keep checking on you, but you must stay here in the staff room. Are you listening? Carter? Carter?" She unzipped the overflowing backpack. Hot Wheels and Sharpies spilled out, skittering across the floor.

She was extracting him from his helmet when Rachel walked in wearing neon pink tights and a tie-died shirt that hung to her knees. She held a cookie tin painted with cherubs and roses.

"Oh," Rachel said, as she surveyed the chaos. "I've brought cookies for the staff. Oatmeal chocolate."

"Mrs. Brandon has a toothache," Sarah said stupidly, wanting to cry. "This is Carter. I had to bring him." Rachel stood, unmoving. Disgusted, perhaps.

Sarah played tug of war with the helmet now in Carter's sticky hands. "Look, it can go right here, on top of the fridge, beside Billy's. This is Rachel, Carter. She's the one who gave Billy his helmet."

This helmet news impressed Carter. "Billy is my best friend," he told Rachel, who smiled and nodded as he blathered on. "Billy's an artist and I am too, and my mom is an artist, but she only draws monkeys. Did you know there's murals around here? I can show you if you want."

"Carter, scoot down there and pick up those toys. Hurry, please." She should have had Edith's room cleaned by now.

Carter slid along the floor like a flapping seal. Rachel burst into laughter, a rusty sound that filled the room. Then she clapped too, which caused Carter to exaggerate his gyrations on the linoleum tiles. "This is better than a basket of puppies," Rachel said between snorting fits. Carter obligingly yelped.

Sarah felt woozy and bleak and put off by the pair's exuberance. This was never going to work. Carter had been overjoyed to ditch the dreaded Mrs. Brandon, but he couldn't sit quiet and alone with his toys all day. It would be like cramming the rabbit into the tortoise shell.

She must flee the building. She must exit right now.

Rachel strode over and placed her hand on her arm. "Sarah, you go do your rounds. Carter can help me with my mother. I'll take him to her room with me. And the cookies too."

Carter brightened. "Can I, Mom?"

He had no idea what this meant. Neither did Rachel. "I can't let you do that," she said firmly. "He's a handful."

"Nonsense!" Rachael squeezed her arm. "He's a breath of fresh air. And besides, I could use a handful. My mother has been rather dull lately."

She was quite sure Rachel had no children of her own. Quite sure she hadn't the vaguest notion of a five-year-old's brain, especially a brain like Carter's, that leaped and bounced and zigzagged every which way.

Yet Rachel pressed harder. "You'll know where to find us and can pop in and out. Carter, what do you say? Should we go through my makeup bag."

Carter shot off the floor and stood in breezy solidarity beside his new friend. "Can I, Mom? Please."

Rachel whisked him away before Sarah could object. She had regrets within seconds of their leaving, a running diatribe of imagined calamities in her head—Carter frightened of the skeleton under the covers, Carter, not frightened, jumping frenetically on the poor woman's bed. Carter in a tantrum, peeing his pants, breaking Rachel's lipsticks, blurting out wildly inappropriate questions, driving her mad.

She swallowed her panic and jumped into her rounds. The hallway filled with the usual pacers trundling along. The congestion started near the train mural. Billy and Evie were at their posts, spectators lined up across from them. More chairs had been added since yesterday, a bigger crowd, even Violet, who never sat still, not even for meals.

It was an astonishing sight, not just the mural, which could have rivalled a museum piece, but the joy of the residents, who sat as if posing, as if they too were being woven into the scene.

Billy perched on his ladder, focusing on the skyline. Evie stared intently at the wall, a brush in one hand, her pallet in the other. Sarah waved to them both as she flew by. She would start at the far end and work towards her boy. She might have an hour before all hell broke loose in Rachel's room, and by then she'd be close by and could intervene. With luck, Dorothy would stay off the floor and be none the wiser.

She vacuumed, dusted, polished. Opened curtains and windows. Gathered laundry, hung shirts and dresses, returned underwear to drawers. Redirected residents stuck in closets or lying on the wrong bed. Fished dentures out of the garbage and soap bars out of the toilet. As each explosion-free moment ticked by, she felt a swelling debt of gratitude.

By the time she had worked her way down to Violet's room, her forehead was shiny with sweat, and that sudsy sludge of trepidation in her stomach had all but disappeared. She looked in on Rachel and Carter who were across the hall. She wished she could take a picture, the image opening her heart and blooming like a flower. There was her son with a cookie in his hand, a pirate now, painted moustache and eye patch, a jagged scar crisscrossing his cheek. Rachel had given him her bright green scarf for a bandana. They sat across from each other, the contents of the endless backpack dumped on the table between them. He was describing every little thing, *This is a smelly marker, this is a Skywalker, this is a Minecrafter book.*

Carter turned and saw her in the doorway and said, simply, "Hi, Mom," as though she bore witness to nothing extraordinary.

"You're a pirate, buddy. That's so cool."

Rachel turned and waved. "Ahoy, Matey."

"Want to play with us, Mom?"

"Afraid I can't, buddy. I have to keep working." She glanced at the bed, Victoria blissfully sleeping, gumming her lips like a newborn infant. "Are you doing okay, Rachel?"

"Arrr," she said in her pirate growl. "We're perfectly fine. Did you know that an Apatosaurus swallows plants whole, without chewing a bite?"

Sarah laughed. "I can't thank you enough. You're an angel."

"She's not an angel," Carter said indignantly. "She's my prisoner."

"Shiver me timbers," Rachel said. "Be ye gone and let meself get about me business."

Sarah felt teary for no reason. "I'll be right across the hall. And then I'll grab Carter for lunch so you can have a break."

Violet's room was empty. She had few of the knick-knacks that the others seemed to collect—no photographs in cheap plastic frames, no decorative plates on her walls. Violet had no family, at least none that came around. Dorothy had told her that she'd arrived before the carpet, cooped up in here for nearly a decade.

Her wrinkled blanket pooled on the floor. Sarah stripped off the sheets and blanket and started over. She was fluffing the pillows when she heard a familiar shriek.

She turned to see her boy peering in behind the armchair, hands on hips, face flushed. She hadn't heard him sneak into the room.

"There's a baby in the corner!" Carter thrust out his moustached lip. "I think it's dead."

"Why aren't you with Rachel?"

"She's in the bathroom. I think it's really, really dead."

"Let's see then, Carter."

She marched over to the heavy armchair, pushed it away from the corner, and reached in.

"It's Violet's new doll," she said, handing him the doll in its lacy pink dress and bonnet.

"It's a girl." He took it from her carefully and held it inches from his face.

Sweet Rachel had brought in the new doll for Violet after her other one went missing. She'd dumped the doll in the staff room without fanfare, a note taped to the box that read, For Violet. It was exquisitely made, so soft and baby-like. The staff took turns bringing it to their noses to breathe in its talcum scent.

Carter delicately placed the doll on Violet's just-fluffed pillow and ran his finger across its eyelashes. "Maybe the lady who lives here forgot she lost it."

Violet hadn't lost it; she'd hid it. She wanted nothing to do with her new doll. When the staff tried to put it in her arms, she pushed it away and made deep growling noises. If she could still use words, she would have demanded what she wanted—her old doll with the missing eye and bald patches. It was heartbreaking.

"That's a good place to leave Violet's doll, Carter. She can find it there for sure."

He pulled back the blanket, dragging the doll under by its neck. If she didn't get him out of there, he'd have the whole bed unmade.

She took his arm and tugged gently. "Come on now. Let's go back to Rachel. Then we'll have lunch."

Carter darted out and across the hall and through the wrong open door. Sarah sprinted behind him into Audrey's room, only to find Dorothy with her back to them, rifling through one of Audrey's open drawers.

"Where are we?" Carter yelled.

Dorothy turned with a start and dropped her hands to her side before slamming the drawer with a bang. "Sarah. What's this?" She stared at Carter, her expression as blue-black and threatening as the roiling sea.

Sarah instinctively reached for her son, but he'd flattened himself against the wall. Dorothy glared at his smeared eye patch and sooty face. The woman terrified him and rightly so.

"Can I go to Rachel?" he stammered in his faint little boy voice.

"Yes, go," Sarah said. "Rachel is right next door." She pointed, pushing him away. Carter ducked around her and bounded out of the room, leaving the two women face-to-face.

Dorothy stepped closer, blowing air through her nose. "Yours, I presume."

"Yes, that's my son. His name is Carter."

"So now you're bringing your preschooler to work with you?"

"No, no. Of course not." But that's exactly what she'd done. "I can explain," she started, though it seemed stupid to try. She took a deep breath and spoke slowly, grasping for notes of credulity. "There was an emergency with daycare this morning. This meant I was given no notice, nor could I give any to you. I didn't want to leave the unit short-staffed and have you and my colleagues scrambling for coverage. Rachel Moss kindly offered to watch Carter."

Dorothy shifted from one giant foot to another. "It's highly inappropriate. You can't expect family members to look after your son all day. And Rachel Moss? Her mother palliative, no less. We have rules."

Sarah stood tall, chin high, though her insides were flopping about like a caught fish. "I know there are rules, Dorothy."

"Well obviously you're willing to break them."

Sarah could feel heat rise from her chest to her ears, a raging fire that she needed to douse. "Bringing Carter here this morning seemed like the best solution from a list of few choices. As a contract worker, I'm not entitled to personal days, as you know."

"Of course, I know!" Dorothy narrowed her eyes, her expression hard and impenetrable. "I hired you. And you accepted the terms. Eagerly, you might remember."

"You're right, I did, yes, and this job is important to me." A roof over their heads required any number of humiliations. "I want to do my best. I'm truly sorry. This will not happen again, I can assure you."

"Go home. Get yourself straightened out." Dorothy turned away dismissively, a great swirling of stale air. "Now!" she added, before stomping off.

Sarah leaned against the door frame, feeling small and beaten, a prisoner of war. Rachel and Carter stared at her from their doorway. When she got to them, Rachel said, "We heard the whole thing."

"Heard what whole thing?" Carter clung to Rachel's tie-died shirt.

Rachel whispered in her ear, imitating Dorothy's cutting voice. *"And Rachel Moss. Her mother palliative, no less.* I'd like to bitch-slap that woman until her ears bleed."

"I'm sorry," Sarah said. "I should have never put you in this position."

Rachel scoffed. "Sorry? I've had the best time in ages. I'm thinking of changing careers, taking over a pirate ship. Carter can be my first mate."

"Can I, Mom?" Carter asked. "What's a first mate?"

"We've got to go, buddy. Say thank you to Rachel. And let's give her back her scarf now."

"Nonsense," Rachel interjected, before Sarah could untie the knot. "Every pirate needs a bandana. Let him keep it."

"Can I, Mom?"

"Not unless you say thank you first. Now, go grab your toys."

He wrapped his grateful arms around Rachel's neon leg, grinding his painted face into the shiny pink fabric before skipping to the table.

As he crammed his treasures into the backpack, Victoria stirred, a slight fluttering of sheets and the mewing noises of a little blind kitten.

Rachel looked at the deathbed and sighed, a sadness in her eyes. How unfair and random, the burdens for some and not others. Soon, she and Carter would walk out her door, leaving her stuck there.

Rachel's eyes glistened, a far-away look. "I wish you didn't have to go. I was doing good with Carter, wasn't I?"

"Of course, you were. He adores you. You've been so kind, and I can't thank you enough."

Victoria choked and sputtered, a wet rattly sound. Carter spun around from the table, startled to find a dying woman lying there.

Sarah needed to get them out of that room. She grabbed Carter's hand and left Rachel alone with her mother and the wounds still between them.

Chapter 13

Nick spent until after midnight getting his computer sorted. Deleting the cached images, running virus and malware scans, removing toolbars and extensions. The kid's search was innocent enough. Big titties and happy thumpers. Normal even, if not behind schedule.

Nick got why Billy didn't confess to the porn. What he couldn't understand was why Billy didn't tell him about his parents. How hard could it be to pass along that tidbit? *Your mom and pop stopped by. The end.*

How had he let it get this far? This distance with his parents. It was their hope he couldn't face. Their unrelenting willingness to take his dropped crumbs of decency and turn them into a banquet. He'd rehearsed his confession a hundred times. A thousand times. His mantra before sleep and upon waking. *It was me who started the fire. Me who was drunk. Me who destroyed the world you created.* But the lies he told himself had long since taken over. Why hurt them this way? Why ruin their image of their perfect, only son, the boy they'd raised to be good, when the living, lying version was so pathetic in comparison?

Weekends together or how-you-doing phone chats had become too painful. He hadn't even bothered to pass along his new number. He wanted them to give up.

The call came at a quarter past nine. He'd been barrelling towards Neesley at thirty kilometres over the speed limit. He'd already be late for his ten o'clock.

Your dad phoned, head office told him. *An emergency, you need to call home right away.*

Nick swerved into a farmer's field access, picturing the worst. Ways their bodies could have betrayed them. A heart attack. Brain tumour. Breast cancer. Or a more sudden tragedy. A terrible fall. A collision with a freight train.

It hadn't occurred to him the emergency could be his tight-lipped boy.

They were not dead or dying. Not fragile as they pelted him with a hailstorm of questions, their speaker phone clicking in and out as they talked over each other. *Why didn't you call, Nick? We've been waiting for your call. Why didn't you tell us about Billy?*

So they'd met him then? When?

It took some time to untangle the specifics. Apparently, they'd had a brief visit with Billy a few days before. Surely Billy told him they'd come? Surely Nick could have shared the news himself?

He had planned to, he assured them, but everything happened so fast. Billy was a surprise; he was still sorting it through.

His parents were now live-in caretakers for a large apartment complex in Edmonton, his dad patching drywall, changing furnace filters, fixing electrical and plumbing issues, while his mom organized socials in the activity room and soothed resident squabbles. Nick had an open invitation—*We'd love you to come anytime, son*—but he'd still never seen the place.

He answered each of their questions. No, he hadn't kept in touch with Billy's mother. No, she wasn't that blonde girl from BC. Yes, he had money. Yes, he had milk in the fridge. No, Billy didn't spend his days cooped up in the house. He had a summer painting job, nine to five most days, strict supervision. Yes, Billy had his own phone. Yes, he'd give them his number.

You were still a child, his mother said, removing any blame from his seventeen-year-old self. His father agreed.

They were seeing him as they knew him, playing out his back-to-school special, the one where his bright future stretched across the screen. They'd stayed stuck in the past, same as him, because of him, their feet cemented to the floor of their front-row seats.

It was a painful and awkward inquisition that lasted over an hour. He owed them that much.

"Billy's a good kid, an excellent artist." He found himself explaining Billy's love for his grandma, his love of art and food, his quick wit and quirky sense of humour. The sun beat down on him in the cab of the truck, but he refused to open the window, as if he couldn't bear for the cows to overhear.

His mother wanted to know what they had done to be shut out like this, a weariness in her voice that shamed him deeply. How many times had she asked herself that same question?

"Maybe you could come down," he heard himself saying. "A Sunday sometime. Spend the day with us. Get to know your grandson."

He could hear her sharp intake of breath. "Oh, that would be lovely, Nick. So lovely. We would love that."

"When?" his father asked. "Which Sunday?"

He immediately regretted his guilt-driven invitation. "August sometime?"

"Which Sunday?" his father repeated.

The inevitability of it, their lives intersecting around his table, Billy tossed into their family's baggage like a forgotten backpack. It scared the bejesus out of him.

"Which Sunday?" his father repeated for the third time.

He could hear static over the phone line, his mother's voice cheery and far away. "I'm looking at the calendar. We're free all Sundays in August except the nineteenth. We've got Sid and Margaret's fortieth anniversary party. You remember them. The Jorgensons. Campsite eighteen. What about the seventh?"

Nick scrambled for more time. "How about the twenty-sixth."

"It will be hard to wait that long," she said. "But I'm writing it down now."

His head pounded by the time they were done sorting dates and promises. He honked at the cows as he pulled away. He needed to reschedule the Neesley inspection, mumble some apology, but he rang Billy instead.

Billy picked up after a dozen rings, "Yeah, what's up." He sounded breathy and curt, like he had better things to do. Nick recognized it as that same holier-than-thou tone he'd used when he took his own parents' calls.

"I'm on the ladder. Busy right now."

"How's Evie doing?"

"She's busy too." Muffled voices, likely residents bunched beneath his son to watch the paint dry. "You need to back up, Harvey, okay," Billy was saying. "There's a chair, see? Over there. That's right."

Nick gripped the steering wheel, tamping down his irritation. "Why didn't you tell me my parents stopped by?"

Billy said nothing. A woman yelled in the distance, "Bingo in five minutes!"

"You still there? What the hell, Billy. Why didn't you say anything? My mom and dad stopped by, and you couldn't bother to tell me."

Billy snorted. "Tell you? Maybe you shoulda told them about *me*. About your big mistake."

Nick stared straight ahead at the empty road. Of all the mistakes he had made, Billy was the least of them.

"Yeah, I shoulda told them. That's on me. And I was planning to, but you beat me to it. And you're ass-backwards about the mistake part. You're not that."

"Whatever," Billy mumbled. "That it?"

"Thinking we'll have the leftover chicken for supper. With rice and broccoli."

"I already ate the chicken."

Nick sighed. He should start buying turkeys. "Your grandparents want to get to know you. We've got a date. I've invited them over."

"Tonight?" Billy sounded alarmed. Like he could fall off his ladder.

"No, not tonight. Not until August. I'm giving you notice—courteously communicating—which is what people do when they live together. Tonight, we need to go over a few things with the computer. Stuff you should know before you do another search."

"Um. Yeah. Okay," Billy said, all cockiness gone.

Nick hung up, not satisfied exactly, but not torn up either. They could muddle through this, whatever this was.

Nick's face lit up when he answered the ring. It was Sarah. Billy wanted to eavesdrop—maybe they were planning another Full Moon Pizza run—but Nick headed outside, letting the screen door slam. He held the phone to his ear, pacing back and forth in the yard like a dog on a chain.

Billy watched from the sink, scouring pots and the grunge around the faucet, giving himself reasons to stay at his post. At least it wasn't Candace. Billy would just as soon not see her again.

Nick finally strode back in and handed Billy the phone, smiling. "Sarah wants to ask you something."

Billy wiped his wet hand on his jeans. "What's up, Sarah?"

Could he babysit? It would be a huge favour, she knew. But the daycare lady had a tooth infection, and she couldn't afford to miss more work. Could he manage one day away from his painting? He could watch TV if he wanted, and she'd have lunch in the fridge, and she would pick up snacks tonight, and Carter had a bike and of course a helmet and they could go bike-riding, but it would be up to him, and Carter could be a handful, but Nick said it was okay, and she'd pay going rates, and she'd rush straight home.

It poured out of her in one long string, and she was panting by the time she was finished. Nick looked on intently, mouthing the words, *Say yes*.

"Sure," Billy said, wanting to laugh. She'd sounded so desperate.

"Really? Carter will be over the moon. His dream day come true."

He could laugh at that. "Better than Lucy?"

"Way better. He adores you. And unlike Lucy, you're toilet trained. So's Carter, by the way."

They talked through the when and where and the ways that Carter would try to bend the rules. No space diving off the headboard. And the apartment was a no-helmet zone. Sarah promised to keep an eye out for Evie and find ways to keep her busy.

After their goodbyes, Billy tried to hand the phone back to Nick, who clutched his wrist and wouldn't let go.

"Thanks, Billy. You're doing a good thing here." He sounded as desperate as Sarah, like Billy had agreed to donate a kidney. What was up with the adults in his life? Although he did feel a bit off himself, a rumble in his gut. He'd never babysat before.

"And don't take money from her, okay." Nick finally gave him his hand back. "I'll pay." He dug into his back pocket and pulled out three twenties. "I'll find you some toonies too. Travel allowance for incidentals. Slurpees and whatnot."

"Yeah, okay." Billy took the money happily.

"And Billy. Stay away from Prairie View tomorrow. Sarah's got some shit going on over there. Carter needs to be out of the picture. Right?"

"What shit?"

"It's just hard for her right now. Being a parent is hard."

Like being a kid was a piece of cake.

Billy stuffed his backpack with markers, paints, brushes, sketchpads, and the flattened Tootsie Rolls that Candace had given him. He'd never been in an apartment building before. The stairwell was dank, and the fluorescent lighting buzzed and popped in her second-floor hallway. All it needed was that creepy music from a horror film, that *um-dm-em*, before the alien slithers down the wall.

But Sarah threw her door wide and Carter, still in his pyjama bottoms, dragged him noisily into their bright and lemony room. Sarah handed him her list of Helpful Hints and Contacts, a full page, front and back, while Carter yelled, "Go, Mom, you can go now."

She hugged them tightly in turns, kissing them on their foreheads before she ran out the door.

Carter was off-the-charts excited. He hauled Billy from room to room, showing him where he slept, where his mom slept, where they kept the cornflakes and spoons, where they peed and brushed their teeth. He pulled out every toy in the box.

They battled behind the couch and hunted for treasure in the pillow caves, switching from bad guy to good guy for no reason.

Carter paused often to correct Billy on his sound effects. "You have to go like this when you shoot the laser—*pew, pew, pew, pew*," or, "Bo doesn't talk like that. Her skirt is her cape you know."

Sarah called on her coffee break to see if they were both still alive. Nick called twice before lunch to find out the same thing.

By the time he got Carter wrangled into his chair in front of Sarah's sandwiches and veggie dip, the apartment looked like a bomb had gone off—pillows, blankets, toys scattered everywhere.

Carter hadn't shut up for a minute, even as he chewed through the carrot stick disappearing into the side of his mouth. He was still in his PJ bottoms, food scraps and milk drips plastered to his skinny bare chest.

Billy's phone beeped between the ice cream and cookies. Another video from Nick's mom, this one of Bear curled into a ball on a pillow, snoring loudly. The caption read. *He's bored. He wants you to come play with him.* Cathy had sent a dozen videos: Bear dragging a frisbee out of a leaf pile; Bear in a top hat prancing on hind legs; Bear wearing sunglasses in the kiddy pool. He'd been a rescue dog, and Cathy and George loved him like a kid. Cathy had texted several times since Nick gave her his number, and while he sometimes laughed at her jokes before he meant to, he hadn't asked for this family.

He pictured his real grandma, her lunch in front of her, surrounded by people wearing bibs, saying nothing at all. Until that moment, he hadn't thought of her once all morning. It shocked him to think that he could forget about her so easily. Bit by bit, he was being pulled away. Now someone else reminded her to take her pills and brush her hair and open the curtains and look out at the world. Even Nick was in on it; he bought her toilet paper. *Diapers.* He found it confusing, all that relief mixed with guilt, like blending wrong colours and ending up with mud. He'd check on her on his way home, get right in her face, remind her he was Billy, and they were family.

After lunch, he had Carter dry dishes before they dismantled the war zone. He got him into shorts and a shirt. Got him to pee. Got him into runners instead of rainboots. Got on sunscreen and bug spray, despite Carter's protests as predicted on page two of Sarah's list. The helmet was no problem.

The kid was decent on a bike, slow and steady and old-man serious, and Billy only had to remind him a few times to keep his eyes straight ahead. They stayed on the sidewalks, stopping at every intersection whether there was a car or not, walking their bikes through the crosswalks.

The skate park was empty, like he'd hoped. It was a small concrete space with stairs and launch ramps, a concave bowl and snake runs, bright graffiti scattered in patches. They rode in a big circle along the outer edge of the concrete lip, then practised going in and out between the graffiti lightning bolts of the dips. Carter wanted to launch himself off the big ramp, but Billy said no, definitely not, small ramp only, which was barely two feet high. Billy's stomach flipped every time Carter went up and over.

Carter loved each turn and twist, every small burst of speed. He was a superhero, a motorcycle cop, a cowboy on his stallion. They were both sticky with sweat by the time Billy forced a timeout.

He plunked them down in the grass beside the skateboard park sign and dug through his backpack, pulling out drinks and granola bars, sketchpads and markers.

Carter refused to take off his helmet as he sucked his juice box dry and crumpled it in his fist.

"See all the art around here?" Billy pointed to the graffiti balloons. He could do better. "Let's do our own designs."

He opened the sketchpad and drew Carter's name in giant bubble letters, adding zigzags and borders and fishlike characters with huge eyes and teeth. "Why don't you colour these, add your own shapes."

Carter lay on his stomach and got to work, feet stuck in the air, mouth never stopping. Billy sketched a keyboard with skateboarders in poses on top of the keys.

They stayed at it a while, Carter's page a rainbow of scribbling, his face spotted in every colour marker. A couple of teenage boys came rolling towards them, the plywood tail of their skateboards snapping against the black tarmac road. Billy stiffened as they wove in and out, flipping their boards into the air, as easy as breathing. He didn't want to be caught colouring with a five-year-old.

"Time to pack up, Carter," he said quickly.

But Carter waved frantically at the boys. They jumped off their boards and got up close. Billy stood slowly, ready to pull Carter behind him. But he found nothing menacing, just wide-eyed grins, normal teenage cluelessness and curiosity. The beefy one had an angry patch of road rash on his thigh and a smudge of dirt on his cheek. Billy guessed they were about his age.

"I like your helmets," Carter said, looking up from one to the other.

Beefcake smiled. "Thanks. Yours too. Where's your board?"

"I got a bike."

The skinny guy with glasses took a long swig from his water bottle, then wiped the back of his hand across his open mouth, a railway track of metal braces glistening in the sun. He offered the bottle to the group. Carter started to reach out his hand, which Billy grabbed hold of.

"You guys brothers?" the skinny guy asked.

Carter laughed like the question was ridiculous. "No. He's babysitting. Mrs. Brandon has a toothache."

Beefcake nodded in sympathy. "I'm Ben, and this is Leo."

"I'm Carter."

Carter pointed to Billy, who had not yet managed to say a word. "That's Billy. I can do jumps with my bike. I know all the traffic rules. I rode over here from over there. I'm a good drawer too. I can do my own designs."

Leo laughed, holding up his hands in surrender. The kid could talk paint off a wall. The sketchbooks lay open on the grass, and he bent down and squinted at Billy's skateboarders doing tricks along the keyboard. "Cool. I like your drawings. You're really good."

It was not an asshat observation. "Thanks," Billy said, still unsure.

"Billy's an artist," Carter added helpfully. "That's his job when he doesn't have me. He paints murals. At Prairie View."

"Prairie View?" Ben said.

Leo hit him in the ribs. "Duh. The old people's home. Where Jacob's grandma lives." Then to Billy, "Really? You got a job?"

"Yeah. Well, just for the summer." He hated his cracked voice. He sounded like a hamster.

"My mom works there," Carter added. "She doesn't paint. She vacuums."

Ben picked up the sketchpad in his giant hands and studied it closely. "So you paint this kind of stuff on the old people's walls?"

"Not exactly." He checked for snark in Ben's big face, couldn't see it. "It's more realistic. Like scenes. Hills, trees, trains, that kind of stuff."

Ben nodded. "Cool."

"So how come we've never seen you around?" Leo asked. "What school do you go to?"

Billy shrugged. "Just moved here."

"So, Thomas Berkley Junior High," Leo said. "It's your only choice. It's okay. As long as you don't get Mrs. Deacon for homeroom. She's a hardass."

"I'm in grade one," Carter interjected loudly, getting the focus back where it belonged. "Not now 'cause it's summer. I've seen my room. It has the whole alphabet on the wall. And numbers too."

Leo laughed, tapping the top of Carter's helmet. "My mom runs a daycare for rug rats like you. I bet you're five, right?"

Carter nodded, beaming.

"You should come round and meet the boys. We got a trampoline and a frog sandbox in the backyard."

Carter tugged on Billy's shorts, nearly pulling them down. "Can I, Billy?"

They all laughed.

"Fifth and Main," Leo said. "Can't miss it. Kids bellowing out back. Purple front door. Purple bench. Purple trees. Mom's a purple freak."

"Trust me, it's a whole lot of purple," Ben said, handing Billy the sketchpad. "See you around. Bring your board next time." He backed away, Leo behind him.

Billy and Carter stood under the sign as the boys jumped on their boards and glided into the bowl. It was like watching a dance, from their flip tricks to their soaring air off the ramps. Billy could feel his fingers sketching their movements. Carter gawked with his mouth open.

They watched for a long time before Billy called it a day. They pedalled back to the apartment, mostly silent, Carter likely dreaming about skateboard tricks, Billy still going over the particulars. He'd met some kids, and despite his fumbling, it wasn't awful.

Chapter 14

"So are you coming or not?" Billy wanted to know. He was at the front door, wearing his best striped shirt buttoned to the top, hair slicked back and glossy with God knows what.

"I said I'm coming," Nick grumbled, although he wished he'd said no. There was baseball on TV and beer in the fridge. He couldn't fathom why the kid was so riled up. It was the Sweethearts Dance for a bunch of old ladies, not prom with a shiny-lipped girl. "What time is this thing over?"

"Eight o'clock."

Nick laughed. At least there was that. And Sarah would be there. There was that too.

"That's what you're gonna wear?" Billy demanded.

Nick looked down and shrugged. He had on jeans and a T-shirt. Same as every other day.

Billy sighed, exasperated. "The invitation says semi-formal." He sounded like a disgruntled old man. "We're gonna be late."

"All right. All right. Give me a minute." He rummaged through his closet and came back wearing a musty-smelling suit jacket over the T-shirt.

Billy rolled his eyes and marched out the door, the screen banging behind him. Nick winced. He stood, staring at the empty space, wondering if he'd ever be more to his son than the deadbeat dad in the rundown shack. They'd had their good moments, a few shared laughs, but there was a whole lot of blankness in between. Sometimes he could feel Billy's stare boring into the back of him. He couldn't stand to see his failings through Billy's eyes; on a clear day, he could spot the worst in himself on his own.

The drive took seven silent minutes. Once inside Prairie View, Nick followed Billy down the stairs to where that grim family meeting had been held. They stood in the doorway, the room packed with partiers, mostly old-timers, but family members too, even a few kids dressed in their Sunday best. The transformation was remarkable. The whole building must have been invited, not just the dementia group, as old lady pairs strode past having perfectly lucid conversations. The lights had been dimmed, and foil stars fell from the ceiling on ribbons; helium balloons bobbed from strings on chair backs. A table had two giant red hearts attached to the front of the tablecloth, plates of squares and cookies, a punch bowl and tiny cups with handles. A dance tune blasted from the speakers while old ladies swayed in front of the chairs that had been arranged in a large circle around the perimeter. No sign of Sarah.

Nick turned to Billy, but he'd disappeared. Nick surveyed the wrinkled bodies and silver heads to find him on the far side of the room beside Evie, who sat next to the piano in a sunflower dress. Billy whispered in her ear, then pulled her up. Nick watched in disbelief. There was his awkward teenage boy, leading his grandma onto the dance floor, holding her steady in his skinny arms, two-stepping with ease.

Nick had to sit. He found an empty chair near the door, not taking his eyes off his boy. Billy's face was as bright as the hanging stars. He babbled to Evie, and she tilted her head back and laughed, neither missing a step, sunflowers whirling.

Nick sucked in the party air. He felt an overwhelming need to cry. It came on suddenly, like a fierce bout of nausea, an alien feeling that made him defenceless. He had no idea what was wrong with him. Happiness or hope or a crippling humility in witnessing Billy and Evie and their belonging to one another. He felt dizzy, the music distorted and far off, his chest expanding until his ribs ached. There was something more too, a strange déjà vu, like he'd seen this same dance before.

He was shaken out of his stupor to find Sarah beside him, her hand lightly touching his arm. She glowed, her cheeks rosy, eyes bright. She wore a mauve sundress with tiny straps, one falling onto her freckled shoulder. "You okay?" she said. "Penny for your thoughts."

He tried to smile, slowly coming back into himself. "That'll be a nickel. Inflation and all."

"Thoughts are supposed to be cheap," she admonished, a mischievous look in her eyes.

Nick stared out at the dance floor. A polka had started. Billy knew those steps too. "Just watching my boy."

Sarah looked on with him, her feet tapping to the music. "Isn't he something."

Nick didn't have words.

Sarah said, "He can paint. He can dance. He can sing."

"He can sing too?"

Sarah laughed. "Just guessing. But he has saved our lives. Carter and I will be eternally grateful."

Nick had no idea what she was talking about.

"He didn't tell you? Of course, he didn't. Parents are always the last to know."

She leaned in close, and he breathed her in deeply.

"Billy and Carter made friends at the skate park. Best day of Carter's life by the way. Leo's mom, Amanda—Leo is one of Billy's new friends—she runs a daycare and had one extra space. Carter started today. She's got three other kindergarteners and a couple of four-year-olds. When I picked him up, he was covered in grunge and exhausted and deliriously happy. She's got a trampoline and swings and a huge backyard, and she can bark orders like a drill sergeant. I love her."

Nick thought of Billy at the skate park. Billy making a friend. Billy building a life in this town.

Sarah blinked, looking worried. "Too much information?"

He held up his hand. "No. No. Sorry. It's great that you've got things set up for Carter. He should have the best. It's just, it's all news to me." He'd grilled Billy about his day with Carter but got nothing.

"You haven't honed your interrogation techniques yet. It's a learned skill. Speaking of skills, a rescue is required." Sarah pointed to the snack table, which Carter was glued to, a cookie in each hand, cheeks stuffed.

"I better go." She stood and pressed her skirt creases with her palms. Then she turned and smiled as she wagged her finger at him. "You know you can't just sit here. The girls outnumber the boys ten to one. You have a duty to grab some ladies and spin them around. It's in the bylaws."

Nick watched her sashay away, mauve dress swishing against her beautiful bare legs. Watched as she bent down to Carter's height and gave him a long squeeze.

The music ended to scattered clapping. Billy led Evie towards him, and Nick jumped up so that she could have his seat. Billy plunked himself down in the chair Sarah had just left. Nick took in their shining faces. Evie had on pink lipstick and gold flowered earrings.

"Where'd you learn to dance like that, Billy?"

Billy shrugged. "From Grandma. We've been dancing in the living room since I was a kid."

"You're still a kid." His slicked hair was holding up remarkably well. What had he used? Motor oil? "Well, you're really good. You too, Evie. Fred Astaire and Ginger Rogers."

"Huh?" Billy said.

"Fred Astaire," Evie said wistfully. "That boy could dance on air."

Nick patted her arm. "It's a great party. They've gone all out. The stars and the lights and balloons."

Billy nodded. "Yeah. It's cool. Sarah said it's damage control because of the things gone missing."

A good tactic, families milling and smiling. "Do you want me to get you kids a party drink? A cookie or two?"

The music started again. Another old waltz.

"I would like you to dance with me," Evie said firmly.

"Me?" He was taken aback, unsure how to say no.

But she'd started to stand, leaning into the chair's arms to pull herself up. "Billy, can you hold my seat."

Billy said, smirking. "Sure, Grandma. Go, Nick, go."

Nick kicked Billy's foot before taking Evie's hand and leading her to the floor. He found an empty space, away from the wheelchairs and walkers and Billy's stare.

He looked down at the small woman. "Shall we?" He raised his arm out to the side. Evie placed her palm in his, her fingers cradled between his thumb and forefingers. She rested her other hand on his shoulder, like a small bird perched on a branch. His dizziness was coming back. He stepped out with his left foot, and she followed, the music carrying them away.

"Beautiful, beautiful brown eyes," Evie whispered close to his ear.

Nick felt heat rise in his neck, then more heat still. She was merely repeating the words that were crooning from the speakers.

His dizziness was overpowering, his palms damp, mouth dry. With it came a sudden dawning from deep down, from cellular memory more than consciousness. He'd held this same woman in his arms before. He could feel it in his bones, the pressure of her hand in his, the way she moved.

He tried not to step on Evie's foot or knock her off balance. But it was like he'd left his body and travelled back in time, and if he could only close his eyes, the pieces would fit. He could be right back there, at the Campground Reunion Dance. This same small and fierce woman, clearer-eyed and in charge, pretending to follow his lead. She'd changed so much in ten short years. Everything about her seemed different: her long hair cut short, the way she walked and talked, her looks of confusion.

He held her more closely. "Evie, do you remember that dance? Do you remember finding me?"

"You're such a good boy." She squeezed his sweaty palm.

He wanted to shake her. "Evie, this is important. We danced before. You came and found me. Can you try and remember? Please."

"Here you are," she said dreamily.

But the music stopped. The moment was over. A new tune started up, some staticky jig that Evie wanted nothing to do with. He led her back to Billy, who was beside the snack table, roughhousing with Carter and the crowd of kids circling him.

He dropped Evie there, where Billy would watch over her, and backed out of the room, disoriented. He staggered down the hallway and sat in the empty stairwell, leaning forward, hands on knees, breathing fast as if he'd been chased by his past.

An Ackerman Campground Reunion Dance, five years after the fire, a celebration of the rocking good times had by all during those long, hot summers. He'd wanted nothing to do with it, but his mother had begged. *Please, Nick, we haven't asked much of you since, since . . .* She couldn't even say it.

The dance had been orchestrated by the campers, his parents delighted by *the thoughtful surprise.* It was held at the Lincoln Hall, a creaking wooden structure not built to code. One large room, plus a few ancient appliances and a sink in the corner beside the cramped bathroom. People showed up in droves—the Whites, the Suggetts, the Ponds, the Robsons, and the others. Even the twins made the trip, Randy with a bride on his arm and a baby in a stroller. They came with tents and motor homes, folding picnic tables and trunk-loads of firewood, setting up their temporary camping sites in a circle on the scrub grass beside the parking lot.

By the time Nick showed up, the party was in full swing, people spilling out the front doors, music booming into the night sky, a child's night light of a moon, rosy and round. He'd driven with a bottle between his knees, and he took another long swig for courage before he opened the truck door.

He entered the fray doggedly, like a man going into battle, playing his part as campers swarmed him with wrapped arms and planted kisses and high-fives, Zak grabbing and lifting him off the ground in a bear hug. They were genuinely happy to see him, enshrined as he was in their memory. The carefree boy with the easy smile. The boy who wrestled with their kids and MacGyvered their propane tanks to connect their barbecues to their lanterns. They believed that's who they'd found.

Once inside, he waved at his parents, who were deep in conversation with a group of old-timers. He manoeuvred his way to the coolers table and pulled a beer from the ice. He found a spot on the wall and studied the twirling couples and clumps of campers with their arms around shoulders, relieved to find none of his summer girls, not that they had ever been part of this crowd. Most of the kids his age had moved on, started their careers, embraced their lives. Those who had come clung tightly to the partners they'd brought.

Zak sauntered up and pretended to punch him in the gut. He hadn't changed in five years, still loud and obnoxious and full of trouble. "See that lady over there? She's been checking you out for the past half hour. Hasn't taken her eyes off you. Who is she?"

Nick looked to where Zak pointed. A small and serious-looking woman, standing alone in the crowd, her long braid of silver hair falling nearly to her waist.

"No idea," Nick mumbled. She was in her fifties maybe, a hippie flower child. He'd never seen her before.

She stared back unapologetically.

"Well, she's heading your way." Zak laughed, bending down to grab another beer from the cooler. "Good luck," he said with a wink.

Nick chugged as she made her way over.

"I would like you to dance with me," she said firmly. Just that. No small talk, no nice-to-meet-you.

"My name's Nick. I don't think we've met."

"No, we haven't." She took his hand and he followed.

She was a remarkably good dancer, making him feel more sure-footed than he was. He was relieved to be given this job, saving him from the lies he'd have to tell the others when grilled about his post-campground life. But she had questions of her own. Plenty. Not the usual time-wasters, like where do you work and what are your hobbies. She wanted to know who he admired, if he thought beauty was related to morality, what gave life meaning, could fear be channelled into growth. At the time, it seemed he'd never met anyone like her. But here in the basement stairwell, he knew that wasn't true. Her daughter, Miranda, had that same frankness, that same penetrating gaze. Billy too.

He'd let his guard down while dancing with Evie that night. It might have been the liquor or her reassuring hand in his. He told her his fear of losing his way. Of all his hard stumbling. He told her he'd made mistakes and had no way to fix them.

They stayed together through one dance after another. When the music stopped for a cake intermission that brought whoops and cheers, she patted his arm and whispered, "You're a good boy."

He offered to bring her a piece of cake, but by the time he'd worked through the line, she was gone. He never saw her again.

She was a part of his life now. Evelyn Peat, the harmless old grandma, unrecognizable and most certainly underestimated, ravaged by the throes of Alzheimer's. She must have had a premonition of the disordered attic her mind would become, a diagnosis even, planning the future like a master chess player. She had tracked him down when she still had her wits, her hapless opponent, and made him audition for the role without knowing it.

Up until now, his questions had been unanswered. He'd gone over and over the specifics. How had Evie known where to find him? How long had she been watching him? Why had she named him her power of attorney? How did she know he would say yes?

It filled him with anger the way she'd played him; the way she'd kept him in the dark all those lost years, not once trying to involve him in his son's life. But underneath the heat, a clanking ring of gratitude too. By dancing with Evie, he had been given Billy, if not then, now. He had passed a test that night—shame-filled and slightly drunk—by confessing to who he was.

Nick could hear the click-click of heels from down the hallway. He stood quickly, not wanting to be caught moping in the stairwell.

Sarah came towards him, a lace shawl draped over her bare shoulders. "There you are. Party's almost over." The muted music echoed through the wall.

Nick shrugged. "I needed some air."

"I wanted to thank you again for lending me Billy. This summer would have been a disaster without him. Mrs. Brandon and her stolen cigarette breaks. The craziness with everybody's treasures going missing. Billy has brought the colour back. And I don't just mean the walls."

Nick kept quiet as they walked slowly back towards the party room.

"Carter has been dancing with the little girls," Sarah added. "It's so sweet."

When he still didn't say anything, she stopped and placed her hand on his arm. "Are you okay?"

He must have looked unhinged. He was unhinged.

"No. No. I'm fine," he said, trying to turn it around. "Sorry. It's just that it's been nice. This dance. Evie. Feeling like a part of the family."

Sarah smiled and wrapped her arms around him. He held her tightly, the soft fabric of her shawl bunching under his hands as they swayed to the faint thump of the drumbeat, her warmth seeping into him. They locked eyes, their lips dangerously close.

But the music stopped before they could close the gap. A muffled announcement over the microphone. People filing out the doorway at the end of the hall.

He untangled from Sarah, disoriented. Her cheeks crimsoned as she held his gaze.

The night was ending, but this might be a beginning too. He did not have to be a bad human; he could damp down his feelings of failure and try for goodness instead. If Evie had been willing to take a chance on him, he could step up and meet her halfway.

Nick waited until Billy had gone to bed before heading to the Ploughman. He chose a quiet table near the back, far from his usual window spot and away from the rowdies clustered around the pool tables. Candace had her head down, filling the popcorn tray, and hadn't noticed him come in.

The room was packed for a Thursday. Men mostly, rough looking. A burly guy he'd never seen before sat at the bar, tapping the side of his sweaty glass. One half of his face looked as though it had been badly burned, the skin over his cheek puckered with silver-white lumps, swallowing his eye. Nick had to look away.

Billy Joel blared from the jukebox. Nick watched Candace shimmy around, doling out change for the old men on the VLT chairs, pouring rounds from pitchers, slapping away reaching hands. She was competent, remarkably so, thoroughly in charge of her place in the world. She deserved her name in neon above the door one day. She deserved more.

He was losing his nerve, about to back out, but she caught his eye, squinting in surprise, and strode towards him.

"Hi there, stranger. About time you showed up." She leaned close, her breasts spilling from her tight tank top. "What are you doing hiding back here?"

Nick swallowed. "We need to talk."

Candace laughed, her eyes opened wide, and Nick couldn't be sure what she thought.

"So serious," she said, tsk-tsking. "Got a break coming up. Bring you a Johnny?'

"No. Just a ginger ale. Thanks."

She raised her eyebrows before turning away.

He waited rigid in his dark corner, sliding his sweaty palms down his thighs. She took her sweet time before sidling into the chair across from him, plunking down a pitcher and two chunky stemmed glasses.

"Margaritas." She poured them both a glass and leaned in for a toast, her just-smoked cigarette smell filling his throat. "For old time's sake." She clinked her glass with his, took a long swig, then puckered her lips.

He put his untouched glass down. "I want to apologize for the other day," he said.

She raised an eyebrow, took another drink. "You already did."

"No, I mean after. Back at your place."

She dipped a finger in her drink, swished it around and sucked on it slowly, in and out. "Apologize for what," she said.

It occurred to him they weren't on the same page. "I took advantage of you."

She laughed throatily. "Jesus, you can be daft. Don't get your panties in a twist. I'm a big girl."

He pictured her glassy Sunday eyes, her dead weight as he dragged her to her bed. "I'm sorry anyway," he said.

She relaxed, a grin on her face. "Have a drink. Chill."

He couldn't keep stalling. "I can't see you anymore, Candace."

She stared at her drink, lips tight. He rested his hand on her arm, but she yanked it away.

"Things have changed. I've got Billy now."

She took a long, slow drink.

"I'm sorry." He didn't know what else to say. She might not care one way or another, all his worry for nothing. "Say something, Candace."

"What do you want me to say?"

"That I'm a dick, and you deserve better."

She snorted. "That make you feel better? You're too good now, is that right? You're a daddy all of a sudden, can't be fucking a girl like me?"

He felt a deep wave of shame for the pair of them, but he had to finish what he started. "You can't show up at the house anymore. And I'll stay out of your hair too. I won't come back here. You'll never have to see me again."

"Well, aren't you Mister Generous. What did you think we had going? A love story? You expect me to be all shook up, crying in my beer." She was raising her voice, making a scene. "You want to keep your tiny pecker in your pants, go right ahead."

She stood, knocking her glass to the floor.

Nick stood too, slipping in the sticky liquid. "I'm really sorry. I'm an asshole. It's not you."

It was the wrong thing to say. She hurled the pitcher at him. He sucked in air, shocked by the icy cold hitting his face, stinging his eyes, dripping sticky down his neck and in his ears.

The guy with the caved-in face lumbered to their table. He reeked of booze and old sweat.

"This guy bothering you," he asked Candace.

"He's bothering me greatly." Candace hugged her chest.

The room quieted as Nick dripped and blinked. He could feel a dozen pairs of eyes hoping for a brawl. He widened his legs, planted his feet, and waited.

It came as a one-two punch, a left hook to his stomach followed by a blow to his cheek. The back of his head slammed hard against the floor, his teeth piercing his lip. It took him a few minutes to get air back in his lungs. He raised himself on an elbow, head spinning, ears ringing. He cupped his hand under his chin and worked his jaw, his cheek fiery hot and shredded, a line of red mixed with margarita syrup dripping down his shirt.

A drunken group had circled. He looked up, recognizing some. No one extended a hand. Candace stared, arms crossed, eyes fiery. What had he expected?

He shakily got to his feet. "I don't want trouble. I'm going to go."

Sunken-face kneaded his knuckles. "Yeah, I'd say that's the right idea." He looked pleased in a grotesque, lopsided way.

"You forgetting something?" Candace said.

What more did she want?

She spat the words, "Your tab."

His whole body shook as he awkwardly pulled two twenties from his pocket. He extended his hand, but she kept her arms locked under her breasts, so he dropped the money on the table. Fight over, the group of disappointed onlookers parted to make room.

He felt better and worse by the time he pulled into the driveway. He was done with the Ploughman crowd. Done with Candace's kind of comfort. Since Billy, his wasted years had become painfully clear, now stamped all over his battered face.

It was after midnight. He tried to be quiet as he stumbled around the kitchen. He leaned heavily into the sink, sopping the blood off his face and neck with wetted paper towels, dumping ice cubes from their tray onto a tea towel.

He turned to see Billy in his underwear, hair dishevelled, eyes wide.

"Sorry. I didn't mean to wake you," Nick said sheepishly.

"Are you drunk?" Billy asked, refusing to come near.

Nick shook his head.

"You smell like you're drunk," Billy said.

"I wish." Nick smiled, which hurt the side of his mouth. "I had a pitcher of booze dumped on my head."

Billy stood there another moment, taking him in, then hopped on the kitchen counter and stared him up and down. "Why?"

"Candace did the pouring. I went to where she worked tonight and told her I didn't want to see her anymore."

Billy's eyes widened. "She did this to you?"

"A guy at the bar helped her a little."

"You were in a fight?"

"Nope." Nick wrapped the sides of the tea towel and held the ice gingerly to his face. He'd been a willing target, a man craving that kind of sweet release. "It was a one-way thing. I took a couple punches. The end."

Billy scrunched his eyes. "Does it hurt?"

"Like a son of a bitch."

"So how come you don't want to see Candace anymore?"

What could he tell his son? That Candace was a distraction? That he gave nothing away when he was with her?

He chose his words carefully. "Candace and I don't have a lot in common. We weren't a couple, we just hung out sometimes. It seemed like a good time to part ways."

Billy nodded, his skinny legs dangling over the cupboards. "You really stink."

Nick laughed, then flinched. "Margarita special."

"Maybe you should get stitches. I could go with you to the hospital."

"Nah, I'm okay." The ice had numbed the sting, and there was no fresh blood on the towel. "We better call it a night. I gotta work tomorrow."

Billy grabbed an apple from the bowl and jumped off the counter. "Yeah, I gotta work too," he said, as if they were a couple of stubble-faced grunts on the clock.

Nick watched him traipse to his room, taking comfort in his boy, feeling one step closer to deserving him.

Chapter 15

Billy and Nick packed bologna sandwiches and pickles and cookies and headed out.

They rolled down their windows in the Sunday morning heat, to-go cups of black coffee between their legs. "So how far?" Billy asked.

"Not far."

They were heading to the lake. Nick wanted to show him where he'd snapped the cattails photo now painted on his grandma's wall. Billy would start the alarmed door next. It was Sarah's idea to turn it into a flower shop, with baskets near the floor and poking out from behind a pretend window. Tricky business to paint a door with family and staff coming and going. Dorothy was dead set against it, but the staff convinced her that a disguised door would stop the residents, especially Mazie, from setting off the alarm every fifteen seconds. Dorothy caved under the condition that he work at night. It would be his first solo project, and freehand, no projector, which scared the crap out of him. At least everyone would be in bed.

He was to start Monday night. Nick grumbled about the schedule and child labour laws but insisted he'd do the pickup—no matter the time. *You're not riding your bike home in the middle of the damn night. You either call me, or the deal's off.*

Billy let the cool air blow over his face through the open truck window. Nick drummed his fingers on the steering wheel. He'd been in an unusually good mood for days, which was weird since he looked like he'd been dropped from the roof of a tall building. His face was an interesting mix of purples and reds, a crusted gash curving down his cheek like a sharpie swipe.

They glugged their coffee and stared out the window at the farm buildings, horses circled around hay bales, tails swishing, cows dotting the fields, the sky big and cloudless.

"Is that the lake up ahead?" He pointed to the long line of aqua blue separating earth from sky.

"Yep," Nick said.

"It's big. I was thinking more like a slough. Something you could paddle across."

Nick laughed. "Well, you could try, but it would take you a while. The lake is eighty square kilometres, give or take."

They followed the turn in the road, slowing to a crawl at the flashing light. Signs popped up for bait shops and boat rentals, minigolf and ice cream shops. Traffic picked up too, and they got wedged between two motor homes. Billy had never been on a boat or played minigolf. He leaned out the window to get a glimpse of what was coming.

But Nick turned onto an empty gravel road, away from the crowd. They bounced along, spitting gravel and dust, and Billy closed his window to keep from choking. They came to a cluster of rundown cabins scattered among the trees, an empty playground with a few rusted swings. From there, Nick turned off on a narrow, unmarked road.

"Looks like nobody comes this way."

"That's the point," Nick said.

Billy wondered if they were lost. There was no sign of water. A farmer's potato field had sprouted along the side of the road. "So was your campground around here?"

"Nope. That's on the other side of the lake. I'm taking you to the cattails."

Nick parked the truck in the ditch. Two rows of overgrown trees led through the field like a canopied walkway. A thick metal chain looped around the end tree trunks, blocking the entrance. The weathered sign tacked into the ground read Absolutely No Trespassing.

Nick cheerfully jumped from the truck, swinging the backpack. Of all the places he could choose, this was it?

Billy slid out his door, expecting a guy in camouflage gear to pop out of the potatoes and shoot a round. "What about the sign?" His voice croaked.

"Don't worry about that." Nick sidestepped over the chain. "That's just to keep the ATVers out. We can get down to the lake this way."

Billy followed reluctantly. It was like a secret world past the chain barrier, cool and dark under its lid of overlapping branches from the towering trees. The path was overgrown with tall, wet grasses that pricked his bare legs. Bugs flew up every time he stepped down.

Nick had gotten ahead, and he turned back and said, "Farmers created this road allowance to move machinery around. But now it's just a highway for animals."

Billy sped up so they were walking side by side. "What kind of animals?"

"Deer mostly. Squirrels. Porcupines. Birds and beetles."

"Bears?"

Nick looked at him oddly, which made him feel stupid.

"We're heading into the wetlands. There's no bears here. Just sasquatches." He slapped the back of Billy's neck. "And mosquitoes."

They walked in silence, taking in the sounds and smells. Billy had never been in a place like this, cocooned by the trees, life teeming around him. He slowed his breathing and took in the rich colours and lack of town noise, wishing he'd brought his sketchpad. A ladybug on her climb up a reed; a butterfly, its stick legs attached to a leaf as its black and orange wings opened and closed.

He was concentrating on the tree moss, their greens and greys, when Nick shot out his arm, forcing him to stop. He pointed to a spot up ahead.

Billy squinted at the chocolate-coloured chicken, not much bigger than a pigeon, standing on a stump. He smiled at the way its tufted head perked right, then left, as if trying to solve a problem.

"Ruffed grouse," Nick whispered. "Go slow."

As they approached, the chicken puffed to twice its size. It stood tall and beat its wings, faster and faster, making a deep thumping sound that went on and on. It brought its wings down, then did it again.

"Keep going," Nick said quietly. "He's just protecting his women."

They moved past, but when Billy looked back, the bird followed, running back and forth along the path like a drunk roadrunner.

Billy grabbed Nick's arm. "It's chasing us."

Nick turned and smiled. "Escorting us out of his territory."

They kept walking, Billy backwards, until the bird rushed into the trees and didn't come out.

"What was that bird called again?"

"Ruffed grouse."

"What women?"

"Huh?"

"You said he's protecting his women."

"He's probably got a couple of hens hiding around here. Grouse are territorial."

Nick knew a lot about birds and ecosystems and things Billy had never spent two minutes thinking about. He wouldn't mind learning.

The road allowance ended with dense bush, and Nick entered a skinny path barely wide enough to squeeze through. Billy followed him down a long winding hill, clumsily swatting at the branches that snagged his T-shirt. When they got to the bottom, the view opened, a vast meadow with grassy rivers, the blue of the lake in the distance.

"This is the wetland," Nick said reverently.

Billy shielded his eyes from the bright sun. There was the rickety boardwalk, a thousand cattails rising out of the soupy marsh like hot dogs on sticks, birds with red wings and others with yellow heads perched on top like they were waiting for lunch, calling to each other, fluffing their bright shoulder patches and spreading their tail feathers.

He'd painted this scene. Nick had taken the photo. But in real life, the picture was so rich, so busy, and he could smell the water and crushed shells and hear the gulls screeching above his head and the sum of it made his heart buck in his chest.

They carefully made their way along the bog, avoiding the soggiest patches. When they stepped onto the boardwalk, the planks bounced under their feet, causing blackbirds to fly up from their perches. They clomped down, stopping in the middle. There was no one else in this part of the world. Just the two of them.

"It's pretty cool," Billy said.

"Yeah. It is." Nick eased the backpack off his shoulders and dropped it onto the weathered wood. "Cattail Lane. That's what I called this when I was a kid. The whole shoreline used to be like this."

Cattails sprang up from the marsh, taller than Billy. He reached out and ran his finger along one of the velvet cigar-shaped heads.

"That makes an excellent fire starter," Nick said. "Survival tinder if you're stranded. And you can eat the stalks. Fry 'em up in a stir fry. Or you can dry the roots and pound them into flour."

"You planning to dump me here, Nick?"

Nick laughed as he stripped off his runners and socks and dangled his feet off the edge, making ripples in the murky water. Billy kept his runners on. He didn't want to know what lurked beneath the surface.

They unzipped the backpack and pulled out their picnic and ate their sandwiches. One by one, the blackbirds came back to their posts—making a hell of a racket.

Billy could feel the allure. The air smelled different. He was glad they hadn't stayed on the main road, wedged between the motor homes. "So you want to save this place?"

Nick nodded. "This is the last of the untouched part. You can feel how spongy the earth is under your feet. Imagine ATVs ripping through here. Wetlands can't spring back from that."

Billy thought back to that day in the county office, Nick spitting mad. All those photos of track marks, huge ruts cracking open the ground.

"That's why you met that guy in the county office. Peter, right?"

Nick whistled through his teeth, nodding. "Yeah. That was a bad day. Peter's an asshole, and he doesn't want to hear about it. At least I can't get him to listen. Or anyone else."

Billy leaned back on his elbows and took in the colours. He could see the point; this was a place worth saving. "At least you're trying. You have to fight for what you believe in."

Nick stared at him until it became uncomfortable, so Billy busied himself with cleaning up their lunch remnants, stuffing baggies into the backpack, chugging the last of the water.

"I've been thinking about Miranda lately," Nick said, breaking their silence.

Billy looked at him sharply. Nick had never mentioned his mom before.

But instead of saying more, Nick swung his legs out of the water and stretched flat on the boardwalk to drip dry. He cupped his hands under his head and stared at the cloudless sky, his battered face looking sorry and lonesome. Billy felt sorry too, for what he didn't know, and he turned away so he wouldn't have to think too hard.

"She liked playing games." Nick closed his eyes to block the sun. "She had this one where you pretend you got dropped from a plane into the wilderness. You could only bring one thing and had to decide what to take."

Billy couldn't imagine his mom playing games. Couldn't imagine her at all. "What did you tell her you'd choose?"

"My *Watchmen* comics. Stupid, right?"

"Really. *Watchmen*? I've seen the comic series online. Nine-panel grid. Pretty cool graphics."

"Still got the single-volume edition. It's yours if you want it."

Nick owned *Watchmen*? "I've been working on a graphic novel too. A concept, mostly."

Nick turned his head, propping it in his hand, and fixed his gaze directly on him. "I know. I wasn't snooping. I found your sketchpad under the couch. I think it must have slid out of your backpack. Your images are really, really good, Billy. Like everything you do."

Billy could feel his cheeks flare. "I haven't thought about the graphic novel much lately." It occurred to him he hadn't thought about the story in weeks. If he got back to working on it, he could imagine a whole different ending. Fig leaving his planet. Settling in on Earth. "So you didn't finish. What did Mom pick when she got dropped from the plane?"

Nick laid back down flat, not bothering to swipe at the fly crawling up his leg. Billy waited, impatient. He was about to kick him in the hip when his phone buzzed. "It's probably Cathy," he grumbled, digging it out of his pocket.

Not Cathy. He blinked at the text. He read it once. Read it again.

"So?" Nick leaned on his elbow.

"It's Leo." Billy felt jittery and out of balance, like his body was drifting away from him. "He wants me to come to his basement tonight and play *Split/Second*."

"Leo?" Nick sat up and wiped the dried pond sludge from his feet. "The kid whose mom runs a day home?"

Billy nodded.

"Well, that'll be fun."

Billy had bumped into Leo on his way home from Prairie View yesterday. He would have kept pedalling, but Leo waved him over to fill him in on current events, like the Friday Night Teen Swim, with inflatables and water volleyball and a rope swing and tons of girls. *Wanna come?* He mumbled, *Yeah, maybe,* knowing he wouldn't. Leo asked for his phone number, which Billy never expected him to use.

Billy read the text a third time. "What's *Split/Second*?"

"I think it's a video game." Nick pulled on a sock. "Racing maybe."

"I don't know how to play video games." He could feel a breath-squeezing panic rise in him.

"Billy." Nick reached out and put his hand on his shoulder. "Video games aren't hard. You'll do fine."

But it was more than not knowing video games. It was not knowing any of it. It had been years since he'd been invited to a kid's house. There might have been a few invitations after Jason left, but when he kept making up excuses, they'd petered out pretty quick. Instead, he'd gone to school and come home and gone to school and come home. He didn't know anyone else's house rules, like if he was supposed to take off his shoes or shake hands with the parents or blurt straight away that he wasn't one of the cool kids or give Leo ten minutes to figure it out.

The phone felt hot in his hand. "I can't go. I have to see Grandma tonight. She hasn't had visitors today."

Nick leaned in close. "You like this kid, right? Leo. You like him?"

He shrugged. "I don't know. We hung out at the skate park with Carter that day. And I accidentally saw him for like two seconds yesterday."

"Well, he must like you or he wouldn't have invited you over. Maybe he knows more about video games, but you'll catch on in a minute. And I bet you a hundred bucks he can't paint a mural."

For a flashing moment, Billy considered Nick's words. Leo didn't laugh when he'd examined his drawings at the skate park or stare at him like he was a dimwit loser. Nothing had forced him to send the text.

Nick stood, dragging Billy up with him. "Look, I'll make you a deal. You go to Leo's, I'll go to Evie. I'll spin her around the dance floor. Serenade her with old country tunes."

Billy rolled his eyes. Nick couldn't even whistle on key.

"Text back," Nick said with seriousness. "Tell him you'll go."

He took a couple of jerky breaths, typed OK, and stabbed send. Leo replied instantly, *See ya*, with a string of racing car emojis.

So that was it. He had a time and place, and if he didn't blow it, maybe even a friend.

They headed back the way they came, walking single file up the skinny deer trail and into the cool grasses of the shaded cut line. Nick got ahead as Billy scanned the edge of the trees for the drumming chicken. It had disappeared, probably out chasing hens.

Nick asked, his back to him, "Since we're spilling secrets today, can I ask who the hell is Cathy?"

"Huh?" Billy said distractedly. A monster beetle puttered up a dead branch like a shiny black car.

"Leo's text. You thought it was Cathy. You're not hiding girlfriends in your closet, are you?"

Billy harrumphed. "Um. No. That would be your mom."

Nick stopped abruptly, causing Billy to bash into the back of his legs. "She texts you?"

Billy grinned. "Every day."

Nick looked so stunned that Billy laughed out loud. He pulled out his phone, found Cathy's message thread and handed it over. Nick scrolled through video after video of Bear doing tricks, his face doing its own set of contortions.

When he gave the phone back, he said, "That's good, right? My mom staying in touch?" He didn't look sure.

"Someone has to keep this family together." Billy hoped his words might make Nick laugh, which they didn't. He looked like his world had been flipped upside down.

They walked side by side down the road allowance, Billy keeping his mouth shut. He didn't know what Nick had going on with his parents, why he got so wound up. They were friendly people who gushed over a little dog. Maybe Nick didn't like dogs. Maybe one day he could get a dog. Maybe his mom had been a dog person.

They were coming to the road up ahead, and he could hear tires crushing gravel in the distance. "You still never finished your story. Mom's game. What would she take if she got dropped from the plane?"

"She didn't say."

Billy scrunched his eyes, disappointed, thinking that's all he would get, but then Nick added, slow and quiet. "After she was gone, I thought about it. A lot actually. I went through a whole list of stuff she might bring. In the end, I figured she wouldn't take anything. She was perfect, just as she was."

Nick put his hand on his shoulder and kept it there as they approached the chain between the trees. Billy liked the weight of it pressing against him. He imagined his mom looking down, seeing them heading in the same direction.

Chapter 16

Nick sat on the porch step under the darkening clouds and gulped in the moist pre-rain air. He needed a minute of relief from the kid to get his head screwed on right. On Thursday, Billy had invited Sarah and Carter for Sunday dinner, which meant Evie too. They would arrive any minute. It was supposed to be casual, but he'd been in a near panic for three days straight. He was ashamed for Sarah to see how they lived, and Evie too, in a dilapidated old house that he'd neglected for years.

He and Billy did their best to spruce up the place. On Friday night, they trimmed the sagging hedge, raking the dead stuff onto a tarp and hauling it to a bin at the end of the block. Then they threw the yard junk onto the truck—old boards and broken chairs and shovels—and drove to the dump in the dark. It wouldn't win a Rigsbee Yard in Bloom award, but at least it looked as if the squatters had moved on.

The house had its own problems and needed to be torched. There was nothing he could do last minute about the shabby couch and rickety table and the on-again-off-again oven and curtainless windows and grungy walls. But yesterday, they scrubbed floors and cupboards, wiped grime off the baseboards and the stove top and around the toilet base, removed the old runners and boots from the front closet and added hangers. Billy was uncomplaining and remarkably helpful, upbeat as he waltzed around with a rag in one hand, Mr. Clean in the other, which made Nick feel like a shitty human. Why hadn't his kid been reason enough to get his act together by now?

They fought over what to feed their guests. Nick wanted hamburgers and a salad (he could competently flip patties and throw lettuce into a bowl), but Billy thought a home-cooked meal would be better, especially for their first try. He argued the forecasted rain could make the barbecue a fiasco. And Evie couldn't get a burger into her mouth. And girls didn't like burgers as much as boys. The kid won.

They decided on roasted chicken. Billy diligently texted with Cathy, gleaning tips for how to cook it. Nick took comfort in how easy his mom seemed. She passed on cooking times and temperatures like love notes between a mother and her boys, like there had been no empty decade between them. She even sent a video showing how to position the vegetables around the chicken in the roasting pan, which he and Billy watched twice.

They drove to the Foodmart and filled their cart with everything on their list, starting with napkins for the table and nice-smelling soap and new towels for the bathroom. Billy kept checking his phone and barking out orders—*not red onions, white; not those potatoes, the yellow ones.* They argued over which Brussels sprouts to choose and the size of the carrots. Before heading home, they stopped at the liquor store for wine, which Billy thankfully didn't have an opinion on. Then they both shouted *Dessert!* at exactly the same time, so they drove back to the Foodmart and argued over what type of cake. Billy won. Black forest and a tub of marbled ice cream. Nick picked up a bouquet of flowers wrapped in plastic before ringing the items through, hoping he had a vase stashed in a cupboard.

He did. And a roasting pan. And an extra chair in the shed. They rearranged the couch so that the table could be centred in the room and set for five, and while the water glasses didn't match, and they were missing one spoon, it looked happy and welcoming. Billy had painted name tents using the same swirling colours of the napkins, which he'd folded under the forks. He gave Nick the rickety shed chair in his seating arrangement, putting himself between Evie and Carter. The flowers looked like they'd been jammed in the vase by a clumsy fist, a few drooping in defeat, but they added extra colour. And the oven worked too, thank God. That sizzling poultry smell filled the house, overtaking the bleachiness of all the products they'd tried. They were ready.

Nick stared at the menacing sky and replayed his Sarah moment from the Sweethearts Dance—a memory he had relived over and over. The light in her eyes when she looked up at him, the softness of her shawl, the warmth of her body pressed into his. Their lips so close when the music stopped, leaving him shaken with a mix of regret and hope.

Billy yelled from inside, "Are they here yet?" which Nick ignored since it was obvious they were not. Billy opened the screen and plunked down beside him on the porch step, wearing his best shirt, hair slicked back. He jiggled both knees, full of nervous energy.

"Rain's coming," Billy announced, like he was ninety years old. "It's almost four. We said four, right?"

"Calm down, Billy," he said, though his stomach was doing flips of its own. He touched his bad cheek, not as fat as it was last week, tracing the dented line that would leave permanent evidence. He wanted badly for this to go right; to not be diminished in her eyes.

"Do you think grandma will like our house?" Billy wondered out loud.

"You'd know better than me."

Billy pondered his question a minute. "I think she will."

Nick asked, "Do you think our chicken will turn out all right?"

"Yeah. Smells good. I think it will."

The air went eerily calm, the birds silent. Then a crack of thunder as the wind picked up. Nick could feel a fat drop of rain wet the back of his neck, then the *tap, tap, tap* of drops landing on the step.

"Here it comes."

They dashed inside and then crowded behind the screen to watch the clouds open. It came in sheets, deafening loud, whipping sideways in the wind, gushing out the drain spout along the side of the house.

"Grandma can't walk through that!"

"It'll let up in a minute," Nick said, not sure, wondering if he still had an umbrella in the truck. His phone rang from the kitchen counter, timed to another ominous clap of thunder. Imagining the worst, he strode over to retrieve it.

"Nick? It's Sarah." She sounded breathless. "Evie's had a fall."

Nick turned to Billy, who still stood in the doorway, taking in the storm with boyish innocence.

"Is she okay?" Please God, let her be okay. He could hear the Prairie View door alarm blare, then shuffling noises.

"She took quite a tumble," Sarah whispered nervously, the background noise fading to nothing. "It just happened. Right before I came to pick her up. The nurse is in with her, but we think we should get her to the hospital. She'll need X-rays."

Nick stared at the five chairs around the table, feeling in his pocket for his keys. "We can be there in five minutes."

Billy quick-stepped towards him, eyes huge. "Is it Grandma?" he yelled.

Nick held up his arm, holding him back.

Sarah said, "Carter and I can drive her. We're here anyhow. The staff will help me get her into the car. Meet you at the hospital?"

"You sure?"

"Positive. I'm so sorry, Nick."

He filled Billy in as they grabbed raincoats and ball caps. They ran to the truck, desolate and wet. Billy leaned his head against the foggy window, saying nothing, as they hydroplaned through the dark streets.

They beat Sarah to the hospital, parked the truck, and dodged the swelling puddles in the parking lot, Billy carrying the unopened umbrella at his side. They waited under the overhang by the Emergency sign. When Sarah pulled up, Nick helped Evie from the car and into a courtesy wheelchair he'd snagged, Billy shielding her with the umbrella until they got her through the glass door. Nick insisted he park Sarah's car and when he got back to them, they huddled around the emergency desk, all talking at once, including Carter, who helpfully piped in with, "She's really hurt," squeezing his eyes and cradling his arms, as if he were in pain. Sarah provided the injury details. Evie slipped on a piece of paper in the dining room, falling forward not backward, her body cracking against the pillar edge before crumpling to the floor. The recreation staff had witnessed the slow-motion fall. She did not hit her head. She did not lose consciousness.

Nick felt some relief in hearing it laid out. It was only a piece of paper, a benevolent slip, not the beginning of the end. He'd read about what to expect as Evie's brain cells kept dying: loss of muscle strength and balance; a shuffling gait; fall after fall until limbs went on strike. This was not that. But when he looked at Evie, as pale as death, her breathing seemed laboured and too fast. One eye watered, which she kept dabbing with a Kleenex from her purse. Her arm shook as she raised it to her face and brought it down again.

The nurse led them to a cramped room with an examination table and two chairs. She said, "Maybe a few of you could go to the waiting room. There's a TV there."

But no one wanted to be without the other, so they squeezed in and circled around Evie's wheelchair. Sarah rested one hand on Evie's shoulder and held tightly to Carter with the other. Billy rocked on his wet runners, making squeaking noises on the tiles. They looked like they'd fallen into the lake, the room too close and steamy.

"Maybe we should take off our coats," Nick suggested.

They were in a state of half dress when the doctor stepped in. He was basketball-player tall and had to shoulder his way through to get to Evie. He folded into a squat and gently took her hand.

"Hello Mrs. Peat. I'm Dr. Tarris. I hear you've had a fall."

"Don't be silly." Evie pulled her hand away. "What is all this fuss about?"

The doctor gave a practised smile. "Can you tell me where it hurts?"

Evie repeated, "Don't be silly." Her eyes darted about as she breathed in short, shallow puffs.

"We're going to take X-rays and run a few tests, make sure you're all right."

Her lower lip quivered. "Where's Billy?"

Billy squatted in front of her, dwarfed beside the huge doctor. "I'm right here, Grandma." She leaned towards him and winced. Billy turned to the doctor, as frightened as Evie. "Can I go with her?"

"Sorry, not for this part. You came at a good time. The ER is dead this afternoon." He frowned at their solemn group. "Well, that was not a good choice of words. What I meant is that your grandma will have my undivided attention. We'll be back in a jiffy. Mrs. Peat, maybe you'd like to leave your purse here?"

She pressed her purse to her stomach as he wheeled her away.

They stood frozen, staring into the hallway. Sarah broke the trance by gathering their coats, shaking them out, and bunching them on the hook near the door. She wore a pretty polka-dotted blouse, soaked around the neckline and where her hair fell onto her shoulders. She dropped into one of the chairs, and Nick sat beside her.

Carter crossed his arms, pouting. "There's only two chairs. Where do I sit?"

"You can sit on the bed," Sarah said. "But take your boots off first."

Carter kicked off one boot, then another, and grunted and huffed as he hauled the stool over and climbed onto the paper-covered table.

Billy paced. "I hate hospitals."

"Nobody likes hospitals," Nick said.

"I do," Carter shouted, spread-eagled on the crinkled paper.

"The last hospital nearly killed her," Billy said.

"But it didn't." Nick pictured Billy back in Chetville, behind the curtain in Evie's hospital room, getting himself to school every day, stewing about what would come next and where he'd get dumped. Those memories moved to Rigsbee with his boy.

The minutes dragged on, Billy frenetically pacing, Carter getting antsy. He'd been colouring the paper underneath him with a crayon from his pocket, but the novelty of the examination table was wearing off. Sarah passed him a plastic water toss game from her bag. Carter crossed his legs and bugged his eyes and frantically pressed the launch button.

Nick could think of nothing helpful to say to Billy, so he chatted with Sarah, who wanted to know what had happened to his face, if he'd also slipped on a piece of paper. He shrugged sheepishly and changed the subject. She answered his questions in short clips, her worried eyes following his son. *Yes, Carter was still loving his new daycare. Yes, the rednecks upstairs were still blasting their music all night. Residents' belongings were still disappearing. And Lewis Clifton, well, he'd disappeared too. Left a scribbled "I quit" note on his desk and walked out the door.*

Billy stopped in front of them, hands squeezed into fists. "What if they want to make her stay?"

Sarah reached out, but he shook her off and backed away.

"Billy!" Nick's anger flared and died in less than an instant.

"We'll have to wait and see," Sarah said patiently.

"Whatever," Billy spat, heading towards the door.

Nick grabbed his shirt sleeve. "Where are you going?"

"To the bathroom. If that's all right with you."

Nick sighed, his lungs filling with the hospital air. He turned to Sarah, who was staring at him intently. "Sorry about that. Billy's not usually rude."

She nodded. "Don't apologize. It's scary not knowing. He loves her a lot."

Nick covered her hand with his. They sat motionless. He could feel his blood roar from his heart to his fingertips.

Then Carter shrieked, "Got 'em all," which separated them jerkily. They both laughed as he furiously hunched over his game, paper shredding under his squirming bum.

"I'm sorry about dinner," Sarah said. "We were so looking forward to it. I hope you didn't go to much trouble."

"No, no trouble at all," Nick lied. "Hadn't even ordered the pizza yet."

Sarah laughed. He loved the sound of it. "Raincheck?" he asked.

"Hopefully on a sunnier day."

"I'll hold you—"

Dr. Tarris wheeled Evie through the doorway. He and Sarah stood and leaned into each other. Carter's game pinged to the floor as he climbed off the bed.

Evie clutched her purse, blinking. She had colour back in her cheeks, her look of terror replaced with mild surprise. "Oh," she said pleasantly. "Is this a party?"

Dr. Tarris smiled. "Why not."

They could hear running footsteps. Billy burst into the room, forcing the doctor to step aside or get bowled over. "Is she okay?" He bent and kissed Evie's cheek.

"Is she okay?" Carter repeated, edging beside Evie's wheelchair and fiddling with her brake lever.

Both boys were right up in her smiling face, firing questions like bullets. *Does she need surgery? Did she get a bandage? Did she break her bones? Can we take her home?*

"Enough," Nick warned, holding out his arm. Then more calmly, "Enough kids, okay? Give Evie some room and let the doctor tell us what's going on."

Billy held Evie's hand and stared at the doctor. Sarah grabbed Carter and made him stand beside her.

"There's good news and bad news," Dr. Tarris addressed Billy directly. "First the bad. Your grandma has a broken rib. That's going to hurt for a while—she will experience chest pain if she breathes too deeply or bends over or laughs too hard. There's not much we can do other than give her body time to heal. We've ordered some Tylenol to be added to her meds at Prairie View. She'll be bruised for a week or two, and bowling and tennis will be out. But as for the good, there are no signs of concussion. No internal injuries. We practised walking in the hallway and her balance is fine. Her vitals are great." He smiled at Evie, who smiled back. "Besides the tumble, you're fit as a fiddle."

"Not too bad for an old lady," she said.

It was embarrassing the relief Nick felt, stepping forward, weak in the knees. "Thank you, Doctor."

"So that's it?" Billy said. "She can leave?"

"Uh-huh. But she'll need to rest and take it easy for a few days. And the Tylenol might make her more sleepy than usual. I'll have their resident doctor look in on her tomorrow."

"Let's get her home, Billy," Nick said.

Dr. Tarris patted Evie's hand. "Now remember what I said, no bowling for the next few weeks."

Carter escaped Sarah's grasp and pushed forward. "I don't think Grandma likes bowling," he stated helpfully, then added, "I do. I'm a really good bowler."

"I bet you are," the doctor said, bending way down and shaking Carter's hand. "Great meeting your family," he added to the group. Nick smiled, noting how others, even the doctor, assumed they belonged to one another.

Once Dr. Tarris was gone, there was a scramble for coats and Carter's wayward boots and the plastic game that had wedged under the cabinet. The table looked like it had been torn apart by a pack of wild dogs, so Nick scrunched the paper and stuffed it in the wastebasket.

Outside, the sun peeked through scattered clouds, its rays glistening in the leftover pools of water. It was comfortably cool, no wind, so they took their time getting to their vehicles, Carter skipping ahead, stomping in puddles, Billy solemnly pushing Evie in her wheelchair, he and Sarah following, strides matching, bodies touching.

Nick wanted to take her hand. He didn't know what to call this burst of emotion thundering through his body. Today was a victory for Evie and Billy, for the time they had left together. He could sort the rest later.

They said their goodbyes in the parking lot, Carter pouting because he couldn't go to Billy's house, Sarah promising she'd come see Evie first thing in the morning. It took some finagling to get Evie into the truck, so Nick jerry-rigged a stool ladder from toolboxes in the bed, and Billy held tightly as she climbed into her seat. She was more concerned about her purse than her ribs, which they took as a win.

The staff fussed over her at Prairie View, administering the Tylenol, helping her into flannel pyjamas. A nurse cheerfully brought her dinner to her room, the tray arranged with a rose in a plastic vase. Evie was content to eat dinner in bed, propped up with pillows, though she didn't understand why, her fall long forgotten. Nick and Billy sat on either side, watching for signs of distress. Billy did the talking, carefree musings, no trace of his dark thoughts from before. He was thankful to have her back, his world righted again. Every time Nick chimed in, Evie glanced curiously at him—*who are you and what are you doing here*—but she was too polite to inquire and carried on as if a stranger at her bedside had to be endured.

They stayed with her until after eight. She was ready to sleep, so they turned on her night light and quietly backed out of the room. Nick stayed near the exit while Billy zipped down the empty hall to let staff know they were leaving. While he waited, he studied Billy's latest project, the one that had consumed his last week of nights. The alarmed double doors were now a storefront with baskets of flowers topped by a striped canopy. Billy had cleverly disguised the doors' push bars as window frames; cleverly hidden the security keypad in a cluster of ivy leaves. The design was brilliant, and it was all his own.

Nick pictured his son in front of the looming project, residents down for the night, his imagination transforming the puke-green doors into something beautiful, his body parts working in unison, his heart directing his brush strokes.

Nick had been the one not paying attention. Billy had texted for a pickup around one every morning. After four nights their new rhythm had lost its charm, and the minute Billy climbed into the truck, Nick grumpily demanded to know when he'd be finished. Billy was chill, nonchalant, like he'd just gotten off a shift slinging fries at McDonalds, his paint-splattered fingers the only evidence of his masterpiece. *I'm done*, he said, like it was no big deal. Nick didn't even ask how it turned out.

Billy came back down the hall and whispered, "They're going to check on her through the night, make sure she's okay."

Nick laid one hand on his shoulder, pointing to the flower shop doors. "Billy, this is such fine work."

Billy grinned. "Yeah. It needs a few coats of varnish, but I can do that when everybody's up. No more night shifts." He cocked his head, examining his work critically.

"Maybe we ought to think about art school."

Billy scrunched his eyes, but if he had a question, he didn't ask it. Nick didn't care what path his son chose. Anything he set his mind to would turn out.

"I'm starving," Billy announced on their drive home.

Nick realized he was too. "Damn it," he said, remembering the chicken.

By the time they got to it, the chicken had morphed into a wrinkled turtle, the vegetables a sooty mush that had glommed to the roasting pan. It looked nothing like the happy platter at the end of the cooking video. But at least the house hadn't burnt down, and with the windows open, the scorched smell was bearable. They left the table as it was, set for five, and ordered pizzas, eating in front of a National Geographic special about wolves. Nick thought about phoning Sarah just to hear her voice, but he didn't want to break his connection with Billy, whose socked feet lined up with his on the coffee table. He decided to call it a good day.

Chapter 17

Sarah had been preoccupied with Nick all morning. She couldn't shake the memory of their almost-kiss at the dance. The way his eyes softened, the warmth of his hands on her back, the tenderness in his touch. But his bruised face and absence of an explanation had her concerned. If it were a simple accident, he would surely have said so. No, a black eye said nothing good about this man she barely knew, a man she had willingly let waltz into her son's life. And wasn't it her job—perhaps her most important job—to stay vigilant? And yet. There in the hospital, she saw Nick as a man rock solid, so present and patient with Billy, so gentle with Evie. She'd watched from the parking lot as he'd held onto Evie's purse while helping her into the truck.

A ruckus down by Mazie's room pulled her away from her thoughts, so she hurried to head it off. Mazie was yelling at Ruth, who'd wedged her wheelchair in front of Mazie's door, blocking her entry. Mazie had had a rough morning, refusing to call *Bingo* when her row was filled, refusing to accept a cookie from the snack cart. Now she was winding up to slap the top of Ruth's head.

Sarah managed to nudge Ruth and her chair out of harm's way. Mazie slapped Sarah with the force of a slip of paper brushing against her uniform sleeve.

"You're a stupid woman," Mazie yelled. "Stupid, stupid, stupid."

"You want to go into your room, Mazie? Let me help you."

Mazie shuffled through her doorway, Sarah following, closing the door behind them to keep the others out.

"This is my room," Mazie glowered.

"It certainly is. It's a lovely room."

Mazie looked blank. She'd already forgotten her spat with Ruth and had moved on to this new fight. "This is my room," she barked. "Get out."

"Of course, Mazie." She helped her settle in her chair by the window. "You have a nice rest here in the sunlight. See if you can spot a robin. We'll come get you for lunch soon."

Mazie was asleep by the time Sarah got back into the hallway. Such a difficult morning, the latest uproar over Violet's missing hummingbird. It had dangled from a frayed string in Violet's window, big as a fist. It looked nothing like a real bird with its faded green velvet and broken wing, but Violet used to bat at it every time she looked at the sky. First her doll, now her bird. It was so unfair. And with all the other disappearances, the staff were increasingly on edge, turning trivial matters into all out wars. Just the other day, Angelica and Leslie yelled at each other over whose turn it was to fill the hand sanitizer dispensers. They laughed about it later, but they all agreed it was becoming harder to stay focused.

Sarah had time before lunch to check on Evie, who'd quickly become a favourite among the staff, everyone watching out for her since she'd broken her rib. Evie had a sunny disposition and seldom complained, and her skills as an artist were brandished all over their once-dreary walls.

Sarah parked her housekeeping cart at Evie's door and found Billy and Evie squeezed together on the small couch in her room. "Two of my favourite people. How are you doing this morning?"

"Oh, hello," Evie said. "Can I help you?"

"We're playing X's and O's." Billy pointed to the sketchpad on his lap. "Grandma's won five out of seven."

She sat on the edge of Evie's bed across from them. The sun streaked the dappled linoleum, the room as warm as Venus. Like most residents, Evie preferred it greenhouse hot, her sweater buttoned to her neck.

Sarah smiled at the pair. "No painting today?"

Billy shook his head. "We're taking a break. Grandma's rib still needs healing."

"Good idea. But I'm excited to see what you come up with next." The bulrushes and train were lovely, and now the flower shop door.

"We're gonna hold off for a while." Billy added an X, passing the felt marker to Evie. "I got canoeing camp next week. With Ben and Leo."

She was thrilled that he was finding his place, finding new friends.

"Canoeing," Evie said, catching that fragment of their conversation. "That's wonderful, Billy."

He turned to Evie and said, "It's not overnight or anything. I'll still come visit after supper, but I'm gonna be on the water most of the day."

"Got any lunch plans?" Sarah asked.

He dramatically slashed a line through his X's and yelled, "Booya!" which made Evie laugh. "I'm eating with Grandma. They're bringing lunch to the room and sneaking extra for me. A cracked rib goes a long way around here."

She laughed. "Well, carry on. I'll leave you to it then."

"Sarah," he called out before she got to the door. He loped over and whispered confidentially, his voice throaty and nervous. "There's something wrong with Rachel."

She leaned in, whispering too. "Rachel? Why do you say that?"

"She's been crying. A lot. We hear through the wall."

Sarah's heart lurched. The poor woman, her mother's fight for breath so excruciatingly drawn out.

"Oh, Billy. Rachel's mom is near the end."

He crossed his awkwardly long arms. "You mean she's gonna die here, like next door?" His cheeks reddened. "They're not going to take her to the hospital for that?"

"That's right," she said calmly. "Mrs. Moss will stay here with us until the very end. Her breathing will slow down and become irregular, and it might stop and then start again or there might be long pauses between breaths until her breaths stop altogether. It will be peaceful for her. And after Rachel has said her goodbyes, the funeral home will come and move Mrs. Moss onto a stretcher and take her away so she can be buried."

Billy rocked slightly, arms crossed, a fixed look of concentration as he stared at the floor.

"It's a sad time for Rachel, so it makes sense that she might cry. Are you okay, Billy?"

"Yeah," he said, though she wasn't sure. "What should I say to her?"

"Just be yourself."

"I thought she was crying for the bunnies," he added.

"Sorry? The bunnies?"

"She's been feeding them at her house—well I guess technically it's her mom's house, except her mom doesn't need it anymore, obviously, so it's up for sale."

"Oh," Sarah said, confused.

"They're chewing through the flowers. Not Rachel's flowers; she doesn't have any. The neighbours told her to cut it the hell out with the feeding, gardens torn up and turd piles everywhere, but Rachel said she'd never met an unkind bunny and she could do what she wanted with her own front lawn. They're pissed. Really pissed. They won't let her walk their dogs anymore. Some guy put a letter in her mailbox and called her a lunatic Peta-phile and told her to go back to where she came from. Like he has a clue. That house is exactly where she came from."

Poor Rachel, this shitty town conspiring against her yet again.

"I'll go see her right now."

He nodded, his face uncreasing in stages, relieved perhaps, as if she had the power to fix this.

"Nice to see you, Evie," she called out with a wave, then pressed her open palm against Billy's chest. "Don't you go eating your grandma's lunch. You leave some for her, you hear?"

She was glad to step back into the air-conditioned hallway and let the cool air blast down on her. Rachel didn't deserve to be shunned by her neighbours, not now, and not all those decades ago.

She pushed her cart into the Moss room. Rachel slumped in the chair beside her mother, a shrunken, faded version of her fireworks self.

"Thought I'd pop in to see how you and your mom are doing." She went first to Victoria and busied herself with adjusting pillows and blankets, checking the sheets for signs of wet, the frail woman eerily translucent, her skin a silvery sheen, like broken down rock in a desert creek bed.

Rachel watched, despondent, her nose a brilliant red, raccoon rings of mascara under swollen eyes.

"Rough day today?"

Rachel shrugged. "More of the same."

"I know this isn't easy. Why don't I bring you a cup of tea? A few cookies?"

Rachel shook her head.

Sarah ran her duster along the ledges and light fixtures, prattling while she worked. "I've got Carter into a new day home. He's thrilled to bits to run around with a pack of boys in a huge backyard. Even a trampoline. He keeps asking about you. *When can we see Rachel again?* He's asked a hundred times."

Rachel slumped in her chair, her face pinched and shiny. The longer she sat without moving, the more Sarah could see the lost girl she had been. She moved on to the sink and countertop, using liberal squirts of disinfectant. She could hear the staff in the hallway, coaxing residents towards the dining room. "And Billy's new door mural has been such a godsend," she said, her voice light and breezy. "It feels a lot calmer down on this end. The alarm hardly goes off anymore. The whole lot are bamboozled into thinking it's a real flower shop and not a way out. I caught Edith with her nose to a rose."

Sarah was worried by Rachel's silence, a fog settled over her. Her mother remained as still as a faded painting. "Is there anyone we can call? Anyone who can be with you?"

Rachel stood slowly and went to the window, arms crossed, swaying as she looked out. "I know what they say about me."

"Who?"

"Everyone."

Sarah felt her heart thud. Of course, Rachel knew. All the gossip and innuendo about the long-lost Moss girl come home. The nasty neighbours trying to run her out of town. "Well, you're certainly admired here at Prairie View. The way you've tended to your mother all these long weeks. The way you strong-armed management into letting us have the murals."

Rachel remained with her back turned, posture rigid. "People love to hate poor white trash," she said to the clouds.

"They don't know you like I do."

Rachel turned, her gaze intense. "You don't know me at all." Her voice was like the snap of an elastic.

Sarah tensed. "I think you're a saint," she said quietly.

"A saint?" A bitter laugh escaped her lips. "You think I've been the stoic dutiful daughter? I've been leaking resentment. It's been pouring out of me like boiling oil. I've been whispering in my mother's ear. Telling her every little thing she couldn't hear when I was a child."

Sarah's heart sank, her sympathy swelling. Of course resentment would be part of the mix.

Rachel crossed the room, stood over her dying woman, and lightly touched her cheek. "Mother wasn't the mean one. But she didn't get us away either. She let it go on and on and on and on."

Sarah rushed to stand beside her. "Rachel, I'm so, so sorry. It's not fair. None of this is fair."

"You think I'm a saint," she scoffed. "Some days I still want to strangle her."

"But you haven't. You've sat by your mom and watched over her and told her what you needed to say. That doesn't make you bad. You can judge the heart of a person by the way they treat the weaker among them. Isn't that how the saying goes? Bunnies. Little children. Struggling teenagers. The dying. That's how I judge you. I've seen it and felt it. You have a good heart."

Rachel turned her mascara-streaked eyes towards her. "Billy told you about the bunnies?"

Sarah nodded, hoping she hadn't just broken a confidence.

"One of the neighbours has threatened to smash their skulls with a baseball bat. I think he wants to smash mine too."

Sarah's stomach clenched. "That's horrible."

Rachel sighed from deep within her chest, radiating a dreadful kind of angst. "I thought when I came back here this could be a fresh start. But everything's the same."

"Don't let them do this to you. This town is insufferable. You're dealing with so much right now. Too much. I'm amazed you're still standing. You're a good person, Rachel."

"I want to be," Rachel said, her voice trailing off like a piece of string.

Sarah could feel the grief shimmering in front of her. She wrapped her arms around Rachel and held her close, counting the seconds until she could feel the stiffness leave Rachel's body and her arms reach back.

Chapter 18

S arah walked blindly into Dorothy's office, unknowing and uncon-
cerned. Nothing out of the ordinary; she'd been in and out at least
a dozen times, adding her signature to a birthday card, signing off on
tweaks to the schedule.

Dorothy sat woodenly behind her desk, not a hint of a smile, which
also wasn't unusual. But when she barked, "Shut the door," a demand
she had never made before, Sarah felt a strong urge to leave it open.

Dorothy's eyes glared. "I've asked you here today to tell you that
your services will no longer be required. By law, we are obligated . . ."

Sarah heard individual words—contract, rights, notice—but she
couldn't put them in sentences that made sense. She sat on her hands,
which had started to tremble. Was she being fired? Her scrambled
thoughts galloped forward. Back-to-school clothes, birthday parties,
Christmas. How would she take care of Carter?

"Do you understand?" Dorothy finished.

"No." Her cheeks burned. "I don't. Why?"

Dorothy cleared her throat, a phlegmy, rotting sound. "There have
been issues. We're choosing to terminate your contract."

"Issues? What kind of issues?" Her heart thumped ferociously.

"For one, you brought your son to work, left him unattended. You showed extremely poor judgment. While bending the rules, I might add."

That was weeks ago. Sarah knew she had crossed the line and had apologized profusely, her indiscretion well behind her. "And I am so sorry," she said now. "It will never happen again."

Dorothy crossed her arms and leaned back. "I could let one slip-up go, Sarah, but there are other concerns."

"What concerns?"

Dorothy clapped her bicep with the palm of her hand. "You are too chummy with the residents. Your socializing gets in the way of your work."

Sarah sucked in her cheeks and bit down. "I always get my work done. And I'm the same as I've always been." Being kind was not just cause for termination. The woman was grasping at dust. "What is this about, Dorothy?"

Dorothy worked her jaw and stared. Sarah studied her back, waiting. They faced off for some time, until Dorothy spat the words, "You know exactly what this is about."

She didn't. She could not lose this job.

Dorothy narrowed her eyes. "You were rifling through Ruth's purse this morning. I saw you myself. And you can't deny it. It's clear as day on the security footage."

Sarah rewound her busy routine, trying to zero in on what Dorothy might be talking about. Ruth? She couldn't remember talking to Ruth all morning. She sifted back through her steps until she found it. Ruth's wayward purse left in the dining room. Yes, that was all this was. She could innocently explain. Laundry day, Ruth's extra bra missing for a second week in a row. When she saw the purse under a chair, she whisked it out and peeked inside. A logical calculation–Ruth stuffed her purse with all sorts of things. No bra. Nothing but a ball of crumpled newspaper, some wool bits, and a few rancid meatballs which she fished out with a Kleenex and dumped in the garbage.

"I can explain, Dorothy." She was about to when she covered her mouth with her hand, the horror of it sinking in. Her mind wavered between murk and razor-sharp clarity. All that had been stolen from those dear people. Mazie's pearls. Violet's doll. Harvey's watch. Edith's quilt. Dorothy was accusing her of causing all this pain. Sarah found it difficult even to formulate the words. "You think I was stealing from Ruth?"

Dorothy blinked with a flash of uncertainty before her face went blank.

Sarah's body jerked with adrenalin, jolting her forward, slamming her fists to the desk. "You honestly think I'm the thief. That I could steal from these people?"

"Ruth's daughter told me her wallet is missing. So, you explain it then!"

A few of the residents had irrelevant, moneyless wallets. But Ruth? "There was no wallet in her purse."

Dorothy refused to look at her. "I saw you!"

Sarah seethed inside, a violent rush that reached the pit of her stomach, the lunacy of this talk making her want to laugh hysterically. She splayed her fingers on the desk as if about to pounce, Dorothy unable to look her in the eye. Sarah pitied her. Her failure to lead, her failure to grasp any true sense of what had value.

"You are making a very big mistake here. You won't get away with this."

Dorothy reached jerkily for her desk phone. "Are you threatening me?" Her eyes looked frightened.

Sarah stood as tall as she could make herself. "You disgust me. Your incompetence is staggering."

Dorothy studied the phone in her hand, the wind knocked out of her. "I suggest you go now. You're done here. And you'll be hearing from the police. Antonio will see you out."

Antonio from maintenance was standing sheepish and sorry-eyed outside Dorothy's door. She had thought him a kindred spirit, always whistling while he changed lightbulbs or pulled socks out of clogged toilets. But he couldn't look her in the eye either. He solemnly escorted her to the staff room so she could collect her sweater and purse and solemnly escorted her out the front door.

He held on to her arm before letting her go. "Lo siento mucho, señorita."

There were no other goodbyes. She managed to hold back tears as she walked dazedly to her car, hair whipping across her face in the wind.

She held them back into the next day, keeping upright for Carter's sake as she see-sawed between damp despair and white-hot anger. This morning, she made his favourite breakfast of pancakes and sausages; didn't nag when he talked with his mouth full or slopped juice down his shirt; answered each of his questions. He was a different boy since starting at his new daycare. Now he sprang out of bed in the mornings and came back each afternoon equally enthused, babbling about his missions and sword fights and trampoline tricks.

Her whole body felt numb as she drove to Amanda's house, Carter in the back testing his newly learned expressions. *Man oh man, there are a lot of humans out there.* He wore runners, not boots, same as the other boys, insisting on his Thor T-shirt for a second day in a row.

When she stopped the car, he raced up Amanda's sidewalk and disappeared into the sea of boys behind the door. It broke her heart. Carter loved this place, and she did too. And now she had to take it away.

Seven in the morning, the sun trying to break through the early fog, the air oppressive inside the closed car, pressing in on her like the end of the world. She had nowhere to be, so she drove back home without seeing the roads, trudged up the apartment stairs, and locked herself behind her door. She slumped at the table, still littered with the breakfast debris. It was deafeningly quiet—she'd never once been alone here before. She needed a plan, but the part of her that took charge had shut down. Her groceries could be stretched for a few weeks. Her daycare expenses were paid until Friday, then Carter would have to say his goodbyes. She had one month's rent tops. Even less emotional reserves.

The accusation felt like a knife wound, a deep and oozing cut over her heart. It was the unfairness of it more than anything, that her colleagues could think so little of her. The memory would remain as permanently a part of her as Carter's first newborn wail.

She looked around the empty apartment, wishing the tenants upstairs would blast their insufferable music. She used to long for the day when she could steal a few minutes and do nothing at all. Now the empty black hours felt like torture.

She needed a plan. She could start with the breakfast dishes, stretch out her scrubbing. But she couldn't muster the energy to stand. Why hadn't she just stayed calm and forced Dorothy to understand? She could have turned Dorothy around, made her see how ridiculous she sounded. Instead, she offered no defence. Called the woman names. *You disgust me*, she'd said. Look what her wounded pride had done. Left her jobless in a town with big ears. She'd have to uproot Carter, again, start over somewhere else, another dingy apartment, another Mrs. Brandon, another godforsaken town.

She drew figure eights with the tip of her finger on Carter's gooey plate. She'd been penniless and hungry before. Carter was two when she walked out of the meat-packing plant, so affected by the blood-bleach smells and the crowded lines of knives that she felt as if she too was being skinned and chopped into pieces. It took three long months to find another job. Three months of watering down the milk jug and letting Carter run barefoot because his runners squeezed his toes. It took years before she could wash that stink off her.

She was afraid of her muddy thoughts, afraid of Carter's future. She reached for her phone, hesitating, not wanting to show him this pitiful part of herself, but her need was too strong, and she pressed his name with her sticky finger.

Rivers of salty tears poured out of her when she heard his voice. They ran down her neck and splashed onto Carter's plate.

The connection was spotty, cutting in and out. "Sarah. Sar . . . What's wrong? Where are . . ."

"I'm at home." She could barely manage to form the word, gulping and snivelling, unable to catch a breath.

"Sar . . . I'll be . . . stay there. . . . I'm coming."

The line went dead. She held the phone to her heart and kept sobbing.

Nick headed north on Highway 31 to Winsdale for his first inspection, a thermos of coffee and sandwiches by his side, rock 'n' roll cranked, the last of the fog pooling in tufts along the gullies. He'd just dropped Billy off for his third day of canoeing camp. The kid had taken to it like a duck to water, his eagerness infectious as he showed off his paddle strokes with the broom.

Nick had waved goodbye alongside the other canoe parents, as if he too belonged to their secret club, his deadbeat dad persona dissipating with the fog. He couldn't remember his life so complicatedly simple. Work, home, Billy, repeat. His son the engine now propelling him forward with meals to plan, and a house needing fixing, and school to think about in the fall. It had become easier for him to fall asleep each night. Easier to breathe.

The highway was empty when he dipped into a valley, not yet eight in the morning. He was surprised to see Sarah's name flash on his phone, his body reacting with a rush of heat. But something was off. The reception was bad in the valley, and he couldn't decipher the quick, rising, strangled noises. She cut in and out. His heart bounced as he listened to her choppy gut-wrenching sobs.

He screeched to a stop, burning rubber as he turned the truck around. He had the address she'd given Billy, and he careened past everything that moved to get back to her. He tore up the apartment stairs, pounded down her hallway, and banged on her door. She stood on the other side, small and wrecked. He grabbed her with outstretched arms and examined her from head to toe. She was puffy eyed but intact, and he allowed himself to breathe again as he drew her close and wrapped himself around her. She was not injured. This could be fixed, whatever this was. He felt her heart against his, her chest rising and falling in rabbit breaths, and he held her tight, not knowing what else to do. They stayed like that for a long time.

"Where were you when I called?" she said finally.

A tear spilled down her swollen cheek, and he brushed it away with the tip of his finger.

She'd told him nothing, and he needed to take extra care. "Highway 31. On my way to Winsdale for an inspection."

"Can I come?" she asked.

"I'd like that," he said.

She smiled weakly. "I'll have to be back in time to pick up Carter."

So Carter was okay, safe at Leo's mom's place. "I can have you back whenever you need."

They walked hand in hand out of the apartment, down the hallway, down the stairs, and into the truck. The morning mist had disappeared, the sun clean and bright, the sky as flawless as Billy's paintings. She seemed too far away, strapped into her seatbelt, and he cupped his hand behind her neck to assure himself she was real.

It took twenty miles of rolling highway before she started to talk, her voice low and scratchy. He turned the stereo off, straining to hear her words. The story came out haltingly. Dorothy had done this to her. That sack of shit woman had fired her, accused her of stealing.

By the time she was quiet again, his hands fisted over the steering wheel. "Dorothy is batshit crazy," he said.

Sarah sighed. "I could never steal from those people."

"Of course you couldn't. No sane person could think that. You're the best thing that ever walked into Prairie View." He was livid. He wanted to drown Dorothy in a flushing toilet.

Sarah stared out her window. "She told me the police would call. The police!"

"We'll go to them first. Explain your side of the story." He knew he was too loud, but he couldn't get control of his voice. "We'll get this straightened out. Get you your job back."

She looked at him, her eyes sad and unfocused. "I'm not asking you to fix this, Nick."

But he did want to fix this; every molecule in his body sizzled and popped.

"Did you hear me, Nick? This isn't your problem."

"I know, I know. I'm sorry. I'm so sorry this happened. It's not right. Or fair. I just want to help."

He put his hand on her thigh, and she encased it with hers. "You are," she said. "It helps to be with you."

They turned off the highway and drove the potholed road into Winsdale, its main street grey and grim. There were no people about. He couldn't imagine inhabitants, much less renovations.

"Welcome to Winsdale," he read from the faded sign missing half of the *W*. "Population four hundred." All they needed was a tumbleweed rolling past.

He turned onto Third Street, the second story addition easy to spot. The yellow wood sat like a tipped hat capping an old and craggy face. He could tell from the truck that it was a fiasco, the foundation not designed to support that load.

He parked in the shade of an old elm tree. "So this is our first stop."

She tilted her head, surveying the house. "It doesn't look right. The top is too big for the bottom. And it's leaning, isn't it?"

"Yep," he sighed, wishing people were less stupid. "I shouldn't be long. There's coffee in the thermos and sandwiches in the bucket. The keys are in the ignition if you need music or air."

"Or if I need to skip town. I *am* a thief on the lam after all."

"Yeah, but I'm your getaway driver." The inspection was going to take a while. "Will you be okay?"

"I'll knit a sweater while you do your manly stuff."

He laughed, relieved to have this part of her back. He didn't want to get out of the truck. Eventually she pushed him away. "Go. Time is money, Nick."

Chapter 19

S arah watched as Nick gathered his ladder and tools and walked towards the ugly house. The muscles under his T-shirt worked across his back as he moved, his legs all strength and sinew. He was so fully male, yet so boyishly unsure, which made him more beautiful to her.

It frightened her how much she had needed to hear his voice. She seldom cried and never like that, never with a witness, all her sobbing over the phone.

No, that wasn't true. There was that once, when she was just a young girl, barely old enough to do fractions, her mess of hair pulled back with barrettes. Mrs. Dobkins had called her to the front, her turn to display her art project, a golden fish with sparkly fins. It had taken her hours to glue on the sequins. One of the boys hissed, *Carrot head*, as she made her way up the aisle, then another, *Pumpkin patch*, and then all the boys chanted names. She had become used to the taunts, but she was so proud of her fish, so unwilling to let that moment be stolen. Mrs. Dobkins missed it (how did she always miss it?), and by the time she'd turned from the chalkboard, Sarah was lunging towards the first boy, pummelling him with her fists, pummelling the others that jumped in until they were a wild ball of arms and legs, sequins raining down like confetti. Most of the boys cried. She did not. She waited until after the witless Mrs. Dobkins had deposited her in the principal's office, waited until after the nurse had bandaged her forehead, waited until after she was set in the big chair to watch out the window as her classmates poured onto the playground for recess. It was not until her mother rushed into the school, all fire and fury, and scooped her up in her arms. That's when her tears started. They didn't stop until she was tucked under her covers with a hot water bottle and a cold compress and a promise of a million shining sequins to start a new fish.

Her mother was her safe space. Her kind, fearless mother who smelled like their garden, her touch as soft as the peony petals that floated to the ground after a rainstorm.

If her mother were alive, she and Carter would skip to her house for Saturday sleepovers and Sunday dinners, their plates smothered in gravy and grandma love. Sarah would have called her every time she got sick, every time Carter got sick, her soothing voice on the line telling them to rest, to make chicken noodle soup. She would have called her mother this morning, her life thundering towards catastrophe. Instead, she dialled Nick. She barely knew this man, and she could hardly trust her instincts since they had steered her so wrong in the past. Yet his voice was what she needed. His voice. His arms wrapped around her.

He had disappeared into the tilting house. She rolled down the truck window to let in some air. A squirrel noisily argued with an indifferent black cat sauntering down the sidewalk. Two doors down, an old woman with a hairnet and sturdy, white-laced shoes hung laundry on a line that stretched over a thick bed of dandelions. Every time the woman pulled a wrinkled clump from her basket, she shook the fabric angrily until it stretched into the shape of a slip or a blouse.

Sarah pushed her head back and closed her swollen eyes. She hadn't slept last night, moving from her bed to the couch, scrolling through channels and magazines and seeing nothing at all. For a half second, she thought of begging for her job back, but she would never pull it off. Her mouth would twist in rage every time Dorothy's shadow crossed her path. She could not stay in Rigsbee. Not without a job. Not with rumours sucked in with the breeze through every window in town.

She didn't want the plan to form, pulling her away from the safety of the truck and Nick's woody lingering smell. She would move back to the city, start over. Get on with a senior's centre or a nursing home attached to a hospital, maybe even a union job that had benefits. With a little luck, she could find Carter a good school. He'd continue to sprout, learn to escape with a book. She could teach him to skate, and take him to those city places with indoor slides and climbing walls. They still had each other. It was what they were used to anyway, just the two of them, and she could not fail at this one thing.

Sarah heard a door bang and saw Nick extending his ladder against the side of the house. A grubby man in an undershirt and suspenders followed him out and stood beside the ladder, puffing a cigar. Horse dung smoke wafted through her open window. She and the man watched Nick climb, then shimmy along the slant of the rooftop. He seemed surer of himself up near the sky than down on the ground, and she held her breath, willing him not to fall.

By the time Nick got back to the truck, Sarah was asleep, mouth slightly open, head tilting awkwardly. He didn't want to wake her, but the dickwad whose inspection he'd just failed was pacing like a mangy lion, and he needed to get them out of there.

She woke when he opened his door, blinking and confused.

"Sorry," he whispered.

She smiled sleepily, yawning while she fastened her seatbelt. "That's okay. Coffee break's over."

"You're done knitting your sweater?" He started up the engine.

"I knit an entire wardrobe. How about you? Find any holes in the roof?"

"Holes and more holes."

She waved at dickwad, who thrust out his middle finger as they pulled away. "He looks happy," she said.

"I aim to please." Nick turned the truck around at the end of the street, and as they drove by stupid again, still standing in front of his tilting eyesore, Nick honked the horn and gave a thumbs-up.

Sarah laughed. "Are all your customers this pleasant?"

"Only in Winsdale. But now you've seen it. You can't say I never take you anywhere."

"I'll cherish the memory."

She joked, but he really would cherish this memory, Winsdale forever attached to the smell of her hair.

They shared his bologna sandwiches and took turns sipping the lukewarm coffee from the lid of his thermos. He stayed under the speed limit, wanting to stretch the minutes with her. They travelled in a straight line into a patchwork of green and gold, black and white cows and spotted ponies dotting the fields like plastic animals in a farmyard set. Noisy green-winged teals gathered in the pothole sloughs along the sides of the road, diving for food, popping back up like corks.

He'd often driven this stretch without seeing the view, but today, the world seemed new, full of colour and promise.

Sarah slapped her visor down to shield her eyes from the now blaring sun. Nick pulled sunglasses from the glove box and handed them to her. They were too big and kept sliding down the bridge of her nose. He wondered if she still felt shaky and needed to go over it again. The accusation, the fallout, all of it wrong.

Sarah lifted her glasses onto her head and stared at him with bright eyes. "I don't really know anything about you."

Nick laughed. "Um, yeah, you do. Sorry, but this is pretty much it."

"No, I don't really. I want to know more."

"I'm not an axe murderer."

"And?"

"And?"

"Tell me more."

"And I'm a fun-loving single who enjoys travel, long walks, and hanging out with my friends. Redheads preferred."

"Well done. All the clichés."

"Okay, your turn then."

"My mom died when I was fifteen. She divorced my dad when I was five. He's got a whole other family down in California. Didn't even bother to show up for Mom's funeral. Carter's dad is out of the picture too."

"A lot of absent fathers in this story," he said, lumping himself in the bunch.

"Back to the topic at hand. I was asking about you. Tell me about your family."

"Not much to it. Mom, Dad, no siblings."

"I'm not a census taker. What are they like, your parents?"

He kept his eyes on the road. "Good people."

"I knew they would be. Have they met Billy yet?"

"Yep." He felt uncomfortably warm. "My mom texts Billy a lot. They've got a dog. A yappy little thing that likes to do tricks. Billy must have fifty videos of him already."

"I'm glad. Billy needs his grandparents. Sounds like you're close. I love to see that."

"We used to own a campground. The beach. Fresh air. Hard work. Happy campers coming and going."

"It sounds like a fairy tale."

"Yeah. It was."

"And now? Where are your parents now? What are they like now?"

He didn't want her to know the ugly parts of him. He didn't want to lie to her either, so he kept his mouth shut.

"Nick?"

He wished she would drop the subject. When he still didn't answer, Sarah stared out the window, the silence festering. Clouds rolled in from the east, marring the perfect blue skyline. He needed to say something, bring her back to him. "What about your mom? What was she like?"

He put his hand on her knee, but she moved it away.

"Why don't I start where we are," she said. "Yesterday was my darkest day in a long, long time. In my lowest moment I called you. I've spilled my guts to you, literally. And when I ask about you, your family, you brush me off like a stranger, like I'm asking too much of you. Why is that, Nick?"

He was not used to such persistence. "I'm sorry."

"Me too," she said quietly.

The bitter irony was laughable. Despite being innocent, she'd been tried and convicted, and here he was as guilty as hell yet assumed blameless. He could hardly share how pathetic his crimes, how pathetic the life he'd made.

He slowed the truck, his looming inspection just over the next hill, mere minutes away. He could not leave them like this, leave her in the truck alone.

He eased into a farmer's pullout and cut the engine. "You want to know." He kept his hands gripped on the wheel and his eyes focused on the rolling clouds. "I had an idyllic childhood. We weren't rich. I had to make choices. New skates or new jacket, save my allowance for a bike or blow it on Cokes and fries. My parents . . . my parents raised me to believe that I could be whatever I set my mind to. *You dream it, you can live it*, my dad used to say."

Sarah unbuckled her seatbelt and turned to face him.

He sucked air between his teeth to give him courage. "My mom, she liked to seize the moment, break the rules. She'd serve pancakes for supper, make jack-o'-lanterns with pineapples, decorate the outhouses at Christmas. She wore a bathing suit from June to September. Had no problem hauling me out of bed in the middle of the night to watch lightning flash across the sky. *Listen to the music*, she'd say. *God's concert*. Every time I hear thunder, I still hear her words."

"God's concert," Sarah repeated, her voice soft and low.

"She would drop whatever she was doing if you brought out the cards. She had the best poker face and always kept score. Competitive too. Merciless. I must have been thirteen before I beat her in Wizard for the first time."

Sarah laughed softly. He was afraid if he turned to her, he would lose his nerve, so he kept his eyes ahead.

"My dad. My dad seldom lost his cool. He instinctively knew the right thing to do. When Dewy Turner came out of the water sputtering and drained of colour—the kid was terrified, nine or ten years old, almost drowned, his waterskiing tow rope tangled in his feet and dragging him under—Dad dropped his tools and took Dewy and his pale-faced dad up to the house and sat them down at the kitchen table in front of a couple pints of ice cream. I don't know what he said. The next thing, they're back in the boat again, Dad with them this time, skiing tandem with Dewy. He spent the whole afternoon on the water with the kid, until Dewy was screaming like a howler monkey on skis, his heart right back where it started. Dad was always doing stuff like that. The regulars would take a bullet for him. Every summer we had a few bad apples pitch a tent, too much beer in their bellies, itching to stir things up. My dad could break up a fight without raising his voice."

He tried not to sound bitter. "That campground meant everything to them—to us. It brought together all I'd been taught to hold sacred. The earth. The water. The campers. The greater good."

Sarah reached over and peeled his knuckles off the steering wheel. "What happened?" she asked, holding his sweaty palm between hers.

Nick stared at their tangled hands and let the warmth of her fingers seep into his skin. "I torched it."

She squeezed his hand tighter and waited.

"I was careless. And drunk. Started a fire in Campers Hall. It was the hub for campers—my dad and grandfather built it—the place seeped to the rafters in Ackerman history. The hall and everything in it went up in flames. All the photos, my grandpa's vintage radio with the broken dial, the weathered sign with all our silly campground rules. *No synchronized swimming in the puddles.* Even the stupid marshmallow mascot costume. Incinerated."

She looked shattered. "I'm so, so sorry, Nick."

He shrugged. "One thing led to another. My parents had to give up the campground and move on."

"I can't imagine how that must have felt. Was anyone hurt?"

"Not by the flames. No one had to get carted off in an ambulance. But there was plenty of hurt to go round."

"How old were you?"

"Seventeen."

"That's a hard thing for a kid. A seventeen-year-old boy can barely get his shirt on right side out."

"I was supposed to go to university in the fall, but I somehow got it in my head that I could want something different. Something bigger. I was up in the loft, drinking and dumbass dreaming about getting on a plane and seeing the world. At some point, I lit a few candles. Didn't have the wits to extinguish them."

"But you didn't light the fire on purpose. You didn't splash gasoline on the floor and watch it burn."

He shook his head.

She took his face between her hands and forced him to look at her. Her eyes were wide and clear, no jolt of disgust lingering under her lashes. "You didn't mean to start a fire," she said, emphasizing each word. "It was an accident. You can be forgiven an accident."

He took her hands away and held them against his shirt. "It's not that I started a fire. It's that I didn't own up to it. Still haven't. My parents think it was the campground kids partying in the hall, smoking God knows what, letting things get out of control. I never told them otherwise."

He could feel her hand under his turning over, her palm against his. "I haven't admitted it to anyone."

She pulled him towards her. "Until now. Now your secret's out, and the world hasn't exploded. Look at me. I'm not running screaming down the highway. You're not an axe murderer. You made a mistake. You were a kid. We're allowed to make mistakes."

He needed to make her understand. "You know what it's like? It's like tossing a burning cigarette out a truck window and a spark catches hold. You think that you should stop the truck, stomp it out, but you rationalize to yourself that it's just a tiny ember, a small white lie that will die out on its own. But the ember jumps to another patch of ground, and another, and another, until you look back in your rear-view mirror and the whole fucking world is on fire. I've been living a lie since I was seventeen years old. My parents don't . . ." he couldn't finish.

She put her mouth to his ear, "It's not too late," she whispered. "You can turn the truck around. Go back. Douse those flames."

"I've never really left that place. Never got on a plane."

"It's not too late," she repeated.

He felt quieter inside, that relentless hum that lived under his skin turned down. She smiled, cheeks flushed.

"Today was supposed to be about you," he said sheepishly. "Now I've gone and made it about me."

She laughed. "Thank God. Here I thought my life sucked. You've cheered me up considerably."

She buckled her seatbelt. "Don't you have another inspection to go to?"

"Yes, ma'am. We've got three more today."

"Well, enough dillydallying."

"Nobody says dillydally."

"They certainly do. It's big points in Scrabble."

He laughed as he pulled the truck back onto the road. "You know the crazy thing. That's where we made Billy. We met at the campground that last summer. I hardly knew the girl. A spur of the moment, one-time thing that ended up changing me, changing it all."

She whistled through her teeth.

"Wild, right?" he said.

She looked out the window. "Since we're sharing secrets. I want to tell you something too."

He held her hand, knowing enough to keep quiet.

"Carter's father. He was my English professor. In my first and only semester in college. How's that for a classic cliché. The guy was married with kids. Twins, no less. Curls and toothless grins inside the picture frame. I could see their little faces while I lay sprawled on his desk with my legs in the air. I was twenty-three and knew it was wrong, but I was impossibly lonely, and no man had ever paid attention to me like that before. I thought what we had was *special*."

Nick didn't know what to say. Her damn professor. He was the culpable one.

"When I told him that I was pregnant, he begged me to get rid of the problem, so I quit school, my part-time job—him. Left the city and started over."

Nick pictured Sarah driving into the sunset, Carter inside her, Carter now a beautiful boy who made the world brighter. "I'm glad you made that decision," he said. "About Carter."

She rolled down her window and let the breeze blow on her face. "Me too. My mistake turned out to be the best thing that ever happened to me. Your campground gave you Billy. There's grace in this world, don't you think?"

He looked at the honeycomb sky and saw only light, the world suddenly a place where forgiveness was possible.

Chapter 20

B illy waited for his grandma to finish in the bathroom. It dragged
on so long every time he wondered if she took off her clothes. Her
cracked rib didn't seem to bother her anymore, so at least there was
that, but she was less steady on her feet now. There was no hurrying
her, so he stepped into the hallway, wobbling a little, his leg gone numb
from being under his butt throughout all forty-eight pieces of the
basket of kittens puzzle. It was strangely quiet, no residents in sight.
Either the speakers were on the fritz again or no one had bothered to
turn on the hallway music.

Billy peered into the empty room next door. Rachel's mom was
gone, which meant Rachel was gone too. The poor old lady croaked
while he was at canoe camp, and he didn't know if it caused a big
scene or if the stretcher guys quietly whisked her away in the middle
of the night. He was relieved he didn't have to hear or see or smell
any of it, although the place seemed empty without Rachel sitting on
the other side of his grandma's wall in her glowing tights. He missed
her. She talked to him like he wasn't a bonehead kid, like he'd earned
the right to hear whatever she had going on. *Hummingbirds can fly
backwards. Life is just a stack of years. No one can lie like a mother.*

Menopause was a bitch. She'd told him to floss daily so when his hair was gone he'd still have teeth. To never let someone borrow his car, his shoes, or his woman.

He wished he could talk to Sarah, but it had been days without her, and the whole place felt grey. He missed her springy steps as she popped in and out of rooms. Missed hearing her happy out-of-breath laugh. Missed joking with her over sandwiches at the rickety picnic table.

Nick gave him the whole Sarah-getting-booted story the day after it happened. He was so pissed during the telling that his face went from red to more red, sparks popping round his heated head like in a comic.

Billy backed away to a safe distance as Nick stomped around. He'd picked up the details on his own already. It was all the staff talked about. They were on Sarah's side and didn't believe it could be her. Who could? It was the stupidest thing he had ever heard.

Dorothy thought she was in charge, but she was wrong. She had no clue that Sarah was the one who could get Violet to wear shoes or get Ruth to take her pills. It was Sarah they called on when Clement refused to shower because he said the water smelled like piss. There were these little covert operations taking place, like a hidden grid of communications lines. With Sarah gone, the wires got crossed and everything went haywire. He hated Dorothy. She made him want to puke. And while it wasn't brave or nearly enough, he turned his back to her in protest whenever she thundered down the hallway.

He stepped back into Evie's room, but her bathroom door was still closed. He put his ear in the door crack and listened for a flush, but it was dead quiet in there, so he knocked lightly. "You alright, Grandma?"

"I'll be out in a minute, Billy." She sounded annoyed, like he was interrupting an important business meeting. Then she added more generously, "Go ahead and make yourself a snack."

His phone blared in his pocket, causing him to crack his forehead against the door, and he scrambled backwards into the hallway before he could make it stop.

"Want to ride to Ghost Lake?" Leo yelled into his ear.

Billy smiled. Leo was a dork, but it wasn't awful being around him. They'd laughed so hard trying to right their canoe during capsize training that the instructor made them do it again. Twice more, in fact, until their arms screamed, and their mouths stayed shut.

"Where's Ghost Lake?" Billy asked.

"Edge of town. It's not a lake. Just what we call it. More like a slough."

"I'm with Grandma."

"Yeah, I know. I'm with Ben. When you're done. We'll wait."

"Where are you guys?"

"At the front door."

He met them in the lobby of the independent side. They stuck out like trash cans beside the potted plants and plush chairs and the mahogany front desk where no one sat anymore. Lewis Clifton's office was empty too, since no one wanted the manager job, which meant he could slip them in without signing the book or having to invent reasons for their visit. They looked like they lived under a bridge, hair slick with sweat, Ben's T-shirt ripped under the arm pit, Leo's glasses cloudy and splattered.

Leo solemnly held out his hand and placed a dead fly in Billy's palm. "I found this and thought of you."

"Gross," Billy said, dropping it to the floor. His friends were barbarians.

"So can we see where you work?" Ben said. "You know, with the . . ." He stuck his tongue out and twirled his finger around his ear.

"They're not crazy," Billy said hotly. "They have dementia. What's your excuse?"

"Sorry." Ben grinned manically.

"I'll let you in, but you gotta act decent. No horseshit."

Leo sucked his lips into his cheeks and crossed his heart and the pair followed dutifully. Billy turned and glared at them before he swiped the fob. He remembered his first time. The vacant stares, the blaring alarm, the pungent smell of diapers. Leo and Ben huddled together, eyes wide, the door clicking shut behind them, locking them in with the others. The hallway was empty, but they could hear Edith yell, "Help me, help me," from her room up ahead. Edith yelled, *Help me, help me*, no matter what she was doing—eating ice cream, painting a sunset in art class.

"Holy shit," Leo said. Evie's mural was right there. "You painted this?"

"Grandma helped." If Leo turned around, he would have seen the flower shop too.

Leo got up close to the cattails, scrunching his eyes, then backed up to take it in, crashing into Ben, who had one hand under his chin, scrutinizing the wall like an art critic.

Ben whistled. "This is really good, man. Really good. How did you get up in the clouds?"

"A ladder." Billy swelled inside. Leo and Ben were seeing the piece of him he found hard to explain.

"I'll let Grandma know I'm heading out."

The three turned to duck into her room, stopping first to examine the flower shop door they'd just walked through.

"Sick," Leo said. "It doesn't even look like a door."

Ben took a selfie pretending to smell a flower.

When they entered Evie's room, they found her sitting on her bed.

Her eyes lit up. "Oh Billy. How nice to see you." She'd forgotten they'd just done the kittens puzzle.

"I want you to meet my friends." Billy dragged them towards her. They stood in an awkward semicircle in front of her bed. Evie looked frightened of Ben, as would anyone in their right mind. He towered over her and smelled like a gorilla.

"How do you do," Ben squeaked, suddenly tongue-tied.

Leo jumped in, thin and knobby, all manners and couth. "We're pleased to meet you, ma-am. We love what you painted on the wall.

We've never seen anything like it." He sounded so choirboy chirpy, Billy rolled his eyes.

Evie blinked, surveying the room. Her paintings were everywhere. "It's nice to have a bit of colour."

Billy wondered if she was thinking, *What place is this? Where am I?* She still looked dubious of Ben, who was nervously rocking on his heels like a pendulum. Billy thought it best to get them out of there.

"We're going to go now, Grandma. I'll come see you later, okay?"

"Be sure to pick up the eggs, Billy. And be careful. You don't want them to break."

He kissed her on the cheek, and whacked Ben on the back to get him moving.

Billy led them down the hallway to show them the train mural. He didn't need their praise, but a little more wouldn't hurt. As they passed Edith's room, Leo whispered, "Maybe we should go help her?"

"Edith's okay, I promise. *Help me* are her favourite words."

"Your life is weird," Leo said.

"Likewise," Billy said.

They stood in front of the train. He felt small when he stared at it; the reflection in the metal of the wheels, the rust-coloured rumbling, the white-foam clouds.

"That's sick, man," Leo said. "It looks so real."

"Like it's actually moving down the tracks." Ben made his mouth do a train whistle, which sounded like a canary with tonsillitis.

"Harvey is a train man. That guy over there. He used to be a train engineer."

"Is that still a job?" Ben said. "I think it's all automatic now. Like dishwashers. You press a couple of buttons and you're done."

Sometimes it was just best to ignore the crap that came out of Ben's brain. "We're going to do one more. That one." He pointed to the wall adjacent to the nurses' station. "But I haven't figured out the idea yet."

Ben scrunched his great hairy brows. "What about dragons. Fire breathing. Big scales."

Billy sighed.

"How about a canoe?" Leo piped in. "Two canoes. A canoe race. We could stage it." He clapped his hands in a eureka moment. "You can take a photo of Ben and me. We'll be your subjects. I'll be in the canoe at the front, Ben dragging behind."

Ben hip-checked Leo, banging him into the train.

"What?" Leo threw up his arms innocently. "I'm just stating the obvious. You're useless in a canoe."

Billy ignored them, seeing the new wall come to life in his head. Leo's idea could work. Not canoes, but a rowboat. Oars dipped into still water, turquoise and robin-egg blue. Green lily pads scattered around. An older couple in the boat gazing across at each other. The lady could be holding flowers. No, not flowers, a picnic basket with a handle, the weaves in the wood a maple-sugar brown. He would run the idea by Nick, see what they could come up with. Nick had a good eye. Not as good as Evie, but better than these two idiots. Ben now had Leo in a headlock, his glasses skewed sideways, Leo thumping him on the chest with his scrawny arm. They were making too much racket.

"Cut it out," Billy hissed, getting between them. When he looked up, Rachel was striding down the hall, all sparkle and bling. He was so happy to see her he laughed.

"Just here to drop off my fob," she said as she got close. "Got a buyer for the house if you can believe it. They're going to tear down that shitbox and put up an infill. Good riddance." She examined him from head to toe. "You don't look too soggy. So you didn't drown at canoe camp?"

"We didn't drown. These are my friends, Leo and Ben." He wished they'd quit panting. She didn't look as put together as usual, puffy, red-rimmed eyes, no earrings, no lipstick or eyeshadow. "This is Rachel. She bought the paint."

Leo and Ben dropped their arms and stood, mumbling incoherently.

She ignored them. "Have you seen Sarah? I've been in and out of all the rooms. I've got something to give her."

So Rachel hadn't heard. "Sarah doesn't work here anymore."

"That can't be. She loves these people. And she needed this job, I know she did."

"She got fired."

Rachel's hand flew to her chest. "Fired? Why on Earth?"

He was glad he was the one to tell her. He expected her to be fiery mad. Expected her to march into Dorothy's office and raise holy hell.

"Dorothy accused her of being the thief. She thinks Sarah's the one who's been stealing everybody's stuff."

Rachel stepped back, a wild look in her eyes.

"Dorothy got it wrong," he said hotly. "Sarah is innocent. Everybody thinks so." He dared anyone to say different. Instead of breathing fire, Rachel slumped against the train wall and clutched her chest.

Billy had no clue what to do or say. He'd never seen her like this. Ben and Leo shuffled on their feet like they were standing in hot water.

"Rachel?" He worried this might be a heart attack. Her chest heaved in and out, her face turning sidewalk grey. "Do you want to sit down? She grabbed onto a piece of his shirt and clung on. He didn't know CPR. He didn't know shit. "I'm going to get one of the staff," he squeaked. He gently pulled away from her, his shirt knotted where her fist had just been. She shook her head no, eyes fluttering.

"Rachel, what do you—" but she was stumbling away, clinging to the wall for support like an old woman. She turned once and said, "Tell Sarah I'm sorry," sounding desperate and truly bonkers.

They followed her at a distance until she disappeared into her mother's empty room.

"Man, that was weird," Leo said, after they'd fobbed out and gulped in the fresh air. "This place is like a soap opera."

"That's dementia, man," Ben said, shaking his head as if he'd spent a lifetime studying the subject.

"Rachel's not a resident."

"She's not?" Ben said dumbly. "She didn't look all there to me."

Billy felt sick. "Shut up, Ben. Her mom just died. Cut her some slack, will you."

Rachel ate at him for the rest of the afternoon. Later, as Leo and Ben waded into the slough for God knows what, he sat on a rock and stared at the ground.

"There's something wrong with Rachel," he mumbled to Nick that night. They were sprawled on the couch watching another nature special, a mother elephant trying to push her baby out of a mud hole with her trunk, the other elephants along the edge trumpeting her along.

"I think she's having a breakdown or something," he added, stuffing his mouth with more popcorn.

Nick turned and squinted at him like he'd grown an extra head. "What are you talking about?"

"Rachel's off. You were right."

Nick muted the TV. "I never said that."

"Yeah, you did. Maybe not those exact words. But I know you think she's weird."

"Weird doesn't really do the feeling justice."

Now there were three elephants in the mud hole, but the baby kept sliding down in the muck. It was a couple of feet to safety, but the incline was too steep for her.

"So, what happened?" Nick sounded annoyed.

"Ben and Leo picked me up at Prairie View this afternoon. I was showing them the murals and Rachel showed up."

"Rachel's mom died last week. What was she doing there?"

"She was looking for Sarah, and when I told her she got fired, she went nuts. I mean really nuts."

Nick leaned back and thoughtfully threw a piece of popcorn into his mouth. "Sounds like she cares about Sarah. Doesn't sound unreasonable to me."

Billy felt his cheeks burn. "I never even told Rachel I was sorry that her mom died."

"Well, you didn't have a chance. You were at canoe camp when it happened."

"But I could have said something today. I just stood there like an idiot."

"Don't get bent out of shape. It's hard to know—"

"And I coulda told her how to find Sarah. Rachel had something to give her, and I didn't say anything. It's like I just froze. She's done all this great stuff—buying the paint and my helmet and hamburgers. Her neighbours are dicks and now her mom is dead. What are you supposed to say to someone when their mom dies?"

Nick sighed. "I don't know. I guess you tell them you're sorry. Tell them you care."

"I didn't say any of that."

"You don't just get one chance to tell someone how you feel."

"But she's done with Prairie View now. I might never see her again."

Nick sucked air through his teeth. "There is that."

Billy perked up. "But I know where she lives."

Nick tilted his head, eying him with suspicion. "How do you know that?"

"We've driven by her place. It's a dump. She used to live there when she was a kid, and she came back to be with her mom."

"You mean she's taken you in her car? The two of you? Outside of Prairie View?"

Nick could be dense. He was missing the whole point. "She came back because she's a good person. She sat with her mom until the end because that's what good people do."

Nick clenched and unclenched his fists. Billy stared at a piece of popcorn on the floor and waited for something to happen. When it didn't, he said, "What's wrong with you?"

"Yeah, okay," Nick said, a little less stunned. "So, if you know where Rachel lives maybe you could drop off a card."

"You think?" Billy chewed on the idea. Rachel's house was sold, but she couldn't have moved out already. "And what about flowers?" he blurted. "Flowers would be appropriate, right?" He imagined knocking on her rattletrap door, a bouquet in his hand.

Nick smiled and reached into his pocket, pulled out some twenties, and handed them over. "Get Rachel something nice. Then she'll know you're thinking about her."

They stared at the silent TV, both gnawing their lips. He could feel the heat radiating around their bodies. But then out of the blue Nick said, "Billy, you don't have to paint more walls, if you don't want to. The place looks great and I'm proud of you. If you've got other stuff to do, that's okay." Billy was confused by Nick's sudden softness. "You can hang out with your friends, hang out here if you want. Maybe spend a little less time at Prairie View. What about it?"

Billy nodded, not sure why. The elephants finally managed to hoist the baby out of the water by getting their trunks under her legs and pushing from behind. It took the whole family to get her up on the bank and not one stomped on her head.

Chapter 21

Billy picked up the card and flowers at the hole-in-the-wall shop beside the Peavey Mart. The bundle came wrapped in a polka dot cellophane cone, the flowers as loud and bright as Rachel. The card was simple, a couple of pussy willows, painted blue, with the hand-drawn words, *You're in my thoughts today*. On the inside, he wrote, *Love Billy*, with a pen he borrowed from the blushing cashier. For sure, he should have brought his backpack. He felt like a dweeb, riding one-handed with the bouquet in the crook of his arm. One lady honked and gave a thumbs-up as she drove by.

As he skidded to a stop in front of Rachel's, he realized he'd come too late. A work truck was parked where her car should be. A dumpster nearly as big as the house had been dropped onto her patchy brown grass. No sign of bunnies. So, this was it then. She was gone.

A couple of beefy guys backed out of her propped-open door, struggling with a humongous sagging couch. They shuffled and scraped their way to the dumpster, counted loudly back from three, heaved the couch up to their shoulders, and tipped it in. The thing landed with an echoing crack. One yelled, "Jesus fucking Christ."

Billy stood beside his bike on the sidewalk and watched as the men went back and forth from the house to the dumpster, trip after trip, hurling chairs and mattresses and tables and lamps and bookcases and mirrors and curtains and dishes and pots and pans. He couldn't move, couldn't look away, although it felt wrong, like he was seeing Rachel naked, her private life being chucked into the trash. Thuds and bangs, splintering and shattering, grunting and swearing. He wondered why there was nothing she wanted to keep.

The men finally wound down and sat heavily on the porch step, guzzling from giant water bottles. The shorter guy lit a cigarette and hunched over his phone.

The big one stood and sauntered towards him, wiping his sweaty brow with the back of his hand. Billy swallowed and stood his ground.

Big guy stopped inches from his face. "Are those for me?" he said, pointing to the flowers.

Billy looked down, embarrassed. "They're for the owner. I came too late."

He shrugged. "Maybe not. The lady's coming back later today. She left some crap we're not supposed to touch."

"Oh," Billy croaked.

"Seems like she could use flowers." He smiled. He had surprisingly gleaming white teeth under his out-of-control moustache. "You might as well go inside and drop them off. Put them on top of the big box under the window. But you better do it now while we're on break. If you get in Sid's way, you'll end up in the dumpster."

Billy stood there brainlessly, not sure what to do.

Big guy squinted his eyes. "So are you coming?"

He followed him obediently past the dumpster to the porch. "It's the box beside the pile of clothes," big guy said, plunking down on the stair beside phone guy, who didn't bother to look up. "Go on in then."

Billy wove around them and stepped inside. He heard big guy yell behind him, "Don't steal anything," then smoky laughter. The house was mostly empty, the air heavy with Rachel's hairspray colliding with mildew and mould and generations of dust bunnies and cobwebs and the grassy vapour of rabbit pellets in an open bag.

He panned the room, found the box beside the clothes pile under the window where big guy said it would be. The box lid was open. He peered down, curious to see what Rachel had chosen to keep. His stomach flipped, knowing in his gut a second or two before his brain kicked in. Violet's doll, crammed on top of the rolled-up quilt. No mistaking it. The doll's once-rosy cheeks faded to a ghostly hue, its missing eye, hair matted and tangled. He squeezed his eyes shut, breathing fast, the discovery pulsing through his veins like a shot of adrenalin. The rest would be stuffed into that box too. He didn't dare look more. He dropped the flowers and ran.

Billy peddled furiously, careening down Main Street, over the tracks, past the skateboard park, past the last house in town and onto a gravel road that dipped and curved.

He rode and rode, until there was nothing but fields and cows and the blistering sky and the sound of crunching gravel and rattling handlebars and loud wheezing. Still he kept going, minutes, hours, lungs screaming, legs mush. He didn't plan on stopping, ever, except a gopher popped out of a hole and darted in front of him. When he swerved to avoid it, he lost control, pitching forward into the ditch, his head bouncing inches from the barbed wire fence.

He threw his bike off of him and sprawled out like a dead man in the dirt, gulping to get air back in his lungs. The light was a dusty yellowed white, the air full of cow shit and decomposing earth smells. This was as far as his plan took him: to get on his bicycle, get away from her house, get to a place where he couldn't be seen. But now here he was, God knows where and utterly alone. What was he supposed to do? It took him several minutes before he could think in full sentences. It was stupid to try to outrun this. He'd seen something that he couldn't unsee, and for once what he did next was important. There was a label for this. A moral dilemma his social studies teacher called it—*feed your family or your cattle*—the crapshoot between two wrong choices. Shitty option one: He calls Rachel out as the thief and she gets punished, hauled off to jail, the good in her erased. Shitty option two: He keeps his mouth shut and Sarah is out of a job, blamed for something she didn't do.

He lay there a long time, breathing in dust, eyes clapped tight against the glaring sun. He wished he could tell his grandma what he knew. She would ask, *What does your heart tell you, Billy?* Nothing, his heart was as heavy as mud. He'd looked up to Rachel, her bright colours and "grab what you want" attitude. He thought she saw him as a human being, not just a dumb kid in the wrong town. What a sick joke. He didn't care why she did what she did. There could be no excuse big enough. Her stolen life was a big fat fake. The squeaky toys in her car. The crap in her house. Probably his helmet too. He was the chump with his head stuck in a lie.

His thoughts swirled round and round like flies on a carcass until finally the voices faded and a floating feeling came over him and all he could hear was his angry body. It needed to pee and drink and eat. His stinging right arm had taken the worst of the fall, and when he raised it to his face, the angry road rash from elbow to wrist made him queasy. He stayed in that wind-whipped ditch, too defeated to crawl his way out, until a blankness washed through him. He dreamed he was in the ocean, its heavy swell lapping at his side.

He came to with a start, a brown spotted head bent in front of him.

"You okay, son? I almost didn't see you down here in the ditch." The old man was small and wiry with skin like oiled leather. He looked ready for a fight, but his eyes were kind. "Seems like you've taken a tumble. Can you sit?"

Billy sat and wiped the drool off the side of his mouth.

"Can you stand?"

Billy stood, flicking away the burrs riding on his shoulder. The man smiled like he was a dog doing a trick. Nothing much hurt except for his shredded oozing arm.

"Where you headed?"

"Rigsbee." He had a sudden and inexplicable need to get back to Nick.

"Looks like you were going the wrong way," the man said. "I'll give you a lift." He manhandled the bike into the back of his pickup before Billy could offer to help.

They didn't talk on the way into town, the local radio blaring country music between weather and crop reports. He'd ridden his bike an impressive distance, the ride back bumpy and depressing. The guy passed him an old canteen like from a western movie, and he glugged and gulped until the last drop, warm water sloshing in his empty stomach.

He got dropped off without fanfare at the end of his block and cycled wearily into the driveway, testing the brakes and steering. Nothing shook or squealed. When he walked through the door, Nick came from the kitchen, wearing an apron.

"Jesus. What the hell happened to you?"

Billy thought he might cry. He had a sudden memory of standing in his grandma's doorway, his grandma gone, stolen, carted off to the hospital, his world teetering like a three-legged chair.

Nick led him to the couch and hovered over him like a mother hen, helping him take off his helmet and dirt-caked runners.

"You've got a bad case of helmet head. And you're fried to a crisp." He brought out wetted cloths and tweezers and rolls of gauze and crinkled tubes of antibiotic ointments. Nick worked methodically, as he dabbed and cleaned and dressed his shredded arm. Billy stared at his sturdy face, eyebrows pinched in concentration, his own heart pounding uncomfortably. Nick was as gentle as if Billy were a toddler, which made it seem worse. He couldn't trust what he was feeling. This good man his father, a man kind and right in his head, not the loser he'd labelled him for all those absent years. But what did he know, really. He'd thought Rachel was good too.

When he was done, Nick inspected his bandaged arm and said, "You'll live," as he headed into the kitchen. He came back with a glass of water and an aspirin bottle, popped off the lid, and passed him two.

"So you gonna tell me what happened?"

"An accident." Billy drank obediently, wiping his mouth with his good wrist. "The bike's okay. It landed on top of me."

Nick took back the glass and stood over him on the couch. "Musta been scary. Anybody else involved?"

"Just a gopher, and he got away."

Nick stared into him like he had X-ray vision, like he was challenging him to spill every little thing he ever knew. "I feel like there's more to this story. Would I be right?"

They faced off there in the living room until Billy's ears burned.

"You done talking?" Nick finally said.

Billy nodded and then stopped, because he was still close to crying. He had to sort through the wormhole that was Rachel before spilling her crimes. It was surprisingly easy to stay quiet for once, his decision made, without knowing how he got there.

"Then let's get you fed." Nick pulled him off the couch by his good arm and kept his arm around his shoulder as he walked him to the table.

After three bowls of spaghetti and two bowls of ice cream and time spent crammed together at the kitchen sink doing dishes, Nick said, "I was thinking of driving out to the campground tonight. You don't want to come, do you?" He looked as if the answer might hurt him.

"Yeah. I'll come," Billy said, not wanting to leave his father's side.

Chapter 22

C arter yelled from his bedroom.

"What, Carter?"

"Can I go to Amanda's?"

He'd asked this twenty times since breakfast with a litany of variations. *Can I get a trampoline? Can we get a hose to shoot water? Can we get a basement with a ping pong table?* Sarah felt ridden with guilt, treating him yesterday to lunch and a movie that she couldn't afford. A play date was impossible. His friends were at the daycare, paying customers, happily somersaulting and chasing each other with water guns. She'd taken him to the pool instead. At home, they'd dressed like pirates, played Go Fish, painted rocks. But there was a resignation in him that she couldn't deny, a growing recognition that his life had been taken away. All he really wanted was to be back where they were.

Still, she had a job interview on Friday, by video conference. She had applied without hope, not yet in possession of the nursing credentials they asked for, and when the exuberant woman from HR called, she nearly dropped the phone. *I'm sorry, who is this,* she made her repeat twice, Carter bellowing in the background for another cheese string. *Yes certainly, Friday morning at ten*, she managed to stutter before the woman could change her mind.

It was a large company with a fancy website, boasting of care and compassion towards clients and a loyalty program for employees, the position full-time and at eight dollars more an hour than she'd been making. The job description centred around daily living activities—toileting, bathing, dressing, feeding, visiting, socializing, sorting out medication—no mention of dirty floors or dirty laundry. Over a thousand bucks more a month to focus on what she was good at, enough to buy Carter decent school clothes and before and after school care.

She'd rehearsed the interview while she pushed Carter on the swing and cleaned behind his ears in the bathtub and scrubbed the grass stains out of his sweatpants. If they asked why she left her last position, she would smile brightly and lie, tell them she was moving back to the city so that her son could enrol in French Immersion.

She hoped it would be enough. She would do the interview in her bedroom, set up the card table near the window where the light would be best, make it look like she was behind a proper desk. She would wear makeup and a freshly ironed blouse, tame her out-of-control curls, plunk Carter in front of the TV with a lapful of snacks and pray that he would leave her alone for however long it took to talk her way into their new life.

For now, she had trouble catching her breath. "Let's go to the park," she announced, making it sound like it was exactly where they should be.

Carter stopped in his tracks. "Again? Really?"

"Why not."

There were no other cars in the parking lot. Two boys, older, nine or ten perhaps, were swinging along the overhead bars, thatches of unruly hair white from the summer sun. Carter ran ahead and stepped onto the balance beam, turning to the boys every few seconds with a proud *look what I can do* smile.

She knew enough not to hover when there were older boys to impress, so she sat on the steel bench. The heat was oppressive, the sky shiny grey, the sun a hazy disc hidden behind the sheet of smoke that had travelled across provinces from the latest forest fire. It was so dry and hot she could light a match and set the whole world ablaze.

A Volkswagen lurched to a stop in the spot beside hers. Sarah recognized it from Prairie View. Rachel. There she was, slamming her door, hurrying towards her, a blur of wild colour against the dull backdrop.

Sarah stood wearily and waved. Carter barrelled towards Rachel, took her hand, and dragged her towards the bench, her sandals slapping in the gravel, her floppy purse slapping against the folds of her hallucinogenic blouse. By the time the two got to her, Rachel's face was shiny with sweat, her breath coming in short puffs.

"I didn't know how to find you," Rachel sputtered. "I've been searching everywhere. Every place I could think of. Even the post office."

Sarah was confused. "Well, you found us. It's good to see you." Although suffering was stamped across Rachel's face, in the creases around her mouth and beneath her puffy eyes. Sarah's bucket was near empty, and she didn't think she could conjure the strength to do any good.

The bigger boys had moved onto the giant net climber, Carter's favourite, the ropes layered in a way where the child is supposed to tumble down rather than fall straight to the ground.

"Can I go?" Carter said, as if he'd been summoned to the bench in the first place.

"Of course you can go," Sarah said.

When he skipped away to join them, the two women sat. Sarah took a deep breath to steady herself, nearly choking on a lungful of smoke-filled air. "How are you, Rachel? This must be such a hard time with your mom gone."

Rachel dug through her purse for a Kleenex and blew her nose pitifully. "I want you to know that I'm sorry," she said. "So very sorry."

"I'm sure," Sarah said, her throat raspy and raw. She should have kept Carter indoors like the air quality report advised. "I'm sorry too, Rachel. We're never really ready for loss, even when we know it's coming."

"It's all my fault. I'm a horrible person."

So this was the way it would be. "Don't ever say that," Sarah said in her nurse's voice. "None of this is your fault. You've been a wonderful daughter, so kind to your mom when she needed you the most."

"No, it's not that." Rachel's voice was inflected with something Sarah hadn't heard before. Fear, perhaps. She couldn't understand it.

"It's worse." Rachel sucked in her breath as if steadying herself to let out something she'd been holding in for too long. "Much worse."

Sarah crossed her knees and swung her leg back and forth. She felt drained and blank with waiting.

Finally, Rachel started up again, like an old motor cranking to life. "I have something to tell you. It's hard."

So, tell me already.

"I'm the one they've been looking for. All those things that went missing. It was me. I took them."

Sarah blinked several times, as if that would help her make sense of what she'd just heard.

"Sorry?"

"It was me. It was me. It was me," Rachel said, her voice trailing off.

Sarah instinctively shrunk from the woman, unable to look at her. "I don't understand."

"That makes two of us."

She ran through the past weeks in her head. Picking up pieces, dropping them, fragments of conversations, that horrible staff meeting, Violet's lost look without her doll, Dorothy's accusing scowl. "Edith's quilt? Mazie's pearls?"

Rachel sobbed, "All of it."

Sarah leaned over, clutching her knees. She felt like she was going to be sick. She'd left Carter in that woman's care. She looked frantically towards her son to be sure he was still there. He'd made it to the third row of the rope climber, one of the boys reaching out, pulling him higher.

Rachel touched Sarah's arm, and Sarah batted away her hand. "How could you do it? Not once, but over and over. I trusted you. We all trusted you."

"I don't know. I don't know why."

"Well, you must know something. You're the one who's done these awful things."

"I can't explain."

Sarah could feel the flush move up from her chest to the tips of her ears. "Not good enough! A damn hummingbird. What on Earth could you possibly want with it?"

"I don't know how to tell you. It's like it offered itself into my hand. Like it called out my name and it would be wrong to just leave it hanging in another person's window. There's no logic, no right answer. It could have just as easily been something else."

"But you took the things most important to people. That's not random."

"I didn't mean to. Something comes over me. It comes from a place of . . . desperation. A need I can't control—like gulping for air—and if I have the thing, it will fix me. It will stop the despair. And for a minute, I feel a sense of euphoria, like I'm on top of the world. The shame comes later. I can't even describe the depth of it. I hate myself for being weak and giving in and make a promise to myself that it will stop. Only it doesn't."

Carter was at the top of the climber, a dizzying height, yelling wildly. She wanted to run to him with arms outstretched, to catch him if he fell, but her rubbery legs had melded to the bench. And he was safer where he was than near this mad woman. "You've done this before? Stolen?"

Rachel blew her nose, her Kleenex crumpled and soggy. "I was better for a while. I thought it was behind me, I truly did. And it was. I'd finished with all that. Until I came back here."

"I lost my job because of you."

"I never dreamed such a thing could happen. I feel sick about it."

"And what about Billy? You were his friend. This will devastate him."

Rachel started a new round of sobbing, louder this time. It was as if the whole bench shook with the force of her grief. Sarah looked towards Carter, worried he'd rush over like Superman, but he and the white-haired boys were ensconced in their own drama, shouting and laughing as they scrambled down the ropes and raced to the slides, a blur of motion.

Sarah sat rod straight and listened to Rachel's frantic bursts of breath, her breasts rising, then falling, then rising again. It took considerable time before the sobs died out. It occurred to her that this woman had never known happiness. Maybe small moments of contentment, but never for long, never true joy.

"You have to stop doing this," she said more gently than she felt. Hate and pity were hard to hold on to at the same time.

Rachel raised her shoulders, nodding vehemently. "I know."

"And you have to give everything back. You still have their things, right?"

"I do. And I will."

"How?"

"It's all in a box. It's in my car now. I'm going to take it to Prairie View."

She could hardly trust her. "When?"

Rachel closed her hand around her arm and Sarah let it stay. "Today, on my way out. I have to leave this place."

Sarah nodded. If you dug in the dirt, scratched deep, this town shared plenty of blame for the woman she'd become. It could hardly give her what she needed now. It couldn't give Sarah what she needed either.

Rachel dug through her purse and pulled out a small purple satin bag with a ribbon drawstring. "This is for you," she said, carefully laying it in her lap.

Sarah eyed the bag suspiciously.

"I didn't steal it if that's what you're thinking. It was a present from my grandma."

Sarah reluctantly loosened the ribbon and unwrapped the layers of faded cloth to find a teardrop opal on a silver chain.

Rachel stared longingly at the gift she was giving. "I've had this since I was a little girl. My grandma was wearing it when she carried me to bed. She told me I had her eyes. The next morning it was tucked in her handkerchief under my pillow. It was her last visit; my father saw to that."

The opal had a rich pearly lustre, the chain as delicate as silver thread. "Why are you giving this to me, Rachel? This should be something you keep."

"I don't need a pendant to remember her. And I want this for you."

"But why?"

"Because of your kindness. Because of the way you've treated me. Because it's all I have to give."

Sarah looked down at her hands. Slowly, reluctantly, she lifted the pendant to her throat. With trembling fingers, she opened the clasp and felt it click into place.

Rachel's eyes glistened. "It looks beautiful. I won't forget you."

Sarah had to look away, afraid she might cry herself. The weight of the stone near her heart felt too heavy.

"I should go," Rachel said, gathering her purse, pulling herself up.

"Yes. You should go," she heard herself say. She closed her eyes, kneading her temples with the tips of her fingers. When she opened her eyes again, Carter was at her side, sweaty and panting, the older boys whizzing across the field on their shiny bikes.

"Aw," he whined miserably. "How come Rachel left too?"

She gathered her son into her arms and held him so tight he yelped in protest. "Show me how you can climb the pole?" she whispered. She cupped his hand in hers, letting him drag her away from that sad, hurtful place.

Chapter 23

The sky was a sickly shade of orange, the colour of a healing bruise, the air thick with smoke from the forest fires in BC. Nick drove slowly from the drug store to Prairie View, stewing over the specifics. On Monday, Sarah told him she was doing fine, moving on, applying for jobs. She'd been to the police, not needing his help. She said they were surprised to see her at the station; Dorothy had not made a theft charge like she'd threatened. Constable Bob explained that wrongful dismissals were a civil matter and there was nothing he could do. She'd insisted she was not after a lawsuit; she wanted them to catch the thief.

She answered his calls, night after night, staying with him on the line but giving little away while he sat uselessly through their strained conversations, feeling like he needed to say something but not knowing what. He didn't understand it, the hopefulness he'd felt hardening into doubt. It had seemed so real. That day in the truck, she'd swatted away his warnings. She was no pillar of the community either, she'd told him. So what changed between the then and the now?

He opened the truck window and took in the smoke, suffocating on thoughts of inadequacy. At least he could try to do right by Billy. The bike tumble had been simple enough. Boys fell off their bikes.

But it was the layer beneath the road rash that Nick couldn't get a handle on. Billy had stuck close as a shadow last night, pale and quiet, unusually polite, deferential almost. Something about his day had scared him into civility. A fight with his friends? A bad moment with Evie? Nick wanted to shake him by the shoulders until the particulars fell out. He couldn't believe how much it physically hurt to see his boy in pain. He'd rather have launched off the bike handles himself.

The bag for Evie was on the seat beside him. He bought the plastic hangers and garbage bags like the staff asked, plus a few things he'd chosen on his own—a mint lip balm (Evie's lips always looked chapped) and Hershey's chocolate bars. He'd throw Billy's bike in the truck and take them both out for dinner to celebrate her healing rib.

He drove into the parking lot at Prairie View and pulled out his phone. It was three minutes to five, the county office about to close. Peter was a company man, probably at the door with hat in hand, ready to bolt at five on the nose.

Peter picked up on the sixth ring. "You've caught me on my way out. What do you want, Nick?"

"Nice to talk to you too. What's going on at Overdale Developments?"

Thinking about it had been the only bright spot in his crappy day. When he and Billy had driven to the old campground last night, there was not a machine in view, the construction site abandoned like bulldozed ruins.

"What have you heard?" Peter sounded afraid. That was a good sign.

"I'm just a concerned citizen," Nick said politely. "Looks like things are going to shit over there."

"We don't discuss ongoing investigations."

"I got a good look at the stop work order hammered over the permits. From Alberta Environment no less. Looks like they've brought in the big guns."

"Did you . . ." Peter didn't finish the thought.

"I might have made a few calls. So, what's the damage? How much are the fines for destroying an environmentally sensitive area? I bet the county's on the hook too, right? Heads about to roll and all that."

"I can't talk about this," Peter said, his voice faint and morose.

"Of course not. It doesn't matter. It's going to be made public soon enough."

"Don't call me again." The phone went dead.

Nick had gotten everything he needed. Overdale Developments had been stopped. Peter's days were likely numbered, his sticky fingers all over that debacle.

He felt a sick sense of satisfaction as he cut the engine, surprised to find Rachel had pulled her Volkswagen into the spot across from his. The little car looked full to bursting, packages and pillows sprouting like mushrooms against the windows. She was at the back, trying to tug a large box from the trunk.

He grabbed Evie's bag, stepped out of the truck, and walked towards her. They had the parking lot to themselves, no one around, just kids' voices ringing out from a faraway lot. "Hi, Rachel. Can I give you a hand?"

Billy had told him about that weird not-there look in Rachel's eyes the day she stumbled down the hallway asking about Sarah. The same look now stared back at him, woolly and a little frightening.

"Do you need help?" He let his mind drift to Billy. Had the kid bought her flowers? Told her he was sorry that her mom died? So many questions without answers. He was inept at fatherhood, probably always would be.

She stared vacantly, not seeing him, the deep seams across her cheeks caked with red.

"Rachel?"

Instead of answering, she turned her back to him to fight with the box. She frantically dug her painted fingernails into the cardboard.

"Here. Let me get that for you." He dropped Evie's bag, reached into the trunk, and pulled and heaved until the large box came unstuck, scraping against the tailgate on its way up, a loud, grating noise. He stood there holding the box, as big as a mini fridge, readjusting his grip, not sure what to do next. She stared wide-eyed as if a bomb were about to detonate, while he waited a ridiculously long time for her to call the next shot. When she didn't, he said, "What would you like me to do with this, Rachel?"

She ran her hands over her face as if it was all too much. It was one of the saddest sights he had ever seen.

"Are you taking this inside? I'd be happy to carry it in for you."

She blinked several times, as if calculating a risk. "You can take it in for me?"

"Of course. No problem at all." He stared at her blotched face, worried she might melt into a puddle right there in the parking lot.

"You can take it in for me?" she repeated.

"Sure. It's no problem."

"And give it to Dorothy?"

"Sure, I can give it to Dorothy." While Dorothy was the last person he should get near right now, he would shake hands with a grizzly to get this conversation over with. Rachel's distress was contagious, and he was starting to feel a little panicked. "You're not coming in too?"

She shook her head quickly. He glanced through the back window. Her Volkswagen was filled with piles of clothes and an endless scatter of trinkets and shiny objects. It was clear she was leaving. Leaving Prairie View, Rigsbee. Leaving Billy.

"Please tell him I'm sorry," she said, her voice raspy and pleading.

"Excuse me?"

"Billy. Tell him I'm so sorry." Her quivering lips made his eyebrow twitch. He was as disoriented as after a long night at the Ploughman.

She did nothing to clarify things, just stepped falteringly into her car without another word. He watched as she drove away, a sad, mad look in her eyes. He picked up Evie's bag and wrestled the box down the sidewalk. He remembered sitting with her, Billy between them at the Family Council meeting, so chirpy and loud in her sparkly top. He'd judged her harshly that day, thinking her a prime example of why sometimes more is less. Now he only felt sorry for her.

When he got inside, Billy and Evie were in the hallway, following the herd to the dining room.

"Hold up, guys." He caught up to the crowd, relieved to be among their kind of sanity. Billy had a blob of maroon paint on his skinny bicep, which he took as a good sign. The kid was still painting, despite yesterday's spill, his road rash less angry and raw. "I thought maybe I could take you out for dinner."

"Really?" Billy halted abruptly. "Where?"

"Full Moon Pizza?"

"Grandma too?"

"Yeah, for sure. Why don't you help Evie get her sweater, and I'll let the staff know."

They wandered down the hall in opposite directions. Nick dumped the mystery box on a chair in Dorothy's office, glad to be rid of it, glad to have avoided the woman who had caused Sarah such pain. A woman in a uniform raced by, and he told her about their dinner plans.

When he got to Evie's room, Billy was sprawled on the couch with his phone. "She's in the bathroom," he mumbled, not looking up. "This might take a while."

"No problem." Nick hung the hangers in Evie's closet and left her lip balm and chocolate bars on her nightstand.

"What was in the box?" Billy asked absently.

"No clue." Nick plunked down on the couch beside him, picturing Rachel, her leaving. There was no good way to tell it. "I bumped into Rachel in the parking lot. She asked me to drop the box off in Dorothy's office."

Billy sucked in his breath, chewing his lip as he stared at the floor. Nick was alarmed at his mottling colour, a churn of red and white, his face a canvas of emotion painted in vivid strokes.

"What is it?" There was something terribly wrong with the kid. "Billy? Talk!"

He finally spoke, barely above a whisper. "So she brought all the stuff back."

"What stuff? You mean the stuff in the box?"

"Yeah." Billy stood and leaned his shoulder against the window, kicking his runner at the ratty baseboard.

"What was in the box, Billy?"

"Violet's doll and everything else she stole from us."

It came out in a rush, a burst dam of jumbled words, his boy's cracked voice laced with a cynical desperation. He'd been to her house and witnessed the evidence. The betrayal a blast of wind, strong and unforgiving, knocking him off course, and dumping him in the middle of nowhere. The story included a dumpster and a couple of trash men, a stranger who plucked him out of the dirt and stuffed him in his truck. The perils and what-ifs were dizzying. Broken skin, broken innocence, broken heart. All this while Nick had been mindlessly churning out inspection reports.

No wonder Rachel looked half crazed. She was a liar and a thief, nicking stuff from people who couldn't afford to lose more. He let the realization sink in while he stared at his son.

"So where is she?" Billy looked punch drunk and shin kicked, too young for this, like he'd learned Santa Claus wasn't real while he was reaching into his stocking.

"Rachel's gone, Billy," he said, which was hardly adequate. His head hurt as he hunted for better words. "I guess she was trying to make things right by giving back what she took. She wanted me to tell you she was sorry. It seemed important to her that you know that."

Evie called out from behind her bathroom door, "Is that you, Billy? I'll be out in a minute."

Nick kept his voice low. "We'll talk to Dorothy tomorrow, let her see what's in the box for herself." He hoped the evidence would be an indictment of Rachel and everything Dorothy got wrong. Beyond that, he hoped the damage to Sarah and his boy could be undone.

Billy whispered between clenched teeth. "Dorothy better be big time apologizing." Then he added, "Sarah can come back now. We need to tell her. You gotta call her."

"We will. We will. But not right now." Nick stood and joined his son at the window, looking out into the haze at thistle and scrub brush. "Right now, we're going to take Evie to a nice dinner. We're not going to worry her about all this. We'll talk to Dorothy tomorrow. Get this straightened out."

They waited together for the sound of the flush. When Evie finally appeared, she gave them a clear as glass smile and they walked out of the room as though their belonging to one another was as natural as birdsong.

Chapter 24

Sarah muddled through the day in a mist of grief and anger. The smoke from the fires had finally cleared, but she kept the kitchen window closed anyway. Better to be stuffy and airless than put up with the smell of rotting trash from the garbage bin below. Carter yelled for a snack from his bedroom. She needed to feed him, although pickings were slim, and she didn't have the energy to come up with the colours on the plate in Canada's Food Guide. She opened the cupboard and surveyed the shelf. Alphagetti would have to do.

A loud knock on the door startled her into dropping the can. Carter bounded out of his room.

"What was that?" he asked wildly. Visitors were unheard of.

Sarah picked up the rolling can of noodles. It must be Nick. She'd been expecting this moment with both worry and want. "Someone's at the door. Why don't you go answer it."

Carter skipped over and swung the door open. "It's Nick and Billy," he yelled, leaving them standing in the hallway.

She felt a shiver that she instantly pushed down. She glanced at her reflection in the window, dismayed at her appearance, her ragged T-shirt and too-short shorts, hair pulled back in a messy ponytail.

"Well, move out of the way, Carter," she said, striding towards them.

Nick stood there, not crossing her threshold, looking unsure. "Sorry, I know I should have called first. Billy and I bought a bucket of chicken and slaw. Wondered if you could help us with it."

"I've brought something for Carter too." Billy stepped in, making himself at home.

"For me? What?" Carter climbed up Billy's skinny legs, nearly knocking him over.

"It's a surprise," Billy croaked, strangled sounding. "Still in the truck." Carter had himself wrapped around Billy's neck.

"Is it a bucket of chicken?" Carter wanted to know.

Billy bent low and Carter fell off. "Nope. But that's also in the truck. We weren't sure this would work."

Sarah stared at Nick, still in the hall, ball cap in hands, eyes wary. She wanted to kiss his pressed lips and let his scent soak into her. But she could not afford sentiment or hormones or whatever it was that made the heat rush up through her belly and into her throat, so she kept her feet planted at a safe distance.

"Is this okay?" he asked cautiously.

"Of course. It's so thoughtful." She held out the can of Alphagetti. "And you've saved us from this. Come in, come in. We can have a picnic on the floor."

"I'll get the chicken," Billy said on his way out.

"And my surprise," Carter yelled, chasing after him.

Alone, they stood facing each other in crushing silence.

Nick stared at her intensely. "Have I done something wrong? Something to offend you?"

"Of course you haven't." She lay in bed night after night wanting him beside her. It was a cruel choice. She had a son to provide for, away from this town. She couldn't stay. Couldn't afford to start something with an ending so clear. She'd been withdrawn on the phone.

Nick looked at the floor. "I wondered if maybe you've been having doubts about me. After last week. When you were feeling so hurt?"

She felt shame wash over her. She hated that he was questioning himself, questioning the day they had together.

Nick blushed. "Maybe I could have been more supportive. I can be stupid. And insensitive." He looked up again, pleading. "But I can do better."

She'd done this to him, and it was terribly unfair. "If anyone should apologize it's me. I blindsided you with all my blubbering. You were perfectly lovely and just what I needed. I'm better now."

"So you don't need me anymore?"

When she didn't answer, he looked away. Beyond the open door, they could hear the boys tromping down the hallway, getting nearer. He deserved an explanation, but it would have to wait. "Let's just have our picnic," she said quietly.

The boys crashed through the door, Carter proudly displaying a framed painting.

"Look. It's me."

She examined it closely. Carter flying down a grassy hill on his bike, the wind whipping open his unzipped jacket, shoulders hunched, eyes squeezed tight, cheeks apple red, a wild grin. Her boy in a perfect moment, the likeness uncanny.

"Oh, Billy. It's beautiful. It's a gorgeous piece of art. It must have taken you forever to paint this."

Billy shrugged, his arms wrapped around the chicken bag.

"I go that fast on my bike all the time," Carter said, his nose just inches from the canvas.

"Did you even say thank you, Carter? It's such a wonderful present."

"Thank you. Can I put it on my wall?"

If things turned out, Carter would soon have another wall, another room. "Of course you can. Why don't we hang it beside your bed."

He clomped off to his room, painting in tow.

"Be careful with that now," she hollered after him.

"Do you got a hammer?" he yelled.

"Not now, Carter. Come back. We're going to have our picnic."

She found a plastic tablecloth in the hall closet and, with Nick's help, spread it on the floor and divvied out forks and plates. They sat in a circle, the bucket of chicken in the middle. Carter wanted to know when Billy could babysit again and if he could eat a marshmallow in one bite or hold his head under water until he counted to twenty or if he could smash a rock in two with a hammer. Billy answered each one of the relentless questions. Sarah wondered if this was what families looked like. Children nattering. The adults on the sidelines, grateful to leave the difficult bits tucked away.

She glanced from father to son. The pair, so at odds at first, had become more alike with each passing week. Nick rolled his tongue over his teeth when he was skeptical, and now Billy did that too. They both cracked their knuckles for no reason and clasped their hands behind their necks when they were lost for words.

Once the chicken was gone, Carter became preoccupied with chasing a fly with the swatter. She and Nick dumped the dinner remains into the paper bag.

"Well, are you going to tell her?" Billy said.

"Tell me what?" She kept her eye on Carter, who was whacking at the window. "Be careful or you'll break the glass."

One final thump and Carter yelled, "I got it. I got it. I really did. I got it."

"He's never been successful before," she said.

"He's a stealthy hunter," Nick said, cracking a smile that did not reach his eyes.

Carter started towards them, a mushed black speck between his fingers.

"Don't you bring that here. Go throw it in the garbage and wash your hands. With soap." Once he was up on his sink stool, banging on the soap pump, she turned to Nick. "Billy said, *Are you going to tell her.* Tell me what?" She hoped it would have nothing to do with her. Nothing that she would have to turn down.

Nick looked at her closely. "There's been a . . ."

Carter bounced back, hands dripping. He slipped on the tablecloth and crashed into Nick, who grabbed him up in a bear hug. Carter screeched, wrestling madly to get out of his grip.

"Maybe . . ." Nick yelled over the mayhem. "Maybe you and I could go for a little walk?"

Carter stopped fighting. "Can I come too?"

Nick tussled Carter's hair and looked at Billy earnestly.

Billy piped up. "Nah, let's stay here. We can draw superheroes."

Carter sprang from Nick's arms and into Billy's, knocking him over. "I'm going to be Spiderman."

"Would that be okay?" Nick asked her. "Just for a bit. You and me."

She looked a mess, not fit to be out, but it would be heaven to escape from Carter for a few minutes. She turned to Billy, who was on his back, Carter sprawled across his face. "Are you sure, Billy?"

"Yeah, sure," he groaned. "I'm being suffocated, but you go ahead."

So they left the boys in a puddle on the floor and headed down the stairs into the muggy evening air.

"There's not really any nice places around here," she said, appalled to find pieces of chicken coating stuck to her grubby T-shirt. She was a perfect fit with the shabby surroundings.

"I'm in it for the company, not the view," Nick said. "I've always wanted to prowl the streets with you."

"And I've wanted to thank you for your phone calls. I know I've been hard to talk to. I haven't been my best lately."

He shrugged. "No worries. Just checking in."

She nodded, feeling foolish. Maybe she couldn't see straight, imagining what might be, rather than what was. Maybe his courtesy calls had been merely a way to pass the time. God knows, single parents needed the distraction.

Her breasts felt sticky-wet under her bra in the leftover heat of the day, the sun sliding west, her thoughts so tangled that she had to concentrate on staying upright. Nick seemed content to have her beside him, slowing his stride to match hers. They walked along the chipped sidewalk, past the sagging apartment complex, past the long row of matchbox duplexes. Clanging kitchen noises and sharp supper smells reached out into the dead air from behind open windows. They passed an overturned garbage can and half-dead apple tree and turned onto a street she had never been down. The houses here were better taken care of. Real curtains. Boxes of marigolds. Bird feeders shaped like barns.

They didn't touch, but she could feel the heat of his body beside hers, the solid sound of breath and breathing.

"Billy's a great kid," she said.

"I know. So's Carter."

"We're lucky."

"We are."

They continued meandering until she felt more at ease, more in step with the man beside her. She'd nearly forgotten there was a reason for their being childless like this. Nick had something to tell her, and while she'd already guessed, she needed to hear him say it. "So, are you going to keep me in suspense any longer?"

He stopped and turned with a look of concern. "It's about Prairie View. About Rachel." He took a deep breath. "She's been the one stealing things from the residents."

So the word was out. "I know," she said.

"You know?" He stared at her intently.

She nodded. "Rachel told me. She promised to give everything back before she left town. I guess she followed through, then?"

"She made it to the parking lot. I carried in the loot for her without knowing what I had."

"Does Billy know?"

"He found out before either of us. He'd gone to her house to give her flowers. He got inside and saw the box full of stuff. Violet's doll and the rest. It really did a number on him."

"Oh God, the poor kid."

"She took us for fools," he said with disgust. "That woman's evil."

Sarah couldn't bear to think it was that simple. Rachel, evil. The woman she knew had been more than that. Over the past twenty-four hours, Sarah had conjured an agonizing number of Rachels to explain the inexplicable. Trapped, haunted, ill-treated and unloved. She had to believe there was a future for her, some potential for redemption.

"Rachel has demons," she said. "She doesn't know why she does these horrible things."

Nick's face twisted. "Even if she can give a full accounting of the why and how, she's not the one who has suffered it most." He held onto her arm, as if afraid she'd fall over. "This proves your innocence."

"I didn't need proof. I'm innocent."

He nodded. "Of course you are. But now everyone else will know too. You can get your job back."

But there was no going back. If it were the last job on Earth, she would not go back. She could not erase the betrayal, its bitter taste in the back of her throat.

Nick studied his feet, kicking at pebbles, still grasping her arm. "You should demand a raise. And Dorothy better get down on her knees."

His mind was playing out her future. She'd allowed a man to side-track her life once already, and with more to lose now, she could not let it happen again. She didn't trust herself, the things he could talk her into or out of.

"I'm not going back, Nick," she said, more resolutely than she felt.

He dropped his arm. "Okay," he said, leaving her uncomfortably hot under his long gaze. Finally, he pressed, "I get that you're done with Prairie View. That makes sense, they've treated you horribly. But you can find another job."

"There are no other jobs for me in Rigsbee."

"There has to be. Anyone with a right mind would be lucky to have you. If it's money, I can help."

She struggled to find the right words. "I don't want your money, Nick. I want to be a nurse. I want to be the kind of mom who can give Carter the future he deserves. I can't do that here."

He stared at the ground, saying nothing.

"I could so easily be talked into it, you watching out for me, paying my bills, taking care of every little thing. But I need to do this on my own. For me and Carter. I need to try at least."

He clasped his hands behind his neck.

"Are you okay?" she said.

He sighed, a deep final breath. "You're going to miss Rigsbee's Pumpkin Smash Festival. You can't get that just anywhere."

She desperately wanted to hold him but kept her voice light. "Don't lose my number. You can tell me all about it."

"You're still coming for dinner on Sunday?" he asked, almost sheepishly, as if he didn't deserve to know.

"To meet your parents. I wouldn't miss it for anything."

He nodded before moving away, keeping a distance between them. "We should get back," he said.

They walked slowly, pausing to look up as a large flock of black birds littered the sky, sweeping and looping in a single pattern as if they shared the same heart. She wondered how it would feel to be so assured of a direction, to glide so effortlessly.

When they entered the apartment, the boys were hidden under the table, a makeshift fort with draped blankets, Billy's large feet hanging out.

"You can't come inside," Carter yelled, as if her first instinct would be to crawl in. The stereo from upstairs was cranked to full volume, the drum beat pounding through the ceiling, rattling the glasses on the counter.

"Do we got a flashlight?" Carter yelled.

"Do we *have* a flashlight," she corrected. "And no we do not. It's bath time anyway. Come on out now."

Nick was eying the ceiling, his expression grim.

Billy crawled out backwards, hair sticking up, forehead glistening. "Thanks," he said. "It's a sweat lodge in there. Is it always this loud?"

"Not in the mornings," she said. "Earplugs help."

Carter followed reluctantly, dragging his bulldozer. "Can we keep the fort until tomorrow?"

"No way, mister. Now off you go. Get undressed, and I'll get the bath ready."

He grumbled down the hallway, swinging the bulldozer wildly.

"We should go." Nick placed his hand on her shoulder, his light-as-air touch causing a torment to run through her.

"Thanks so much," she said too formally. "For dinner. For the walk. For the excellent company." Then she turned to Billy, kissing him on the cheek. "The painting is beautiful. We'll cherish it always."

Both father and son blushed as they fumbled their goodbyes.

She watched absently over Carter in the tub as he sorted his marbles and dove for the starfish and talked to his captainless yellow boat. She felt sick with loneliness, the ache of something lost. When they heard the commotion upstairs, they both looked up, eyes big. A banging on a door, the stomping of boots, raised voices. She left Carter, wandered into the kitchen, and looked out the window to the parking lot below. Billy was alone in the truck, slumped in the passenger seat, his arm dangling out the window.

It took her a full minute to bring the pieces into focus. The relentless pounding had stopped, stereo strangled mid-scream, her home as still and serene as a sleepy country night.

She waited to make sure he was alright, needing to see proof. She watched as he strode back to the truck, his steps long and sure. Watched as he slipped into his seat, leaned over, said something to his son. Watched at the window until long after he pulled away and out of her sight.

Chapter 25

Nick's parents arrived bearing gifts—tins of chocolate chip cookies, homemade buns, wine, beer—bringing Bear, who leaped from their car, running in circles, hurling his scrappy little paws against Billy's legs. His mom's spark still radiant as she wrapped around him, around Billy, his dad more cautious, shaking his hand too long. He didn't deserve them.

They'd gone to fetch Evie with Billy in tow. He was grateful his parents had insisted on doing the pickup. Billy's newest wall hadn't fully taken shape yet, just the outline of a boat rising out of bucked up swirls of lake blue. They'd spent hours talking about the project, googling stock photos and paintings. Billy took ideas from his favourites and drew up his own design, a man and a woman in a rowboat, their faces still featureless. Nick wanted his parents to see the murals and get an up-close look at the talent of their grandson.

He stood at the bathroom sink, splashing water over his cheeks, willing himself to get this day right. Sarah was coming. (*I can still be part of your life, Nick.*) Bear barked sharply, his claws skittering across the linoleum. A knock. She was here.

And more beautiful than ever. She took his breath away, standing in his doorway, holding out a bouquet wrapped in foil, the fat blazing sun falling out of the sky and onto her freckled shoulders.

Carter threw himself on the floor, the dog on his chest, licking his face.

"We're here!" She laughed, passing him the bouquet. "I hope you have something to put them in."

Why hadn't he brought her flowers? "Who do you think we are? Heathens? We've got a cupboard full of vases." Bear had flipped over, legs in the air, tongue hanging from the side of his mouth. "My parents' dog. Bear. He's a bit shy and standoffish. Like Carter."

"I can see that." She laughed again, blushing as he pulled her towards the kitchen.

"They're with Billy. At Prairie View to pick up Evie. They should be back any minute."

He reached into the cupboard and pulled down the new vase. "It's crowded in here. With Evie, makes seven. We had to buy forks." And a new table and chairs and new shirts and socks.

"The table looks beautiful. And dinner smells delicious. Do you have scissors?"

He rummaged through the drawer, passed her the scissors, and watched as she laid the flowers on the counter and sorted them by colour. She snipped and pruned, adding a flower at a time, crisscrossing the stems until her arrangement was perfect. She was perfect.

"The lily is my favourite." She held out the bouquet with satisfaction.

He would buy her a room full of lilies.

He placed the vase in the centre of the table.

She leaned against the counter, watching. "So this is your first get-together in a while? With your parents?"

"Yep," He sucked air, not wanting to be the kind of man who made excuses. "But they've had a lot of FaceTime with Billy," he added feebly.

Carter chased behind Bear with the water dish.

"Put that down, Carter," she said. "You're slopping water everywhere. Bear will drink when he's thirsty." She retraced his steps with a paper towel.

Nick could hear the car pulling up. Sarah stood beside him. "Big day," she said.

It was. He was drenched in flop sweat.

It started as a happy party, Carter smitten with his mother, his mother smitten with Sarah, his dad wearing a relieved grin, all dishes edible except for the God-awful carrots.

They kept to safe topics, the jarring gap in their family history following behind him like a bleeding white bear shambling through snow. He kept expecting to get caught in a trap, but there was only laughter and silliness and the easy banter he remembered from his childhood. His dad told stories from their campground days—lawn chair waterskiing and marshmallow explosions—Sarah as spellbound as a young girl on a father's knee. Carter interjected with his take on everything from first love to a listing of ways to cook potatoes.

Evie stayed quiet, the voices bouncing around her. She was seated between Billy and Sarah, her purse on her lap, and every time her face pinched in panic, Sarah rested her hand over hers until the cloud passed.

"Your artwork is breathtaking," his mom was telling Billy. "You could have your own art show some day."

"How does one learn it?" his dad leaned in philosophically. "I can understand taking apart an engine, putting it together again. Building a wall. But I don't get paintings. Starting with nothing.

Creating lifelike trees and rocks and faces with a paintbrush. How's it done, son?"

Billy blushed under the spotlight. He'd eaten four of Cathy's buns and was reaching for another. "Grandma taught me mostly. She's a real artist."

Evie smiled when she heard the word *grandma*. "You should have more chicken," she said, patting Billy's arm.

"I think a person must be born with that talent," his mom continued. "But then your father has a good eye too. He takes wonderful photographs. We have his skunks on our bathroom wall."

It was Nick's turn to shuffle uncomfortably, more besieged than embarrassed as his mom told the story. He'd been lucky to have captured the photo without getting sprayed, the mother skunk and her lineup of babies, toddling down the path with their tails up. His parents had kept pieces of him, surrogates for their missing son scattered across their walls.

"You're still taking photos, aren't you?" His mom leaned forward, concern in her voice, as if his watching behind a lens was the most important thing in the world.

When he sat there dumbly, Billy interjected. "That's where I got the mural ideas. From Nick's photos. They're really good."

They passed bowls and refilled plates and clinked glasses. Nick offered twenty bucks to anyone brave enough to try more carrots, explaining how he didn't have the orange juice the sauce called for, so he'd used Tang instead. Bad idea.

"Do I have to eat them?" Carter muttered, which made them all laugh.

"Absolutely not," Nick said. "You don't even have to look at them."

Carter giggled. "Can I be excused?"

"Yes, you can," Sarah said. "You can keep Bear company. Quietly!"

As Carter scampered off, Cathy asked Sarah, "So you met each other at Prairie View?"

"We did. The day they moved in, I knew right away how much I'd like this family. Well, Billy and Evie at least," she added mischievously.

A spray of laughter from his parents and Billy. Even Evie seemed in on the joke, though her gaze was on the upside-down dog and the boy on the mat, six legs and two arms cycling in the air.

"Billy's been such a help with Carter. He's Carter's favourite babysitter." She turned to Nick with a smile. "And your son is handy with the neighbours, who have been unusually quiet these past nights."

Nick's mind raced forward to ways he might still right this ship. He bit down hard on his lower lip and stared at her.

"I don't know where we'd be without you," he said, cartoonishly pleading, as if he could sweet talk her across the line.

An awkward silence followed. Her face changed colours under the harsh power of his stare, her expression landing on a hurt kind of resolve, which embarrassed them both. When Evie asked Billy if there might be a bathroom, Sarah stood quickly, as if relieved to be let go.

He watched them walk across the room, not looking away until they were behind the closed door.

"She's a lovely girl," his mom said.

Nick nodded. She was everything he needed.

"It was so unfair what happened to her," Billy said. "Dorothy is such a—" Somehow he managed to stop before cursing in front of his grandparents. "You shouldn't accuse someone unless you're sure."

"That's a good principle," his dad said. "But what exactly are we talking about here?"

Nick gave Billy a steely look, holding up his hand to shush him. They didn't need to spill Sarah's business all over the table.

"What?" Billy griped. "It's not a secret."

Nick looked at his boy's earnest face. The kid was right. A secret shut out the light, and he wanted no more in his life. And this wasn't Sarah's doing; there was no shame in this for her.

Nick did the telling, cutting clean to the heart of it. "There have been some thefts at Prairie View over the last while. Little things that belonged to the residents. Sarah was falsely accused of the wrongdoing and was fired without proof. Turns out it was one of the family members."

Billy gulped in air, as if he still couldn't believe it.

"One of the family members? A thief?" His dad shook his head in disbelief. "Here in Rigsbee?"

Billy nodded. "Rachel fooled us all. Nobody thought it could be her. I didn't."

His mother kept her eyes on the closed bathroom door, lips pursed. "Oh, goodness. That's terrible. That poor girl."

Nick wanted no poor-girl pronouncements. Sarah would hate their dissecting her betrayal like a splayed frog in biology class. He poured himself more wine. "It's been a shock, but Sarah is strong."

His mother took her napkin and twisted it around her fingers. "But it must have been terribly hard to be fired for something you didn't do. A single parent with a young boy to look after."

Billy scowled. "Dorothy should lose her job."

His dad drummed his fingers on the table, calculating the options. "Sarah should get an apology in writing and added to her employment record. It has to be made crystal clear what's happened so there's no lingering confusion."

No lingering confusion. The only right path. The one Nick had run from all these years.

Billy said, "But now Sarah can come back to Prairie View," as if a happy ending were the only way this could go. Nick hadn't had the gumption to tell his son that she was not going back. He'd been a coward, afraid that if he said the words, they would cause her to disappear.

Evie and Sarah chose that moment to come out of the bathroom, Evie blinking in alarm to find a room full of strangers. Her face scrunched in worry until she spotted Billy, who she headed towards with purpose.

"Where did you go?" Carter yelled as he crawled out of the front closet.

"Just to the bathroom." Sarah helped Evie into her seat. "What on Earth were you doing there?"

Carter brushed himself off. "It's our cave. But Bear won't stay in it. Can we go outside?"

They could see no harm, a boy and a dog tumbling around the yard. Billy followed, promising to keep an eye on them.

Nick stood, remembering this was his house and he was supposed to be in charge. "Does anyone want coffee?" he asked. "Or dessert? Evie, we've got cake."

He and Sarah carried the dishes to the counter, leaving behind the forks. Sarah stood at the sink while he made the coffee, her neck craned so she could get a clear view of the boys. Behind them, his mother kept a running conversation with Evie—the sunny weather, the flowers on the table, Evie's perfect grandson, Billy, who had just stepped outside and yes, not to worry, he would be coming right back.

"I like that they're buds," Nick said, joining her at the window. The kids were at the firepit, Billy showing Carter how to stack wood, just as he'd taught him. Bear at their feet, ripping apart a stick.

She watched them silently. When she turned and smiled, there was a sadness there too, like she was fighting back tears.

"Are you okay?" He worried she might have overheard all their Prairie View talk when she was with Evie.

"Yeah, I'm okay. Dinner was great, Nick. Thank you."

Her eyes seemed glassy, and he didn't trust her words. "Food poisoning can take a while."

She laughed. "So where's this famous cake you've been going on about?"

"In my bedroom."

"Of course it is."

They managed to get the double-layer chocolate cake to the table without dropping it. "Should we call in the kids?" Nick asked once they were seated.

Sarah sighed. They could hear Carter's high-pitched squeals through the screen door.

"Right," Nick said. "Children are loud and sticky. Let's wait a bit. That can't be illegal."

They drank coffee and ate cake on napkins with their recycled forks, Nick tenuously holding onto a feeling of belonging, like he had earned the right to sit at the adults' table. They chatted about the crazy summer storms: gale-force winds scooping up table umbrellas and pitching them down Main Street; great forks of lightning stabbing the black sky; hailstones the size of golf balls bouncing through the northern edge of town, smashing through windows and nearly taking out Martin Brown's left eye.

Not ten minutes out, the boys and the dog bounded back in like they were on the way to jump off a cliff, Carter yelling, "I found a caterpillar. I made it a fort. What do caterpillars eat?"

Billy said, "There's cake," and they scrambled up to the table. The dog barked in approval.

They all watched Carter as he shovelled forkfuls into his sticky mouth. Listened as he described how the caterpillar moves its head from side to side. Cheered as he demonstrated the caterpillar crawl on the floor, Bear on top.

Evie seemed to become increasingly agitated, looking for an escape route, eyes darting about. "It's time for us to go home now, Billy."

"Why don't I take her," Sarah said.

"That would be wonderful." Evie perked up, snapping her purse closed.

"Are you sure?" Nick didn't want Sarah out of his sight.

She nodded, turning to her son, "Come on, buddy. Get your things together. We're going to drive Evie back home."

"Can I bring my caterpillar?"

Nick got an empty jam jar from the cupboard, jabbed a few holes in the lid, and passed it to him. "But you can only keep it a little while. Then you have to let the caterpillar go so it can build its cocoon."

Carter ran through the door holding his jar.

Sarah turned to his parents. "It's been so lovely meeting you."

Cathy hugged Sarah and George patted her arm.

Billy walked up to the group and asked tentatively, "So, when are you coming back to work?"

Sarah untangled from Cathy, blushing deeply. "Maybe we can talk about this later."

"Will you be there tomorrow?"

"No, no I won't."

Billy was not willing to let it go. "So when? Dorothy has to let you back. She got everything wrong and now everybody knows it."

This was Nick's fault. He needed to stop this interrogation. "Give it a rest, Billy." He shrugged an apology to Sarah, but her face was pinched and flushed.

She waited a long moment, and when she finally spoke, her voice sounded raw. "Billy. I'm not coming back. I got a new job actually. I just accepted the offer."

"Where?" Billy said.

"Edmonton."

Nick felt his world tilt. So it was final then. "That's great news," he mumbled.

"Thanks." She did her best to smile. "It's a good job. Better than I'd hoped. I've got my name in for a rental."

"So, you and Carter are leaving?" Billy's face was the colour of potato mash.

"We are."

He backed away and headed to his room, slamming the door. Its bang ricocheted in the dead air, leaving the rest of them bunched like muddied cows.

After stunned silence, Sarah said, "I didn't handle that very well. It's all happening so fast. It's not how I wanted to tell you."

Nick had to work to not garble the words, "I'm really happy for you."

Evie looked about to cry. Sarah put her arm around Evie's shoulder and said, "I'm going to take you home now."

And that was it. She was gone.

There was so much he needed to say, to Sarah, to his parents, but he had a boy who was hurting. There was nothing to do but go to him.

Chapter 26

Billy wandered down the empty hallway. The mural was almost done. He'd put Cathy and George in the rowboat, sketching their faces from a photo that Cathy had sent. In the photo they were picking saskatoons off an overgrown bush, dropping the berries into ice cream buckets strapped around their waists with pantyhose. He stared at that photo for a ridiculously long time before he picked up his brush. He tried to capture their goodness with his brush strokes and hoped they wouldn't freak out when they saw it.

He should haul out his gear and add more shading around the oars. With the hallway so quiet, he'd be done in fifteen minutes. His grandma was on the other side at the birthday party with everyone but Clement, who was locked in his room again with the runs. Cathy and George were at a property manager conference in Canmore. Leo was gone too, camping with his grandparents without cell service. Nick wouldn't be home from work until late, and there was nobody else. He was sick of his dumb, sloshing brain.

Everything got taken away. His old house. His old town. His old grandma. Sarah and Carter. Gone. Even Rachel, who wasn't all bad. She'd skipped town, leaving behind the pile of shit she'd created, in her house, in their heads. The staff hated her. Nick kept telling him to put her out of his mind. *Rachel is not right, not fit to breathe your air.* At least she'd come clean to Sarah and returned the stuff she stole, saving him from turning her in. If the police were after her, a part of him hoped she'd never get caught, that she could hole up with bunnies and stay out of trouble.

Nick had helped Sarah and Carter with their rush move to Edmonton (*We can get a hotel, scream on the rollercoaster at West Edmonton Mall*), but Billy wanted none of it. He figured the drive would be too sad, only now he wished he'd said yes. He wished he'd said a real goodbye.

He'd been mean to Nick for days, giving him the silent treatment. A part of him was sorry, but a bigger part couldn't help it. Maybe he'd been testing his dad, seeing if he'd disappear too. Except he didn't. He hovered. He kept bringing out the crib board. Bringing glasses of milk to his room. Making him bacon and eggs for breakfast. Calling him every day from work. The more Billy pushed him away, the more Nick stuck. It was weird. He wanted to be alone; he wanted not to be alone more.

School started next week, and he didn't know what to call the heat rising from his stomach and landing in his throat. Legitimate jitters? White-hot terror? His past school days had been less than glowy. He'd managed to avoid the mean kids' radar for the most part, but it took diligence, and it had required avoiding everything else too. Raising his hand, opening his mouth, making eye contact. This year he'd have to change tactics. For one thing, he was the new kid, bigger than he used to be, and easier to spot. For another, he'd have Leo and Ben beside him, and they were about as inconspicuous as a pair of braying donkeys.

His heart wasn't into working on the stupid mural. He might as well go home. Evie wouldn't miss him when the party was over. She'd taken to mothering the others—pushing their wheelchairs, holding their hands, buttoning their sweaters—her laugh ringing down the hallway whether he was beside her or not.

He trudged into the staff room to get his helmet. There was Dorothy, a pencil in her mouth, glaring at the papers scattered over the table. He pictured lunging at her, pulling out great clumps of hair, hurling every swear he could think of.

She turned and stared. "Billy. I've been expecting this."

Expecting what? A war? His fingers curled into fists.

"Will you sit down with me for a minute?"

"No," he croaked, all that would come out.

She sighed. "There are things I've wanted to say to you."

There were things he wanted to say to her too. *You are nasty and ugly, and everyone hates you.* He couldn't get his mouth to work. Or his legs or his arms.

She pushed out the chair beside her and pointed for him to sit. He didn't move.

"Well, never mind," she said. "I can say what I need to with you there. Let's start with Evelyn." She opened a file folder and scanned a page with her finger. "I've been studying her charts, and I'm so pleased. Her vitals are excellent. The vitamin D has certainly helped. Did you know she's gained ten pounds this summer? Another ten and she'll be at an ideal weight. And she's healing remarkably well after her fall."

Billy's face burned. He didn't need a lecture about how to take care of his grandma. Prairie View had her, what, a couple of months? He'd had her his whole life.

She snapped the folder closed and stared, not pleasantly. "But mostly, I wanted to thank you."

And he wanted to punch her face.

"I was skeptical at first," she continued, oblivious. "But you have done good work. Your walls have made a difference."

He didn't need a lecture about his good work. Not from her. "You fired Sarah," he hissed.

She nodded slow motion.

He kept going, spitting loud. "You fired Sarah. You are horrible and you wrecked her and you're worse than Rachel. You were so wrong. About everything. And now she's gone, and Carter's gone, and they're not coming back."

She crossed her arms. "Are you finished?" she asked without barking.

"You're an asshole," he said, hot and dripping.

She studied him so long he wanted to run. Finally, she spoke. "I like you, Billy. And your father. And Evelyn. Yes, I was wrong, and I've had my . . . regrets. And I've tried to make it right."

"How?" he yelled. "She's gone."

Dorothy leaned back, the flimsy chair squealing. "I've called Sarah and apologized. Recorded the incident on her file. Gave her new employer a glowing reference. All the stars."

Billy stood there dumbly.

"As Sarah said herself, she's gone to something better. Better pay. Better work. More than we could offer her here." She looked at him sternly. "You want her to be happy?"

He nodded, reluctantly. He wanted Sarah to be happy. Here, not far away.

"Then be happy for her. And be happy for your grandma." She leaned forward, laying her palms on the table. "Have you heard of the Rigsbee Terrific Teen Award?"

He shook his head. Leo had told him about the teen maze and teen pool nights, nothing else.

Dorothy continued, not a whiff of emotion. "It's an award given by the town for young people who have made outstanding contributions to the community. Outstanding potential. I nominated you.

You've won. It's a cash prize. Five hundred dollars to spend as you like. You'll be getting a letter. And the paper will want to talk to you. And get photographs of you and the murals. We'll have an ice cream social in September to celebrate."

She turned back to her papers, all business. "Well, I have a busy day here. I'm glad we've had this little chat."

He grabbed his helmet and fled.

Nick turned off the highway and onto the lake road. September, and the hottest day of the year, the sun searing bright, bleaching the colour from the sky and fields. Not a breath of wind. Even the birds had gone limp.

He crossed the cattle-guard gate and inched the truck up the winding gravel driveway towards the abandoned farmhouse. There was promise for this place, this land, a conservation easement to be slapped on the title. No more dredging or draining or damming or decimating. Front page news in the *Rigsbee Globe*. Ducks Unlimited were in talks with Alberta Environment to purchase the old Ackerman Campground property, and other parcels around Goose Lake. All part of their wetlands conservation program. Nick wanted to believe he'd played a part.

He didn't know why he'd come. Why he'd stepped out of the truck or walked up to the front door or jimmied the old lock. He found himself standing in his childhood kitchen, remembering his mother at the sink, an apron tied over her bathing suit, her bare brown foot tapping to the tinny country music on the radio with the snapped-off antenna. There was the ancient bread box, cinnamon rolls stacked under the cracked glass lid. Lemonade in the happy-face pitcher behind the fridge door. His father, beyond the open window, heading out of Campers Hall in coveralls and his UFA ballcap. The *ringaringaring* song of crickets in the tall grass, the pulse of the campers' voices rising out of trees, the lull of waves washing over sand and rock.

It was everything he'd known. The sweat-soaked skin of summer days. Hard work and hard play. But when he'd come clean at last—his trembling confession in his parents' living room—things weren't as he'd known. So much had been kept from him.

He had driven to Edmonton that morning after he dropped Billy at Leo's place. Billy seemed to be coming out of his funk and had canoeing and a sleepover, a last hurrah before classes started. He wasn't sure who was more nervous, father or son, about the new school year.

Nick wore his best shirt. Slicked his hair back. He found his parents' place with GPS. The towering apartment complex sat at the mouth of a quiet cul-de-sac, big willow trees out front, a red bench with the painted words Live With No Regrets in his mother's lettering beside the main entrance. When she opened her door, she gasped before she grabbed him close. His father and Bear rushed in from another room.

Nick was put on the couch between his mother and the dog, his dad in the old recliner that used to be in the side room in the farmhouse. (The *parlour*, they'd joked.) He handed her his offering, the paper bag that had been clutched in his fist. She pulled out the framed photo he'd kept hidden in his drawer for the past decade. He'd taken the shot from a distance, a wide view of Goose Lake, an explosion of apricot orange from the setting sun, his parents floating together on a giant rubber tube. She held it like it was precious, brushing her fingers against the glass. When she finally passed it to his dad, he said, "You looked mighty good in that bathing suit, Cathy."

They ate chocolate chip cookies and drank coffee and talked about the wonder of Billy. How he ate seven meals a day, could do jumps on his bike, could follow the "How to Make Fudge" YouTube video. His boy: Rigsbee's Terrific Teen. Five hundred bucks for being himself.

For a brief moment he thought, why not sink into the couch fold and carry on like this? Why not simply erase the fault line and pick up where they'd left off? But he'd come for a confession. His voice faltered as he started. It was hard to explain. The stolen beers. The fire. How he hid it. Why.

By the time he was finished, his mother was in tears, his father's cheeks ashen and sunk, hands clasped over knees. He'd broken their hearts. He wanted their anger, but his mom's stifled sobs and the dog's incessant whimpering and his dad's stony silence were worse.

When he could no longer stand it, he said feebly, "I screwed up. Screwed up all of it. I'm so sorry."

His mother leaned towards him, cupping his cheeks in her hands. "You have carried this inside all this time," she said shakily. "This is why—"

He could see the reel play out in her head. All their unanswered calls, all his no shows. He sat perfectly still, held upright between her hands, unable to look at her wet eyes.

She blinked away her tears. "You're not angry with us? It wasn't anger that kept you away?"

Angry at them?

She finally let go, Bear scrambling back into her lap, licking her face to make things right. Then his parents both talked at once. *That place had become too much for us*, he thought he heard his dad say amidst the flood of spilled words, his mother jumping in about the lapsed insurance, how they couldn't afford it.

What were they saying? Their family had everything before he'd ruined it. They'd been doing great.

His dad finally cut through the mud. "Things were falling apart, son, long before the fire. Do you understand?"

Nick shook his head.

"We were holding on by a thread. We wanted to see you off. See you launched before—"

His mother cut in, "We knew how much you loved that place."

"But you loved it too," Nick insisted. He knew that much was true.

"We did." His father looked wistfully at the trees beyond the window. "But its time had passed. The world had changed. We didn't want you to witness the messy business of letting the campground go. That fire just moved up the timetable a bit."

They made it sound as if the fire had been part of a predestined plan, a miracle, a clean break between the old and the new. If Nick had kept things hidden, well so had they, each trying to protect the other.

"You've had your reasons to put up a wall," his dad said, head bowed. "We're just glad you built a door and that you've chosen to walk through it."

They'd been prolonging their goodbyes at the front door when Sarah's name came up again. He'd told them how she'd found a duplex with big windows, nobody above her. A miraculous find. The landlord's new tenant had backed out last minute, which allowed Sarah to slide right in. A boy Carter's age next door. Plenty of worms in the garden out back. He'd helped her with the move, got her cable working, hammered Billy's painting on the wall, put her bed frame back together. He didn't share the part about coming home without her, draining a bottle of Jack Daniels, waking up in the yard beneath the moon. Or about how she called him the next night and said, "There you are. I needed to hear your voice."

"Here's to new beginnings," was what his dad had said.

"Yeah, Sarah deserves this," Nick had agreed, mustering his best self.

His father tipped his head back, eyes drilling into him. "That's not who I'm talking about. This is your new beginning. Hope, son. He who has hope has everything."

Nick stared out the kitchen window of the old farmhouse, skin tingling. How many times had he stood at this very spot, swiping away milk moustaches with the back of his hand? How many dishes had he washed at this sink? How many times had he run out the door and pounded through the tall grass, a bevy of campground kids hollering in pursuit?

Things had come so easily for him once. He didn't have to struggle for high marks or winning goals or packs of friends or summer girls.

But Billy was no come-and-go campground kid. And Sarah was no summer girl. His former self would have run to her and made her his, consequences be damned. But Billy had real friends, a real chance in Rigsbee, and Evie had lost that gaunt look and could find the way to her room by herself.

Things had to be different this time. He had to be different. Sarah and Billy weren't his for the taking. It would require all kinds of hard work and heartbreak to earn their love.

The long hot day had slipped by, confessions taking considerably longer than he'd imagined, his stolen time in the farmhouse more a meditation than a break-in. In disassembling the years, he'd lost track of the hour, the fevered sky now awash in pink. He walked out of the old farmhouse, shutting the door firmly behind him.

His feet led him down the path to the shoreline. The setting sun had drawn a long red carpet across the water, inviting him back in, the same wet he'd worn those hundreds of nights.

What was it his dad had said? *This is your new beginning. Hope, son.* His mom had promised pumpkin pies for Thanksgiving, with Sarah and Carter at the table too.

He stepped out of shoes, first left, then right, and stripped off his shirt and jeans. He felt as fragile as a just-laid egg in a precarious nest. Any number of tragedies could befall him before he'd learn to fly.

Yet the water was warm, the mucky lake bottom squishing between his toes.

What had he done to deserve hope?

Seagulls circled above, squawking in applause as he waded towards the depths. Maybe that was the thing. It comes to you anyway.

Acknowledgements

M y experiences with dementia are where this story began. I
spent countless hours in the Royal Oak dementia cottage in
Lacombe with my dear mom and all the other dear moms. I have been
deeply inspired by our long-term care staff, the angels among us, who
make such a difference in the lives of our loved ones.

I am profoundly grateful to ECW Press for such a joyful and
gratifying collaboration. I owe endless thanks to Jen Knoch, my brilliant editor, who has patiently rescued me from myself more times
than I can count. And I so appreciate David Caron, Emily Ferko, Jess
Albert, Michela Prefontaine, Caroline Suzuki, and the entire team for
creating beautiful books with such kindness and dedication.

A wraparound hug to Leslie Greentree for her invaluable feedback
and for retreating with me among the monks, nuns, and chickadees
to write and talk about writing. My appreciation also goes to Audrey
Whitson for her support and careful reading of early drafts, and to
Richard Harrison and Tashie Deen, my jury duty partners, for helping
tether me to writers' world during our raucous Zoom chats. Warmest
thanks to readers Jimmy Kimmel, Megan Hunter, Judy Howard, and
Brenda and Bernard Parkinson for their encouragement and feedback,

and to Lacombe's Brave New Writers, who keep reminding me why we write in the first place.

I gratefully acknowledge both the financial support from the Canada Council for the Arts and the professional and emotional support from the Writers' Guild of Alberta community.

Love always to my tribe: My beloved daughters, Bre and Megs, their sweet families, and to Jim, my favourite chef and the anchor of my world.

Fran Kimmel is an award-winning author of numerous short stories, plays for both theatre and radio, and the novels *No Good Asking* and *The Shore Girl*. Born and raised in Calgary, Fran now lives in Lacombe, Alberta, and can be reached at FranKimmel.com.

Entertainment. Writing. Culture. ————————

ECW is a proudly independent, Canadian-owned book publisher. We know great writing can improve people's lives, and we're passionate about sharing original, exciting, and insightful writing across genres.

———————————————— **Thanks for reading along!**

We want our books not just to sustain our imaginations, but to help construct a healthier, more just world, and so we've become a certified B Corporation, meaning we meet a high standard of social and environmental responsibility — and we're going to keep aiming higher. We believe books can drive change, but the way we make them can too.

Certified

Corporation

Being a B Corp means that the act of publishing this book should be a force for good — for the planet, for our communities, and for the people that worked to make this book. For example, everyone who worked on this book was paid at least a living wage. You can learn more at the Ontario Living Wage Network.

This book is also available as a Global Certified Accessible™ (GCA) ebook. ECW Press's ebooks are screen reader friendly and are built to meet the needs of those who are unable to read standard print due to blindness, low vision, dyslexia, or a physical disability.

This book is printed on FSC®-certified paper. It contains recycled materials, and other controlled sources, is processed chlorine free, and is manufactured using biogas energy.

FSC
www.fsc.org
MIX
Paper | Supporting responsible forestry
FSC® C103567

For every copy of this book sold, 1% of the cover price will be donated to the Lacombe Performing Arts Centre, which provides accessible arts programming and entertainment to Lacombe, Alberta.

ECW's office is situated on land that was the traditional territory of many nations, including the Wendat, the Anishnaabeg, Haudenosaunee, Chippewa, Métis, and current treaty holders the Mississaugas of the Credit. In the 1880s, the land was developed as part of a growing community around St. Matthew's Anglican and other churches. Starting in the 1950s, our neighbourhood was transformed by immigrants fleeing the Vietnam War and Chinese Canadians dispossessed by the building of Nathan Phillips Square and the subsequent rise in real estate value in other Chinatowns. We are grateful to those who cared for the land before us and are proud to be working amidst this mix of cultures.

ecwpress.com